L. J. EPPS

EXTINCTION
OF
ALL
CHILDREN

To my father, Henry, who always believed I could do anything I set my mind to, and to Aja, who always tried to help me break out of my shell and have some fun. And to Deborah, Wayne, and Craig Sr.

TABLE OF CONTENTS

CHAPTER ONE

TODAY THE WIND IS colder—sharper—and it whips right through my bones. Even so, I continue to run as fast as I can through the wooded area. It smells damp like rain, and mud sticks to my shoes. The air feels thick like sand is choking me. At times, it is hard to breathe; but, I continue on. I have to make it back home before dark. If I'm found on the streets after dark, it means I'm not following orders. And my family might not receive our daily supplies; supplies we need to make it in this land.

Even though I make this trip through the woods at least three times a week, today I feel weaker, more sluggish, as if it is my first time. But it isn't the first time, and it will not be the last, since I'm the one my family counts on.

No, I'm not the boy of the family. Boys are considered stronger, but my brother Theodore—we call him T, for short—is nineteen and not a fast runner; so, he couldn't make the trip that I have to. That isn't the real reason. The real reason is that they say they need his talents for other things, and he can't get hurt.

I have to pace myself. The trees seem thicker and wider, which is odd, since they should be thinning out. This time of year, the leaves should be falling toward the ground, but they aren't. This land is different, and the seasons aren't exactly on point. Sometimes, it is hard to even tell what time of year it is. Ever since our world was taken over and broken into territories, everything seems to blend together.

I know I'm tiring because my thoughts jumble. Why didn't I wear my hair in a ponytail? It is long and thick and reaches beyond my shoulders. I usually know to put it up, out of the way, on days like this. The wind slaps me in my face, obstructing my view. Maybe I should put my hood up; but, it won't stay on, and there is no time to fight with it.

The pack on my back that I used to carry to school starts to feel heavy, as if lead weighs me down. But, I can't soften. I'm almost there, and, not only am I bringing what my mother asked for, but I've also made the most important part of the trip. The part of the trip my mother will ask me about first. She always does; it is always the same.

I need to hurry. It will be dark soon. Normally, I make the trip early, before dusk arrives. But today, I spent more time at the market, looking for what mother asked for. I groan. I don't know how many more times I can make this trip; especially, once winter is upon us.

Not to get food but the other thing, the thing we aren't supposed to talk about, the thing we aren't supposed to mention until we are within the four walls of our small home.

I've been thinking about it for a while now, but how can I tell my parents when they depend on me so? How can I tell them that the last winter was unbearable, and I don't think I can make it through another one? I turned eighteen two weeks ago. Why wasn't I happier about that? Maybe it is because I'm the last child to turn eighteen in our territory, and there will never be another.

My feet are frozen, as if I'm standing in a block of ice, and my thoughts move elsewhere because I hear footsteps approaching. I turn and run in the opposite direction. I'm now going back the way I came to get away from them. My heart is in my stomach. I can't get caught here, or I'll be bombarded with questions. I glance back. Far off in the distance, I see one of the president's patrolmen. He'll probably ask why I'm in the wooded area. He'll probably say it is almost dark.

"I thought I heard something, back here," I hear him shout. "It's probably some kind of animal, but I want to check it out."

I run faster, and my breaths grow jagged.

"We don't have time for that now. Whatever it is, let it go," I hear a second voice shout out.

"We have orders from the president to kill any animals on the loose. It won't take me long to track it down."

He is coming closer, and my jaw clamps shut, like a vise surrounds it. I run even faster than before. I hear his boots *clip clop,* like a horse, behind me. A tree branch crackles underneath the soles of my shoes. I pray he didn't hear it. I'm used to running fast, so why do I feel brittle like I will snap in half? Maybe it's because the danger is right upon me this time, instead of far off in the distance. I need a place to hide.

I come to a stretch of the area that my father tells me never to enter. It is damper and danker, and some say the mud is so deep it is like quicksand. My heart pounds so hard my chest hurts. I don't want to go that way. I can't go back toward the patrolmen, either.

I'll have to chance it. I run straight ahead into thick weeds and tall grass. I stop before I reach the deepest part of the mud—the part like quicksand. I stand still and hope I'm invisible to him, like a caiman, hiding in plain sight. Fear rips through me, and my breaths weave in and out, as if I've just dived into a pond with no water at the bottom.

I try to settle my breathing. His footsteps keep pounding toward me. I don't want him to hear me. If he finds me, I'll have to come up with my best excuse to explain why I'm here. He probably won't believe me.

"I don't see anything," I hear him say. "But, I know I heard something."

If his footsteps come any closer, he'll be standing right in front of me. My throat hardens.

"Forget it, man. We have orders. We're needed somewhere else," the second man yells, as if his feet are standing on hot coals.

I hear the first man grunt, as if he is disappointed he won't be able to kill something today. He turns from the area I'm in and walks in the opposite direction. He didn't notice me, but I fall down anyway. I feel cold dirt beneath my knees. The wetness of the dirt seeps into my skin through the holes in my jeans. I kneel—shaking—while the weight of the moment washes over me.

"I just got a call on my radio about a protest," I hear the second voice say.

"That hasn't happened in a while. President Esther won't be happy."

"They said we should get down to the medical facility and help control the crowds."

I hear the *thump* of helicopter blades rumbling overhead. The president owns several helicopters for her guards and patrolmen to get around in. The fluttering in my chest lessens when I see the patrolmen disappear. Now that my body isn't shaking anymore, I stand. I venture out of the grassy, muddy area to head home. As I walk, I hear talking, but I'm not afraid anymore. They're not deep, overpowering patrolmen's voices. Their voices have now been replaced by townspeople's voices, male and female. The voices sound peaceful—reminding me of my own. I'm curious, so I follow them to see what is going on.

I'm out of the wooded area now, and I keep following the voices until I reach the marketplace. It is about three miles from my home, where all the shops are located. It is neatly placed in the middle of town.

The voices trail off, and I see the market where we purchase our fresh fruits and vegetables. Customers come and go, and I don't see any commotion there. Next to it is the bakery, where they bake fresh bread, but there is nothing going on there either. On the opposite side of the street are the clothing stores, but all is quiet there as well.

I don't know what all the fuss was about. I need to get home before my parents start to worry. I start my stride and I hear a loud voice, yelling, as if through a bullhorn. It is coming from around the corner, near the medical facility, where they hand out free contraceptives to anyone eighteen and over, so there is no excuse for any pregnancy accidents. No one is allowed to engage in sexual conduct until age eighteen, so those under eighteen have no need for contraceptives.

"You people need to go home, right now. Otherwise, we'll have to take you in," a patrolman, in black clothing, yells. "We're trying to give you a chance to redeem yourselves, but our patience is running thin."

I see a group of ten, standing in front of the medical facility. Men and women with grim looks on their faces. Some of the females are crying, and some of the males have tears in their eyes. Some have on tattered and ripped clothing, and others have neater appearances. Some hold signs, while others hold nothing at all. They're chanting, quietly.

The way the two patrolmen reacted earlier, I thought the crowd would be larger. Maybe most of them scattered when the patrolmen arrived, or maybe the patrolmen exaggerated. There used to be protests all the time; but, as time went on, the crowds lessened and lessened. People stopped coming out and demonstrating. They say it is a waste of time, so I'm surprised they're doing this now.

"You give the president a message from us," an older man, with sandy hair, says. "We don't want her free contraceptives. We want our children back."

"Stop putting us in classes," a woman yells out.

"Yes, stop treating us like we're nothing," another man yells. "We're just as good as the people in the other territories."

"We have rights," someone in back screams.

"You people have been spouting this nonsense for years and nothing ever comes of it. You'd think you would've learned by now," the patrolman says with a chuckle in his voice, like he is happy over the fate that awaits them. "Maybe most of you have, since there used to be thousands of you opposing us, and now there are only a few."

I've always wanted to participate in one of these protests, but my parents always refused to let me go. They tell me it would do no good, and I would end up in jail for thirty days for defying the laws. It looks like a peaceful demonstration, and my heart breaks because I wish I could join them.

The backpack, weighing on my shoulders, reminds me that I should go home. I almost got caught in the woods tonight. Do I want to tempt fate, again? But my body won't move, like I'm surrounded by swampy waters. And something in my chest tells me I should join in. Like a lawyer defending his client, I want to support them. So, I move closer and end up standing behind the crowd.

Now that I'm in the midst of things, I see what is really going on. A light-skin woman, a little younger than my mother, stands next to me. She looks to be a few months pregnant. Her stomach has a bulge in it, no bigger than a small ball. A man stands next to her, tightly gripping her hand. The woman's face is tear-stained. Obviously, the patrolmen are here to put her in jail, and later, to take her baby. This small crowd shields her from her impending fate. My face hardens. I'm trying not to cry with her. But my insides tremor, since she probably will not survive this.

"The president said we could have some time together, before turning ourselves in," a dark-skin man with a bald head says.

He is holding on to the woman's hand. I assume he is her husband.

"The president told you that weeks ago, when she first discovered you were with child and hiding it. This is how you repay her kindness? By getting your family and friends together to protest on the very day you're supposed to surrender?"

"We're s-sorry to disobey her." The woman's voice quivers. "B-but we only want to live in peace with our c-child."

"That is never going to happen," the patrolman says.

His eyes are black and beady, like buttons on a coat. His hair color matches his eyes. He pulls a black, metal gun from his holster and waves it around.

"I suggest you disperse. Now!" he shouts.

The crowd stands there. My knees sway, but I stand with them. I hear several gunshots as he shoots into the air. I duck down to the ground with the rest of the crowd. I watch as another patrolman barrels over and grabs the husband. He puts the man in a choke hold, while another patrolman clicks handcuffs around his wrists. I now notice that during all the commotion the pregnant woman has landed behind me. I'm crouching down in front of her, and a patrolman with blue eyes and brown hair is heading straight for me.

"Move, little girl," he says to me. "We need to take in the prisoner."

"Why can't you leave her alone?" I manage to say, although my leg is twitching. "She hasn't hurt anyone."

"Not according to Territory L standards."

He grabs my arm and shoves me aside like I'm nothing.

I fall on my backpack, and the dusty ground wafts up in my face. My body quakes as I watch him yank the woman up by her hair, like she has committed the crime of murder. He snaps handcuffs on her, like she is a hideous criminal. Her cries of help make my skin crawl and my eyes water along with hers.

"Take them down to the launch," he says to the others. "The guards will be waiting there to take them to the president."

He glares back at me and the other members of the protest.

"You should be happy I'm not taking you all in. But I guess you caught me in a good mood today. Now get out of my sight before I change my mind." He rolls his eyes.

I shakily stand and dust myself off. A haze is still over my eyes because I've never been so close to a commotion like this before—let alone been in the middle of one. The others that were involved in the protest walk off looking just as distraught as I am. I can't tell my parents about this. They would be disappointed in me for getting involved, while I'm disappointed in myself for not being able to do more.

CHAPTER TWO

I TURN TO GO home, but before I can start my stride, my heart jumps. A siren blares like a loud horn, meaning it is eight o'clock and every family should be settled in front of their boxes. The blare is so loud, it feels like the sky is falling and it almost deafens me. I would cover my ears if it would help, but it won't. That is why they like everyone to be inside when it starts.

The box is what we call our information system. It is a twenty-four-inch computer screen. It is how President Esther communicates with us. Every Monday night, she takes the podium at the city council building and gives the same speech, with a few little things added. There is never anything good said, but all families are to watch in eager anticipation that something new and pleasant will be said.

It can't be eight o'clock—it is not dark out yet—but the ground is shaking like it is. Buzzards swarm above, squawking loudly. They hate the sirens as I do.

"Alright people," a light-skin patrolman dressed in black yells, "the president is starting her speech early tonight. Those of you still roaming around need to get in here."

He points to a supply store that is a few doors down from the medical facility. It is where my parents were forced to purchase our box, even though we couldn't afford it. If people refuse, they were put in the jail that is kept underground in President Esther's mansion. Those who couldn't afford it, we're put on a payment plan, even if you didn't want to be.

There are only a few of us left from the protest. He shoves me into the supply store with them. I notice several others who were in stores stop paying for their purchases and are ushered in behind us. I've never been out when the speeches start. The law states you're to drop whatever you're doing and find the nearest box to watch. Normally, it is not a problem because it starts at eight when it is dark out, so no one is outside anyway.

The store is dark and there are hundreds of boxes all over. There is a glow of light near the back of the store where one box is on. We stand and wait. I stand in between the tall, older man with sandy hair and the short, blonde woman who had screamed earlier, "Stop putting us into classes."

The awful music, the kind that plays in an elevator, starts. President Esther walks to the podium and takes in a breath. She looks paler than usual, and her scary silver hair looks almost white. Her blue eyes pierce through the screen, as if she is right in front of me. She opens her mouth to speak.

"Hello, people of Territory L. I hope all is well. I will not announce the names of those jailed over the past week. I feel tonight there are other pressing matters that need my attention. I've heard grumblings throughout the territory. My guards and patrolmen always bring any concerns back to me."

President Esther brushes a strand of hair behind her ear.

"Many of you feel, since the last eighteen-year-old has graduated, I may revise my law."

My stomach cringes because I'm the eighteen-year-old she is speaking of.

"Well," she continues. "The law has been in effect since 2080, and I don't feel there is sufficient reason to change it."

Her eyebrow rises.

"I have seen no new changes in the lower-class community that would justify letting them have children again. You all still make the same low wages and most of you still don't have a higher education, which better jobs require."

"Whose fault is that?" I mumble, and roll my eyes.

"This community is still not safe for children…"

I stop listening because I know what she'll say next. She'll say children should not grow up in a world where they can be kidnapped or raped or treated poorly. They should not grow up in an impoverished world where parents have no food to feed them, or where they cannot receive proper health care. Who would want that kind of treatment for their children, she will say.

I glance back at the box and watch as she shifts her eyes from side to side.

"Territory L has no place for children, for babies. You all should be thanking me for my efforts to keep children away from the violence here, instead of whining over the issue. We should rejoice that there are no more suffering children because of the mistakes of our generation." President Esther's voice is rough.

She walks away from the podium and sips a glass of water her guard hands her. She returns to the podium and looks down at the papers in front of her.

Now she will restate the law, as if we haven't heard it a million times. No one in Territory L is allowed to give birth to a child, married or unmarried. It is still not permitted. If anyone is with child, once it is born, it will be taken away and killed immediately. She says having children is an act of selfishness, and if anyone ignores her orders, they will be jailed.

"Some of you have defied me by trying to abort your baby before I can take it away. That is against the law as well. If you find you're with child, you should endure the consequences of having them grow in your wombs before being taken away and killed. Yes, I could have you all sterilized—but that would take away my fun in watching you suffer when you disobey and your child is taken. Like I've said before, sterilization wouldn't be wise, since you can have children if you move on to the upper territories. This is the law as I have written it, and it will remain in effect until I die or decide to take myself out of office."

"That can't happen soon enough for me," I mumble.

The sandy haired man smiles at me as if he is in agreement.

"I shouldn't have to keep going over the law, but I find it necessary since some of you keep defying it. Now that we're done with old business, we will move on to changes. The free contraceptives that are given out as part of your daily supplies will only be available Monday through Friday, not on the weekends. I do what I can to help you prevent pregnancy. You can help yourselves by abstaining from sexual activity. We still have not been able to get our water sanitized properly, so bottled water is still free as part of your daily supplies. Since some of you are still unemployed, I will continue to offer the free block cheese, so you will have food to put in your mouths. If you break these laws, you will not receive your supplies."

Her chest pumps up with pride as if she is proud she has given us a few measly things for free. She swipes her hands together and they sound like shoes scuffing up against hardwood floors.

"Now on to new business," the president continues. "Some of you don't believe me when I say if you work hard you can move up. You don't believe that some have done so well they have earned the right to go on to Territory M, and then on to Territory U—the ultimate goal. I'll show you that I do keep my word."

One of her guards hands her a white piece of paper.

"I normally don't give out the names of the families chosen, but I'm starting something new. We have two families so far this year that are worthy of moving into Territory M. There is the Wessel family: Peter Wessel; his wife, Victoria; and their two daughters, twenty-year-old Leslie and nineteen-year-old Sara. Then, there is the Horton family: David Horton; his wife, Paula; and their nineteen-year-old son, Cameron. I advise you not to ask them what they did to move up. I have shown no favoritism toward them. They worked hard, and they deserve to move on. If I hear they have been pestered, then the person disobeying me might be placed behind bars."

She takes another sip of water and clears her throat.

"Remember, if your family is chosen to go but you no longer reside with them because you have moved out on your own or have married, you cannot move on to the next territory with them. Only those still in the home can go."

Finally, something different is added to the announcements. It isn't sad news but something pleasant I can sink my teeth into. Finally, I can believe I might make it out of this wasteland and move on. I look at the blonde-haired woman who seems to have a glisten in her eye as well.

"Now on to another piece of good news," she says, shifting her weight. "There will be a banquet held to honor the last eighteen-year-old in our Territory—Emma Whisperer."

Her voice seems to get louder.

"Emma is the daughter of Jim and Joan Whisperer."

My eyes bulge at the mention of my name, and my face feels hot. Why should I be honored just because I'm the last one born, who was able to escape this nonsense? My knees shake, and I put my hand on them to keep them steady. The blonde woman smiles at me. I've never seen her before today, but maybe she knows who I am.

"In conclusion, I must add that not everyone will be attending this event. We have eighty thousand people in our Territory, and all cannot fit into the banquet room at my mansion. The event is scheduled for two weeks from Saturday, and those who shall attend will receive letters in the mail. I trust you all understand everything that was announced here. And now, I shall say to you goodnight."

She walks away from the podium, and the silver box immediately turns off.

The patrolman releases us from the store. I walk home with my heart bouncing in my chest. It is unfair that I'm the last eighteen-year-old in our Territory. I would rather not take part in a celebration for that cause.

*

I take in a deep breath before walking into my family's house. Our brick home is around a thousand square feet. My father says since it is on the smaller side, it takes a lot less money to heat and cool. The back of the house is like a forest, and the front of the house is on a dirt road with lots of gravel. As soon as I reach the front door, I notice the stench of beans lingering in the air, making the room smell as if a skunk has run through it.

"You're late," my brother, Theodore, says. "You know dinner is at six."

He shoves my arm. He has on dark clothing that mirrors my own.

"Whatever," I say, rolling my eyes. Another stupid rule. "It's almost eight." I glance at the brown clock on the wall. "Shouldn't you be done?"

"We had to stop what we were doing and watch the box," he says, then he gulps down a bottle of water.

His Adam's apple moves in and out, while the bottle crinkles in his hand.

"Yes, the announcements came early." My father rises from the dining room table. "I'm sure you heard them."

He walks to the living room where I am.

"I did." I lower my eyes.

"Where were you?" Mother asks. "We were worried."

"I know, and I'm sorry, but I'm fine. I watched the announcements from the supply store."

I know they worry about me, but I also know they won't ask how I ended up at the supply store, or ask why my jeans are dirty. There is a more pressing question they want to ask.

"Did you see her?" my mother asks.

"Yes," I reply.

Now that is what they really care about.

"How was she?"

"I guess as good as she can be." I shrug.

"What does that mean?" my mother asks with a frown. "You're not giving me any details."

I sigh. It was the same questions every time I go to the wooded area. Another sigh follows because my heart saddens, seeing how old my mother looks. She is only in her fifties, but I can see the gray strands in her dark hair instantly becoming grayer every time we discuss this. Even when I bring back food, my mother is too tense to eat. Day by day she is growing thinner.

"Emma, answer your mother," my father says, looking at me with slanted eyes.

"If you want to know how she is, why don't you go and see her yourself?" I snap back. I'm tired of the theatrics. But it was a stupid question. I know why they can't go. They aren't strong enough or fast enough.

"You know your mother moves too slowly. She would never make it there," my father says, echoing the very words in my head.

All of a sudden, my heart aches for snapping at them. They're wonderful parents, always have been. My father looks older than my mother. A man in his fifties shouldn't look like he is in his sixties, but my father does. Unlike my mother's gray strands, he has a full head of gray hair. And like my mother, his gray eyes are dim and no life shows in them. He is also thinning because he doesn't eat. He saves his food for hard times, so he can give it to me or my siblings. He often acts as if he is eating, but I'm aware of his hiding place. I see him eat scraps and save what won't expire in his special hiding place.

"Emma Whisperer," he says, using my whole name.

I'm fully aware of what that means. He is upset. He thinks I'm ignoring him and my mother, but I'm not. I'm in deep thought, like always.

"Are you listening to me?" He steps closer to me.

"Sorry, Father," I manage to say. My eyes widen. I know he means business, and I need to listen. "I realize Mother can't make the trip. Please forgive my rudeness."

"Apology accepted," he says, while taking the small brown plastic bag of groceries out of my backpack.

Mother asked me to pick up a few items she had forgotten earlier. I put the groceries in my backpack to keep them more secure. It used to be hard for me to run with the backpack; but my strength and endurance have gotten better, so it is a little easier to run with even heavy objects now.

"Now sit down so we can finish what is left of dinner."

"Yes, sir." I lower my eyes and walk toward him.

"What shall we discuss tonight?" my father asks.

He asks the same question every night at dinner. He still has on his gray lab coat from work.

I look through him at the dark dining room walls.

"I had a productive day," my mother says with sad eyes.

Her day really wasn't productive, but she wants everyone to think it was. Her brown, bleak dress matches her demeanor.

My mother used to be a teacher, until two months ago, when school let out. Now they have no use for her talents. There are no more kids in Territory L to go to school. My class was the last to graduate in our territory, ever. There were other eighteen–year–olds in my class, but they were all born months, weeks, or even days ahead of me. I was the last baby born in the year 2080. Or, should I say, the last one allowed to live. Every baby born after me, in this territory, was killed by President Esther.

My brain checks back in on the conversation. My mother is still going on about her day.

"I was able to pick up some fruit from the market. The apples and pears were fresh. We can have them for dessert on Sunday, along with the whipped cream Emma picked up." She puts on a fake smile. "They don't always have it, since it is only for special occasions.

Thanks for going back to the store to get it. I forgot it when I was there earlier. I hope you didn't have a hard time finding it."

"It is fine, Mother," I say, softly.

Sundays are special in Territory L. It is the day families are supposed to stay in and enjoy each other's company. The day we get to eat chicken or fish, instead of beans and soup. It is the day we play old board games and read old books. Pears and apples are what my mother considers dessert. Maybe this Sunday will be even more special because we're going to have whipped cream on our fruit. We never had it before. I guess whipped cream will make it look more desirable. So, while Territory U has pie and cake, we'll have fruit with whipped cream topping.

"Is there any more milk?" Theodore asks.

"I had your sister pick some up on her way back."

"Yes, T," I say, chiming in. I always call him T, for short. "There is a fresh carton in the fridge. Try not to drink it all. It has to last for at least the next week."

I watch as he narrows his eyes in my direction, then he stands with his glass in hand and goes to the kitchen. He is such a child, sometimes I can't even tell he is nineteen.

"So, how was your day, Emma?" My father turns to me. He just put a spoonful of beans in his mouth. He clears his throat and continues. "I mean, before you ran that errand."

Every time someone talks about the errand, I cringe. It is as if a knife has been put through my stomach because we have such a hard time even saying what the errand is. And the whole thing leaves a sour taste in my mouth. I try to forget about the errand, for now, and dwell on his question—how my day was.

"If you're asking me if I found a job yet, I haven't." I take a sip of water. "There is not much to do around here."

"There is, if you want to be cashier at the market or a salesperson at the clothing store."

"Those aren't real jobs. Sorry," I add, glancing over at him.

He has always said it didn't matter what the job is because any job, even if it isn't glamorous, should be respected. Judging by the slant in his eyebrows that makes the lines in his forehead crease, he didn't take kindly to what I just said.

"What I meant to say," I continue, "is I want to go to college and be a doctor like you, Dad, or a teacher like Mom was. It is not fair—"

"We can't keep having this discussion every night," Mother cuts in, her voice curt. "I know it is disappointing that there are no colleges and no continued education for you. And I also know you don't want any of the jobs the territory has to offer—"

"But that is the way it is, and you have to deal with it," says Father, cutting her off.

"I'm not hungry anymore." I push my plate aside.

I know it is foolish because around here you don't always know where your next meal is coming from, but I can't stomach the same conversation along with the same dry food every night.

"May I be excused?" I lower my head.

"Yes, Emma. You may." My mother's tone is soft. "And Em, things will get better," she says with sad eyes.

She always says that. I think, more for herself than for me. But things never get better. They always stay the same, or get worse.

I walk past the dark living room. We're only allowed one lamp per room—president's rules. I frown at our old, ratty, brown sofa and the two black chairs. One of the chairs is wobbly because one leg is shorter than the other. I guess I should be grateful for what we have; some people don't have any furniture at all.

I make my way to the steps and walk past the five framed pictures hanging on the wall. There is a picture of my father, Jim, when he was young and had sandy hair and bright gray eyes. The next picture is of my mother, Joan, when she was younger. Her hazel eyes were so much more vibrant, her dark hair was so much longer. My brother, Theodore, is nineteen in his picture. He takes after my dad with his sandy hair—although his eyes are brown. My older sister,

Taylor, is twenty. She also resembles my dad with her sandy brown hair. She is so beautiful. Why can't I look more like her?

I continue up the stairs, past my framed picture, stomping the rest of the way. I don't look like anyone in my family, except for my mother. I take after her. My hair is dark and thick like hers used to be. When I was little, she would come in my room and comb my hair and tell me how lucky I was to have hair like I did. But I don't agree. It is so thick and hard for me to comb. My nose is button shaped with a slight widening. And my hazel eyes look big. I'm not exactly a beauty queen like my sister, but I guess I'm all right.

I frown as my door thumps hard behind me. I throw my backpack to the hardwood floor with a *thud*. I plop down on the brown covers on my bed and stare at the dark walls. I know I'm acting like a child, but this is not how I thought my life would turn out. I love my family, but sometimes I feel if I don't get away from them, my head will explode.

Yes, my dad is light-skin and my mom is dark-skin. But out of all of my siblings, I am the only one they call mixed. Maybe that is because I'm not as dark as my mother and not as light as my father, so I'm the only one who looks different. I try not to let it bother me; yet sometimes, I feel like I don't fit in. What bothers me more than that is how my family has no backbone. They bow to all the insane rules that take place here.

Our world used to be one united land. Now, it consists of three Territories. We are in Territory L, which means we're considered lower class.

CHAPTER THREE

I WEAR MY LONG gray knit dress today—the one that falls to my knees—along with my black flats. Since it is a bit nippy outside, I put on my short black jacket with it. I've been wearing my gray dress that lands above the knees the last few weeks, and so far I have not found a job. My mother thought a longer dress would be more appropriate; in her mind, a longer dress means I'll find a job.

I pull my jacket closer because the wind is strong. It roars like a lion as it blows over me, and it rips right through my bones. The sky is gray. It looks like rain—then again, it always looks like rain here. I haven't seen the sun shine in weeks. I know it sounds silly, but I often think President Esther made a deal with Mother Nature to never let the sun shine here again. I understand we're poor, but she likes us to look the part by making us wear drab, dark colors. We're only allowed to wear grays, blacks, browns, and dark blues. She says darker colors keep us in a somber mood, so we can remember our place. We can never wear bright, shiny colors, such as whites, reds, oranges, pinks, greens or even light blues. It is not allowed here, and it makes me wince. If we are caught wearing bright colors, we could be locked up for thirty days, or more.

I stumble over a rock on the ground, making me realize where I am. I've already walked down four blocks, past many houses. I notice that my once black shoes have mud on them.

My chest aches, not from the cold, but from the thought that we're poor. I can't understand how my father makes so little money when he is a doctor. I've been told that he makes under $10,000 a year, while most doctors make over $100,000 or more. Most of the people here with jobs make under $10,000 a year, which has to cover food, clothing, housing, taxes and general living expenses. Every time I inquire why he makes so little, I'm met with sad faces and despondent eyes, so I stop asking. Mother says I should be grateful that we have a home—any home at all—and I am. But I have so many unanswered questions about our world that my inquisitiveness comes off as being ungrateful.

I smell bread baking, which means I've made it down to the marketplace. We don't have cars here. There are a few buses that go downtown, where the main hospital is, near the president's mansion. We mostly walk wherever we need to go, so it is nice that everything is centrally located. The territory is around thirty-six square miles—thirty-five point eighty-six miles, to be exact. We learned that in school. I've heard that the other territories are allowed cars and subways. Cars used to be allowed here, before the territorial division. I have even heard rumors that the other territories have a monorail; but those are rumors, so you can't put any weight in them being true.

President Esther has a car. It is long and black. I remember being seven years old, and it pulled up to our house. But I was rushed into my room; and once I was let back out, it was gone. My siblings and I were never to ask questions about why she came.

Esther allows vehicles to bring deliveries into our territory, and to also bring in the specialists that help out at the hospital. But commoners aren't allowed any type of vehicles at all.

If I'm going to look for a job today, I should look presentable. The shops don't have any bathrooms; instead, they locate them outside for the workers or the customers. I walk to the edge of the marketplace, where there are separate bathrooms for women and men.

The bathroom is tiny and dim like the rest of our world. It

smells of perfume mixed with cleaning products. I pinch my nose before my eyes water. Red eyes will hinder my chances of getting a job.

The water is cool to the touch. I would dab some on my lips, but the water supply was mysteriously contaminated with some kind of toxic chemical. I'm not sure what kind of toxins because the president won't share that with us, but I think President Esther and her underlings contaminated it so we would be dependent on her for bottled water. She likes to appear like she is helping us, while all the while she is the one who causes the problem. I grab a towel from the dispenser to soak it. After I clean my shoes, I walk back outside and look around.

I don't want to work at the furniture shop, or any of the clothing stores. If I continue several miles down the road, I will reach the farmhouses where half the people here work. My heart sinks; I don't want to work there, either. I should walk to the medical facility and fill out an application. But, I'm fooling myself. The only jobs there are for non-urgent matters. There, you can only pick up medicine or get a cough looked at and, of course, get your free contraceptives, which I have no use for since I have no experience with boys. I want to work at a real hospital, where I can really help people.

I take my ID card out of my pocket and stare at it for a moment. It is flat, hard, and made of cheap plastic. The front of the card has my name, date of birth, and eye color on it. The back of the card has my picture on it so, if needed, I can prove who I am. You're to carry it at all times. If you lose it, you can get another one at the information office; but it will cost ten dollars. Most of our drab clothing is lined with pockets, so I keep my ID card in there.

I can't put it off any longer—this is my fate. I turn to head into the market, but I notice my brother T across the street at the pawn shop. He no longer has on the gray slacks and shirt he left the house in. He is dressed from head to toe in all black, including black boots. If I didn't know any better, I would say he was one of President Esther's guards or patrolmen. If it wasn't for the missing silver, circular buttons on his black jacket, he could pass for a guard. The missing emblems lead me to believe he may be a patrolman because they wear no buttons at all.

"Theodore," I shout, using his whole name. I want to get his attention before he disappears into the shop.

His eyes expand and he looks hesitant to come near me. After a few moments, his mouth creases—as if he is frowning—and he walks forward.

"What are you doing here?" he immediately asks, with the wicked frown still on his face.

He is acting as if I'm in the wrong, instead of the complete opposite.

"I'm looking for a job, like I told Father I would."

"If you had started looking for a job two weeks ago, like you told Father, you would have already looked here and moved on to the farming areas by now." His two eyebrows slant into one.

"Maybe I started in the farming areas and moved to the market-place after." My chest tightens knowing I hadn't.

"That makes no sense. You hate all of these jobs, especially the farming." The one eyebrow remains together. "So, if you expect me to believe you started there, I don't. I'm not sure what you've been doing, but I know you haven't been looking for work."

"You think you're so smart." My face feels hot because he is right. "Fine." My shoulders slouch. "I haven't been looking for work. It depresses me knowing this is what my life will become."

"You think you're better than everyone else."

"That is a lie and you know it."

"Emma, people here work hard for less than little money. Do you think they don't want better for themselves? Of course they do. But this is the hand we all have been dealt, and we have to live with it."

Now, he sounds like my father. He grabs my elbow and, like a child, he walks me over to an out-of-the-way spot behind the market, where no one can hear us.

"I don't think I'm better than anyone else. You should know

that." I hate that my eyes are watering. "I know what is right. And, I know what I want. This isn't it. I want to move to Territory M, so I can go to college, like Sara and her sister, Leslie. The president mentioned in her speech that they were approved to go. I want to be a *real* doctor, so I can help people." I bite down on my lip. "Then, maybe move on to Territory U, and have a nice life there," I say.

"You're dreaming. Our family will never move on to those territories."

"Why?" I punch him lightly in his arm, like when we were little and I wanted information out of him. "How do you know so much?"

"Never mind." He turns away. "Forget I said anything."

My throat tightens. Maybe he knows something and is keeping it from me. It doesn't matter now, anyway, because he's shut down, like when we were kids. He is not going to tell me anything. Maybe he doesn't know anything. Maybe this is a way to get suspicion off him, and why he is wearing all black and going into the pawn shop.

"Instead of talking about me and my many faults, why don't you tell me why you're dressed like that?" I can feel my pressure rising, like a cannon, I'm about to explode.

He turns to face me with wide eyes.

"Your clothing suggests you're working for the president," I continue.

His brown eyes stare at me, but he remains quiet. After a few moments, he opens his mouth to speak.

"I might as well tell you." He shrugs. "You're going to find out, eventually. The reason Mom and Dad don't want me going out to take supplies to Taylor is because I can't get hurt."

"I already know that."

"If you would shut up and let me finish," he says, with a growl to his voice.

"Sorry."

I always had a problem with talking too much. I try to keep it under control, but at times like this, it doesn't always work.

"Like I was saying," he continues. "I can't get hurt because I'm in training to be one of the president's guards." His voice is low like he is embarrassed. "If I tripped or fell and broke something, or if the patrolmen saw me going in and out of that house, it would be the end of my new career."

I'm wrong. He is not embarrassed. He is stupid, if he can call working for her a career. His voice is probably low so no one will notice he is talking to me.

"I thought she said she had enough men on her roster already." I step closer to him as if I'm in the middle of an inquisition. "I also thought she didn't want anyone under twenty-one working for her. She always says the young can't be trusted. What happened to that?"

"I don't understand it, either. But I got a letter in the mail, after I graduated, saying she didn't need any more patrolmen, but was hiring a few more guards. And it said she would like me to join her team. I was eighteen at the time, and there was another guy that was nineteen. We are the youngest of the guards. He just completed his internship but I'm still in training."

"How long does this training last?"

"It depends on how long it takes for me to learn everything. Once I'm officially one of them, they add silver buttons to my jacket."

"So, that is why you can't get hurt, because you have to work for the great one." I roll my eyes. "And that is why you've been getting so buff."

His arms are bigger than usual.

"You've been in training." I frown. "So, every day you leave the house with gray on and change to this black ensemble." I move my hand up and down. "Who else know about this?"

My chest squeezes. Maybe I don't want to know. Maybe I won't like the answer.

"Mom and Dad, of course," he says, then pauses. "And Taylor."

"Taylor is in hiding and even she knows." It feels like I've been kicked in the stomach by an angry goat. "I don't understand why no one told me about this."

"Because we all know how you are."

"What does that mean?" My chest tenses even more.

"Emma, you're different. You don't like to follow rules, and we knew you wouldn't understand."

"Is there anything wrong with not following rules if they're insane rules?"

"See, that is exactly what I mean. Sometimes, you just have to go with the flow, so there'll be peace. All our family wants to do is live in peace and make it here. But if it was up to you, we would break down every door because you have to stand up for what you believe is right. That is why we didn't tell you. We knew you would act like this."

"I can't always keep quiet for the sake of peace."

"Well, this time you will." His tone is rough, and his eyes peer right through me. "This is a good job. It pays better than most jobs in this territory. Once I'm fully trained, I will move into the mansion. Then, I'll be able to send money back to the family."

"I hear only her top twenty guards live in the mansion." My jaw tightens. "The other eighty live in their own homes and report in for duty. If you plan on living in the mansion, you must think you're something special."

"I have to get back now." He nervously glances behind him. "I've been gone too long." He walks away. "Em." He turns back around. "I hope you find a job today."

"Thank you," I reply, not knowing what else to say.

I can't believe he is acting as if being one of the president's henchmen is a normal thing. I can't believe the secrets going on in my family, the secrets that everyone believes is best I stay out of.

*

The next morning, I rise early enough so that I can follow T. I want to see where he goes and what he is doing. I wear the same gray dress and the same flat shoes as the day before. Sometimes, I can go two or three days wearing the same outfit, as long as it is not dirty or smelly. I put my hair in a ponytail. I don't want the thick strands to distract me. I follow T down the dirt and gravel road. I try to stay several feet back, so he won't see me if he turns around. I step on a tree branch, and I hear crackling beneath my feet; but he doesn't turn around. He keeps forging ahead, and I keep following.

I follow him down the road to a green, patchy area that is about two miles before you reach the marketplace. He stands there as if he is waiting for someone, or something, to arrive. I feel a cool breeze and hear thumping sounds. One of Esther's helicopters is near. My eyes peer up as a helicopter lands in the green, patchy area. To my surprise, he doesn't get in. I see him talking to someone, and then, like an out-of-control speedboat, the helicopter flies away.

T continues down the road to the marketplace; he is probably on his way back to the pawn shop. I continue following; but the air is thick today, and I start to cough. I see him turn around, and I run behind a nearby tree. Those trips to see my sister have taught me how to run fast. He doesn't catch me—I hope.

Once he reaches the pawn shop, he goes inside. I crouch down below the store window and then peer inside. I smell cigarette smoke, and I can see one of the guards smoking. There are two guards—they look to be in their thirties—inside with my brother. The guards are dressed in all black with silver buttons on their jackets. They wear holsters around their waists with guns in them. And, they carry small radios. I hear them, egging my brother on to do something.

"This is part of your training," the tall one with piercing black eyes and sandy hair says.

"If you can't do a simple task like this, how do you expect to handle something harder, like killing a newborn?" the shorter, huskier one with brown eyes and brown hair says.

My heart races, and I gasp, quietly. How can my parents let my brother be a part of something like this? The storeowner, Mr. Thompson, walks out from the back. He is in his early seventies. His thin frame and bald head show he isn't a threat to anyone. Most shops have been taken over by the president. He is one of the rare few who still possess his own store.

"I'm sorry, this is all I can give you." His voice is shaky.

He opens his trembling hands and a few green bills show. They crinkle as he unfolds them, but by the look on their faces they're not satisfied with what he has produced.

"Look old man," the tall ones says. "Yesterday, you said you would have the full payment. Now, I think you were just messing with us."

"He is right," the short one chimes in. "When you took out this loan from President Esther to save your store, you were supposed to pay her back within a year's time. Well the year is up, and I think she has been reasonable with her demands. The youngster here," he says turning to my brother, "is going to show you a little of what you'll get next week, if you don't have the rest."

They both turn to T, who looks nervous. He is shaking and I can tell he doesn't like what he has to do next.

"Go on, kid," the tall one speaks again. "Show him your training." He pushes T in the back, so he is closer to Mr. Thompson.

My brother bites down on his lip and steps closer to Mr. Thompson. T balls up his fist and punches him in his jaw. Red blood spatters from Mr. Thompson's lips and drips down his mouth. I flinch.

We have known Mr. Thompson all of our lives. Mr. Thompson could just raise his prices to pay off his loan, but I know he won't because he knows the townspeople have little money to pay him.

How can T do something like this? He is like a different person, like someone I don't know.

Mr. Thompson stumbles back into the counter and tries to catch his breath. He holds up his hands and begs them not to hurt him anymore.

I can't stomach anymore, so I quietly crouch down lower on my knees until I clear the window, and then I stand and walk away. As my walk turns into a run, I hear T call my name.

"So, you saw all of that, did you?"

I turn to find him rubbing the knuckles on his punching hand. The skin appears raw and red. I stand there, silently. My stomach feels queasy, as if I have eaten a rotten egg.

"The next time you spy on someone, you need to be more careful." He steps closer. "I saw the top of your head through the window. Good thing the other guys didn't see you. No telling what they would have done."

I am still quiet.

"Please, don't look at me like that." His eyes soften. "I was only doing what I had to."

"Won't they come looking for you?" I ask.

I want the conversation to end, so I can run home and pretend I haven't seen what I did.

"No." He shakes his head. "They told me to leave and come back tomorrow. They're mad because I hesitated back there. Hesitation shows weakness. They don't like either."

He comes up beside me. His eyes look sad, and I suddenly feel sorry for him. Before I can speak, I hear laughing coming from the marketplace. I see two girls. Maybe I shouldn't call them girls. They are older than me, but President Esther doesn't consider us grown until we reach twenty-one. I turn my attention back to the high-pitched sounds.

One girl is Lily. She is laughing with another girl. Lily is beautiful with her long, red hair and green eyes. She went to the same school T and I did; but she is T's age, not mine. Back when the school was open, the boys and girls were in separate classrooms. By the way he'd stare at her in the hallways, I always thought T felt something for her. By the way he looks at her now, I think he still does.

"There is Lily," I announce, as if he doesn't see her.

"I have eyes." He scratches the back of his neck.

"You like her, don't you?" I ask, grinning as if I'm twelve.

"It doesn't matter if I do or if I don't, it is not like we can ever be together."

"Why can't you be with her?" I ask, with annoyance in my voice. "We may not be allowed to have kids, but we can still get married."

"Yes, but what is the point of getting married, if we can't have kids to carry on our legacy?" He puts his hands in his pockets, then takes them back out. "Getting married means having a family. To me, there is no family without children."

"That's not true."

"That's the way I see it. So, I would rather stay single and date with no strings attached. I mean, I've been on a few dates, here and there—"

"I've never seen you with anyone," I say, cutting him off. "Even so, I can tell you really like Lily."

"Look," he says, in a rough tone. "I've heard she wants to get married, so she is not for me." He shrugs. "We're not compatible, but there will be others. It's not that big a deal."

My brother's vulnerability is showing, and my heart aches for him. It aches for our whole territory, and our way of life. Why do things have to be so terrible here because of one horrid woman?

We turn and walk home in silence since neither of us knows what else to say.

CHAPTER FOUR

"So what are we doing here?" I ask my mother.

We're standing in front of the women's clothing shop. Only a few days ago, I saw T across the street, beating up Mr. Thompson. I haven't spoken a word about it since, to him or anyone, and I don't know how to bring up the subject to my mother now.

"I told you we're shopping."

My mother's smile is brighter than usual. Her brown lipstick glistens on her lips. And, she looks happier than I've seen her in a long time. She doesn't even seem out of breath from the three mile walk we endured.

"What are you up to?" I ask, raising my eyebrow.

"What makes you think I'm up to something?" she says, with a small giggle behind her voice.

She is acting like a schoolgirl, and the hairs on the back of my neck stand.

"When you said we were going shopping, I naturally assumed you meant to the market for groceries. So, why are we in front of the clothing store?"

My mom's smile is still wide. Her worry lines have disappeared. She wears a black polyester dress with black heels and a light brown jacket. She looks like she did when she would go off to teach at the school. She had never been one of my teachers, that was frowned upon, but that is who she reminds me of.

A strong gust of wind flows through, and my hair gets caught in my eyelashes. She steps forward and brushes it back.

"If you must know, young lady, we're here to purchase a new dress for you."

"Mother, we can't afford that. Besides, why would I need a new dress? It is not like I ever go anywhere."

"Have you forgotten what President Esther said in her speech?"

President Esther says a lot of things, so I tend to not listen to everything that comes out of her mouth. But I dare not say that aloud.

"Have you forgotten about your big day?"

"I don't want to do this." I shake my head. "I think the whole thing is stupid. Why would anyone want to celebrate me being the last eighteen-year-old in the territory?"

"It may not be a big deal to you, but it is to others."

"The point is we shouldn't be celebrating this day," I say. "We should be horrified that no more children can be born. And the ones who are, will not make it to see their eighteenth birthdays."

I can tell I've said too much because my mother's face saddens, and her whole demeanor changes.

"I understand how you feel." She lowers her head. "I thought this could be something we could do together. We haven't spent much time together lately, doing fun things."

That is because there is nothing fun around here to do. But, of course, I don't dare say that aloud either. I hate the way my family goes around oblivious to the way we live. I know it is an act, and probably the only way they can make it through the day. Still, I don't like it.

Since Mother lost her job, and since all the trouble with Taylor started, this is the happiest I've seen her. I can't take this away from her, so I smile. I act interested, like a kid in a candy store—if we had those here.

"You're right, Mother. Maybe I will get a new dress."

"That's my girl," she says, with a smile, as though I'm five years old.

We walk into the clothing store and everything looks depressing. To the left is a rack of gray and black dresses. To the right is a rack of brown and beige dresses. If you go farther back into the store you reach the slacks and shirts and shoes. Everything is bland. Even the air is stale, like old bread in a freezer.

"Where should we begin?" I ask, with a half-smile.

"The clothes we want are in back." My mother's eyes squint.

Her face looks devious. I watch her walk over to the blonde salesperson. The thin salesclerk walks us to the back of the store, to an area I never knew existed. She takes a key out of a small gray pouch. It clanks as she dangles it and puts it into the keyhole of a door. It looks like we're going into a storage room, but I'm wrong.

I see an array of colors that I have only seen in books. I see reds and greens and light blues. There are red dresses the color of a cardinal's body. And light blue dresses the color the sky should be if it wasn't always so cloudy and dim here. The greens are so vibrant they remind me of fresh-cut grass. My heart beats loudly. I must be dreaming. Even the air is different—it is light like roses.

Where are we? How does my mild-mannered mother know about this place?

"I'll leave you two alone," the salesclerk says. "Let me know if you need anything," she adds.

My mouth drops. Before I can speak, my mother does.

"I know you have a lot of questions. This is an area only few are invited to," she says, "because President Esther has to invite you."

"But how? Why?" My face feels flush.

"Let's not worry about that right now." My mother's eyes are sincere, as she gently rubs my hand. "Let's have a wonderful afternoon picking out your dress for the party. I'll tell you what I can later. You're being honored, so you should have a special dress."

I try on a few red dresses. But they aren't simple dresses; they're more like elaborate gowns with ruffles that flow all the way to the floor. They're beautiful, and I tremble as the fabric touches my skin. I don't feel worthy to wear them. I can tell by my mother's face, she picks up on my hesitation.

"I see you don't care for the red dresses. Why don't you try one of the light blue ones?" She walks to a nearby rack. "This long one with the bow on the side is beautiful." She holds it to my waist.

I stare into the long, silver mirror in front of me. A slow ache is in the pit of my stomach—it always is when I look at myself. My mother holds the dress up to my neck. I frown, because I'd rather not try it on. It is beautiful, but it is not me; maybe none of them are. I have always wanted nice things, and nice clothes filled with bright colors; but now that they're before me, my stomach feels unsettled.

"Emma, what's wrong?" my mother asks.

The worry lines that had left her face have reappeared.

"I don't think the light blue goes well with my skin tone. I look drab."

"Honey, nothing makes you look drab." She rubs my shoulder. "Now what is really going on?"

"Nothing goes with my skin color." I shake my head, and my eyes water. "My skin is olive, and sometimes I don't know where I fit in." I shrug.

"You've never mentioned this to me before."

"I felt like I could handle it. Besides, it's not important when there are so many other things to worry about."

"I wish you wouldn't feel like you have to take on everything. Your father and I are here for you." She continues to rub my shoulder. "We don't like the laws either. We know it is hard to follow them."

"Do you, Mother?" I feel my pressure rising. "Is that why you allowed T to take a job as a guard?" My voice rises.

I know she wants a day filled with bonding and happiness. But all my pent up energy is getting to me. A hurt look crosses her face.

"Sorry, Mother." I glance down. "Let's keep searching. I'm sure I'll find one we both like."

We are both silent as we continue looking. The salesclerk walks back in and shows me a long, gold gown. It has a mermaid silhouette, along with tank straps, and a fitted bodice that gathers at the waist. The fitted bodice is covered in gold sequins.

"It goes beautifully with your skin tone," my mother says. "You should be proud of the way it looks on you."

The heaviness on my chest lessens. I like the way I feel in it, too. We purchase a pair of gold shoes with two-inch, stacked heels, and a small, black velvet purse. I've never owned a purse before. Except for my ID card, I don't know what else to put in it.

I'm sure it costs more money than my family makes in a lifetime. Mother told me not to worry. President Esther is paying for everything. She wants me to look presentable at the party. The whole ordeal makes me cringe, and I don't know what to make of it.

CHAPTER FIVE

"SHE IS GETTING SO big," I say to my sister, Taylor, as my backpack smacks the floor.

I haven't been to see her in a few days.

"I know, it's hard to believe she is six months old." Taylor's eyes sadden. Her brown eyes blend in with her brown shirt and pants.

"I'm sorry it has to be this way." I rub the top of her hand.

My heart sinks as if an anchor is weighing it down. Taylor has been in hiding ever since she was three months pregnant.

We sit on our grandparent's old, brown sofa in the living room of their brick home. Our grandfather died three years ago from a heart attack, and our grandmother died six months after him.

Their house is about a half mile down the road from our family's home. It is only eight hundred square feet. It isn't up near the road where the other houses are. It is farther back, and you have to go through a wooded area to reach it. The wooded area makes the trip seem longer than it really is. Maybe it is because the area isn't kept up. There is mud and dirt and downed branches.

My mother's parents left the house to her after they passed. Father, Theodore, and I boarded up the house. Father wanted to keep the place, in case one of his children ever married; then they could live in it. I guess he doesn't know about T's plan to never marry. Father informed the authorities that he'd still pay the bills—electric and gas, along with the property taxes, and water—so the pipes wouldn't freeze. He told them the house would be empty, most of the time. But now, the house is used as a hideout. Since the house is boarded up it is dark inside. There is no sunlight to bring warmth. On cold nights, Taylor is allowed to turn the heat on low. A high heat bill would look suspicious, as if someone is permanently living here. Since Father pays the bills on both houses now, things are even sparser for all of us.

"Did anyone see you?" Taylor asks.

That question always annoys me, because my family continues to ask it as if I am incompetent. I make this same trip several times a week, so—of course—I know what to look out for. And I am always careful.

The patrolmen normally patrol before dawn and right around dusk, since that is when no one should be traveling on the streets. Everyone has to stay in their homes until morning, when it is time for work. After work you're allowed to go to the market, or shopping, or wherever else you need to go. Once dusk arrives, you should be back in your homes. If you're caught out at the wrong times, you could be thrown in jail.

My father has a more important kind of job. He has to show a work card to the patrolmen if he is out late. The card proves he may be needed at the hospital during unusual hours.

When Taylor first went into hiding, it was decided that I would go straight home after school, pick up food and clean clothes, and get them to Taylor before dusk set in. I would spend as much time with her as I could, and then I would race home before dark. Yes, my family owns the home, but it would look suspicious if I went there a few times a week to check on it if no one is living there. Now that I have no school, I can come earlier—until I find a job.

Abigail starts to cry, and it sounds like a dog howling. The screams of a baby crying is unusual around here. I suddenly realize I never answered my sister's question, but I'm sure she already knows the answer.

"Is she okay?" I stand.

I walk over to the makeshift crib.

My dad chopped my grandparent's old wood bed into small pieces. Then, he enlisted T's help in nailing the wood together to make a crib. I had the job of ripping up my grandparents old bed sheets to make them small enough to line the crib.

Taylor and I were always close. We could tell each other anything. We shared a room growing up. And, when I had trouble sleeping, when I was little, she would tell me stories to help me fall asleep. My parents would ration our food, and she had no problem sneaking food out of the pantry for T and me, after our parents went to sleep, if we told her we were still hungry.

Taylor used to work down at the market. She was a stockperson; but she didn't make much money, so her hope had been to become a cashier. A guy named Nathan would always come in to buy groceries for his mother. They took a liking to each other, and he became her boyfriend. Nathan frequented the store even when he wasn't buying anything, so he could visit Taylor. Her boss didn't appreciate it. Taylor had always been stubborn, and she became even more stubborn once she fell in love. So, Taylor told Nathan he could still come to see her if he wanted to. She never got the promotion to cashier she was hoping for. I think she might have eventually been fired, if she hadn't quit because of the baby.

Once we found out my sister was pregnant, Father said we couldn't let President Esther take away and kill the baby and put my sister in jail for being disobedient to the laws. Nathan's family was accepted into Territory M, so he left her. Father decided to tell people that Taylor had a disease called lupus. She supposedly had fatigue, pain and swelling in her joints, so she had to stay in the house, and was too depressed to have visitors. He is a doctor, so no one questions it. If visitors did drop by, we couldn't let them hear a baby crying, so it was my idea to hide her here.

"Abigail is fine." Taylor picks her up. "She's a little fussy because she's hungry. Did you bring her food?"

"Yes," I say, pointing to my backpack. "I had Mother mix it this time."

Mother urged Taylor to breastfeed because it would save money, and fewer trips to the house would be needed; but Taylor said it was too hard, emotionally and physically. She felt like the baby was attached to her, constantly, night and day. She had a lot of sleepless nights, and she was exhausted. So, while we weren't around, Taylor gave the baby regular milk that was meant for her to drink. The baby got used to it and wouldn't breastfeed anymore. Although my mother was furious, Taylor was fine with it; so my mother had to adapt and make sure the baby had food to eat.

I may not agree with everything Taylor does, but I still love her. I remember when she said she didn't need to stand in line for the free contraceptives because she had no use for them. She wanted to wait until marriage before engaging in sexual conduct. My parents were pleased with her decision—until Abigail was conceived. My sister said she and Nathan were caught up in the heat of the moment and didn't think to use protection. It's funny because they say I'm the one who does things without thinking.

My mother was able to rip some of our old clothes apart and make them into baby clothes for Abigail. The market doesn't supply baby food, so we make our own. Mother mixes together a carrot puree for Abigail. For variety, she takes the carrot puree and mixes it with peas or broccoli. I bought applesauce at the store. It's something a baby can digest without any mixing.

"Would you like to feed her?" Taylor asks.

"Sure," I say, with a narrow smile.

Every time I hold the baby my chest recoils. I'm not used to babies—who here would be? But that is the lie I tell myself. The real reason is that I don't want to get too attached. If anyone finds the baby, and she is taken away and killed, it would break my heart.

I sit on the sofa. The jar of carrots screeches as I open it. The carrots are orange like cheese, and it gives the room a fresh spring smell. Taylor places the baby in my lap, and instantly I fall back in love.

She is precious and chubby, like the babies I see in books. She has on an old gray polyester shirt of mine that my mom sewed into a baby jumper. She has sandy colored hair on the top of her little head, and brown eyes like Taylor. She even has the same birthmark—a light pinkish discoloration that looks like a triangle on the left upper corner of her cheek.

I spoon feed her a mouthful of carrots and she gurgles and smiles back at me. Her brown eyes are so big that my heart expands like a balloon in the sky. She seems happy in this small, dark room. She doesn't know the terror that lurks outside. The spoon slips from my fingers and clanks when it hits the hardwood floors.

My heart jumps when I hear a click as the lamp is turned on.

"Taylor, you know we can't have any lights on," I say. "It has to stay dark in here."

"I know." Her eyes lower. "But I can't see where the spoon fell."

"I don't care," I say, my voice loud. "If anyone notices you're in here, you know what could happen."

My sharp tone makes the baby cry.

Abigail's face grows red like a tomato, and her cries are so loud my skin crawls.

"I'm not an idiot, Emma. I know they could take her away from me." Her voice is rough. "She is my daughter, and I do know how to take care of her. I'm here by myself, without you, most of the time. And it is not a big deal if I turn the light on for five seconds every once in a while."

"It is a big deal to me." I stand and bounce the baby up and down in my arms like a ball to quiet her. "If you turn it on too much it will look like someone is staying here."

I don't mean to be coarse with her; but since she got pregnant, I feel like the older sister. I have to protect her, instead of the other way around.

"I'm sorry," I say, with leaky eyes. "I know you're stuck here, in fear for your lives." I hand her the baby. "You do know if there was any way I could fix this, I would."

"I know. And, I know you sneaking here to bring us supplies is not safe. I do appreciate all you do for us."

"It's okay." I rub her shoulder. "We're both on edge." I see worry lines under her eyes. "I'm sure you're hungry, too. I brought some fresh fruit and vegetables for you. I put them in the fridge. You should eat something."

My grandparent's refrigerator didn't work that well so Father got rid of it. He bought a small 3.2 cubic foot fridge—silver and steel—to put in its place. The new fridge also has a small freezer, big enough for what we need to put in it. I think it is a good idea because it uses less electricity, and it helps with our cover story about the house.

"I will. I need to change her first," she says, laying the baby down on the part of the floor that has blue, scruffy carpet.

I hand her one of the makeshift diapers mother put together for her. It is one of my old cloth t-shirts. She uses old t-shirts and washes them out as she goes along. They are soft and seem to be comfortable for Abigail. The soiled remains are dumped in the toilet. I scrunch up my nose because this is the part I hate. The room stinks like a cat's litter box.

I walk the remains to the bathroom. The toilet roars as it flushes. Once the toilets slows down to a soft hush, I can hear birds chirping outside. It is not faint or even distant. It sounds as if they are sitting on my shoulder, singing in my ear. Air is seeping in past the boarded up window because the nails have come loose. I glance back at the mirror and a small sigh seeps through my lips. My hair is disheveled, and I have an orange smear of baby food on my jacket. But that is not what the sigh is for; the sigh is because this place is rundown and no baby should have to live here.

"Air is coming in from the bathroom window," I say, walking back into the living room.

"I know," Taylor says, now feeding the baby applesauce. "I thought about having you tell Father to come by and fix it, but maybe that is not a good idea after last time." Her eyebrow rises.

"I can bring a hammer, the next time I stop by, and fix it. That way, Father doesn't have to."

The last time he stopped by, he was almost caught. I started coming by every day, once Taylor was almost in labor, and my father stopped by every day, after work. Sometimes, the patrolmen bothered us for no reason, as if it was fun for them to add to our suffering, so they stopped my father. They eventually let him go, but any suspicion gives them grounds to contact the guards and have them check the house.

"How long can we keep doing this?" Taylor's voice breaks my thoughts.

"What do you mean?" I know what she means, but I don't want to discuss it since I can't give her the answers she needs.

"How long can we hide her?" Taylor shifts on the sofa. "I mean, what happens when she is of school age and beyond?"

"Maybe we can make it to Territory M, where children are allowed." I give a half-smile. My throat constricts. I know the words are stupid as soon as they leave my mouth.

"You know only teenagers are accepted into Territory M to attend college. And that is only if their parents are approved to go," she snaps back.

"I know." I plop down next to her and the air from the sofa cushion puffs up in my face. "Maybe we can make it to Territory U. We know people can have babies there."

She knows that is not going to happen, either. But I don't know what to say to make things better.

"Only babies that are born there." Her voice is loud. She puts a spoonful of applesauce in Abigail's mouth. Her cheeks scrunch up and she cries.

I see fear in her eyes. I don't know how she can survive here for the rest of her life. There must be something I can do. But what? I want to curl up in a ball and cry with her. If my parents can't do anything, then neither can I.

"I have to go," I say quietly, while blinking away my tears. "It'll be dark soon." My voice is shaky because I'm lying.

We both know there are several hours of light left; but at this moment, I feel like a failure. I don't know how to help her. And, I feel like a coward. I can't stand to be here anymore. I can no longer look into my sister's sad eyes, or hear the baby's cries. My knees feel weak beneath me.

I kiss my sister's forehead, and then the baby's. Abigail's skin is soft like butter. She yawns, and I see the small creases on her forehead. It reminds me of how much I would miss her, if she wasn't here anymore.

"I'll be back around in a few days," I say.

My sister looks like a deer caught in headlights.

I walk home with a sinking feeling and a knot in my stomach. What if my family is not doing the right thing by hiding them? Maybe we are delaying the inevitable. Many families have gone into hiding because the teenage child or even the adult mother has gotten pregnant. In most cases, they are found out and put in jail, and the baby is never seen again. I always thought since our entire family wasn't in hiding we could get away with it. After all, we're only hiding two people not twenty. But maybe I'm fooling myself, and one day I'll never see them again. A tear nestles on my cheek. Deep down, I know it can happen, and it probably will.

The sky is gray. I hear the pitter-patter of a small, silver kitten go by. Its little, gray-and-white feet make crackling sounds as it steps on some downed branches. It looks well fed; but I can't imagine who could afford to keep a kitten here, when we can barely keep ourselves. It meows, and its green eyes peer up at me as if it wants to play. I shake my head, knowing I don't have time for this today.

*

I'm halfway down the road when I hear meows again. I turn to see the same silver kitten behind me. It is following me down the gravel and dirt road.

"Kitty go home," I whisper.

I wave my hand to shoo it away but it runs up to my leg. Its green eyes stretch open and it is so beautiful that I want to take it home, but I know I can't. I can't afford it, and I know it belongs to someone else. I bend down and pick it up. It feels warm in my arms. Its fur is thick and soft like new carpet, and it purrs at me as if I'm its mother. It is a girl. She does have a collar, but no name tag is attached. I use my fingers to brush through her hair, and the earlier tightness in my chest lightens. If this little kitten can make it here, maybe my family can, too. I shake my head. I can't compare a kitten surviving away from home to baby Abigail who may not survive her fate.

I hear shouting from down the road. My shoulders jerk. I should run the other way, but I can't; I'm too curious about what is going on. I put the kitten down, and instead of walking away, she follows me. My heart races as I move closer to the voices. The tree branches and rocks crackling under my shoes sound louder than normal. The wind blows my hair in my eyes. I'm not quite back to my grandparent's house when I reach the voices. Two of the president's guards are arguing.

I crouch down on some dried up brown grass behind a tree. I chose the tree with the most leaves. It'll hide me better than the others. My heart drops into my stomach while I try to hear what they're saying. I can't help but wonder why they're out here talking during the middle of the day. It is not dusk yet—they're guards, not patrolmen—so they shouldn't be searching the area.

"You need to calm down," the tall one says.

"Why should I?" the short one yells back.

My eyes widen. It looks like the two guards that are training my brother.

"It's not fair that we got stuck training that little punk, Theodore."

I hear a loud *boom* as the short one punches his fist into a nearby tree. It sounds like thunder.

"It's bad enough he's even being trained to be a guard. Why do we get stuck with doing it?"

His face is red. From where I am, his once brown eyes now look black.

"You know, if we don't do this, we'll be demoted to patrolmen," the tall one says, while clenching his fist. "So, pipe down and deal with it."

I heard that patrolmen don't get paid as much as guards do. So, why T would be promoted to guard when he hadn't been a patrolmen yet was something I hadn't thought of until now.

"Maybe if he was strong like the other young recruit, I wouldn't mind so much," the short one continues. "But he is weak, and he doesn't deserve to be here. You know it like I do."

"He is only here because of who his parents are to the president," the tall one says. "So be patient and, in time, he will sabotage himself." He scratches the back of his neck. "If he can't handle himself, he will eventually go running home to Mommy and Daddy."

My stomach feels queasy. Instead of hiding behind the tree, I use it to lean on for support. I hear the sounds of gentle purring again. I look down and see the cat is still by my side. It may sound silly, but I welcome her presence.

I hear rustling. I stop listening to the two guards. My eyes stretch open. There is a brown, beady-eyed squirrel climbing down from the tree I'm leaning on. I'm not the only one who has observed the squirrel; the kitty's eyes turn glassy. She arches her back, and stiffens her tail and legs. Her purrs turn into hisses. The two species sound like a pet store at feeding time as they surround each other. I need them to quiet down before the two guards hear them and come to where I am hiding.

A while back, some of the townspeople tried to kill wild animals for food. It is against the laws, and if you're caught you can spend thirty days, or more, in jail. We can only have the food that is supplied to us at the marketplace. But I've heard that the patrolmen kill all animals on the loose, like it is a sport. My heart races. I panic and grab the cat by the collar. She doesn't like that. Her face squints and she hisses louder.

"What was that?" one of the guards asks.

"I don't know," the other one responds.

My body is still, and my feet are numb, as I continue to crouch behind the tree. What will happen if they see me? It is not a crime to be out this time of day. But they'll know I was spying on their conversation. If they know who my brother's family is, then they'll know who I am. I can hear their boots crunching on the grass and dirt. I know they're getting closer.

One of the voices gets louder. "I think it came from over here."

My hand shakes as I grab the squirrel's tail to quiet it. My hope is if I can get the squirrel under control, the kitten will follow as well. But that is a mistake. Grabbing it only aggravates it more. It takes off in the direction of the guards. The kitten follows. When I hear gunfire as loud as a cannon going off, my shoulders flinch.

"Stupid squirrel," the tall one says. "That's what was making all the noise."

I peer around the tree to see what's going on. They are still about fifty feet away from me. My throat tenses. I see the squirrel, lying dead on the cold ground, with blood as red as a ladybug's body coming from its head.

"And look what is following it," the short one says, picking up the kitten by her tail. "A stupid cat. What do you think we should do with it?" he asks.

Their attention is on the kitten now, and I know this is my chance to get away. My stomach recoils as if I'm an eyewitness to a robbery. Instead of helping the victim, I decide to run away. But I know this is my only chance to escape. If I don't go now, I might not be able to later. I crawl, slowly, over the dried and dead leaves.

Once I think I'm clear of where they are, I stand. I sprint as fast as I can, but it doesn't stop me from hearing the loud blast. The blast is like a bomb exploding; it means the poor innocent kitty is dead.

My lungs feel like fire, and I can't breathe. I run faster and faster while a haze gathers over my eyes. I stumble over a rock, I balance myself and then I continue running. I reach my house, but I can't go inside. Instead, I go to the back shed. Since we don't have cars, this is where my father keeps his tools.

I can't face my parents right now, so I hide in there. I lie on the cold, hard cement floor curled up like a ball. I cry until my eyes are raw and burning. I'm sure they're red like my mother's brightest lipstick—she is allowed to buy it for the president's party. It feels like a dagger has gone through my heart because I couldn't save the kitty, just like I can't save my sister or the baby. My parents knew T had joined the guards, and they were acquaintances of President Esther's.

I notice no more light seeps under the shed door. Through the small tattered window, I see it getting dimmer; but I don't care. I need to let out a few more tears, and then I'll pull myself together and go in the house. It'll be dark soon, and my parents will worry if they think I'm still visiting Taylor without a work card when patrol starts.

CHAPTER SIX

I walk into my room. My mother is sitting on my bed in her black bathrobe. She is ready to fix my hair. I sit down in the chair in front of my dresser mirror. It reminds me of when I was seven, and my mom did my hair before school. It is hard to believe it's Saturday. An entire week has gone by since the cat incident. Every time I walk through the woods to visit my sister now, I think about it and get a cold chill.

She walks over to me with a thick, black plastic comb. It swooshes as she shifts through the strands.

"Your hair is beautiful," she says, breaking the silence. "It is like mine was, when I was young, before it thinned out."

"Your hair is still pretty, Mother." I give a small smile as I look at her through the reflection in the mirror.

Even though there are wrinkles under her hazel eyes and gray in her thin hair, she is still beautiful. It is quiet again, and I watch as she continues to comb my hair. She braids part of my hair, and puts it in an upsweep, while letting the rest hang down in back. There are a few strands, hanging down on both sides of my face, near my ears. I think it is pretty, but I don't look like myself. I look like someone I don't know, and my face drops.

"I know you look at us as weak." My mom walks over to my bed. "Here, come sit beside me." She pats the covers.

"Mother," I say. She is so happy about this party, and I don't want her eyes to sadden again.

"No," she says, shaking her head. "Sit and let me finish."

I plop down next to her and the covers bunch beneath me.

"It is not that we are weak," she says, continuing. "But we feel it is best for everyone if we follow the rules, then we can all live in peace."

It was the same thing T said. My throat squeezes. It was as though they had practiced their speeches.

"But what good is following the rules and keeping the peace if you're not happy? How can you keep up this charade and listen to a mad woman like President Esther? There has to be something we can do."

"Even if we wanted to, there is nothing we can—"

"You see." I cut her off. "That's the problem. You don't want to and I want to know why?"

"Emma," she says, quietly. "Your father and I used to be friends with her, so I know she wasn't always a bad person. I can't go into any details right now. But after the party, I'll tell you everything. Now, we should get dressed," she says, standing.

My body is numb. I want to know more, but I can see by the stern look on her face she won't divulge any more secrets until later.

"One more thing," I say.

I know I should leave it alone, but I have to know this before the party.

"Yes, what is it?" she asks with some annoyance in her tone.

"Is your friendship with President Esther the reason I was spared?"

There is a blank look on her face, so I continue.

"I mean," I pause, and look down and then back up. "I've heard the horrible stories of when the no more children law went into effect. The babies who were born were killed, unless the families went to Territory U. I guess I've always wondered why I was the last one." My face feels flush, and I'm rambling. "I know there were babies born after me, but they all died. Why was I chosen to live and they weren't? Why did the cutoff point stop at me?"

"Emma…that is something you shouldn't worry yourself with." She leans in and kisses my forehead. "Just be glad that you're here," she says, and then walks away. "Now get dressed, we'll be leaving soon."

The door thumps behind her.

I look down at my ratty bathrobe and my chest is tight. I can't help but wonder why she didn't answer my question.

*

I have no idea how we're getting to the president's mansion. I really don't want to trudge five miles to a bus stop in this long, gold gown and gold heels. I walk downstairs fully dressed in the garment my mother purchased—or should I say, President Esther purchased for me.

My father and brother are standing at the bottom of the stairs in black tuxedos and shiny, black shoes. I know they can't afford them, so President Esther must have paid for their outfits as well.

There is a lump in my throat, seeing my mother walk downstairs with a lovely long green gown on. It has a fishtail bottom and spaghetti straps at the neck. The green reminds me of a frog I see down by the pond. Mother looks more beautiful than I've ever seen before. She reminds me of a model in one of the old magazines we have. A black purse hangs over her shoulder. It looks strange since I am not used to seeing her with one. She smells of roses. I didn't know she owned any perfume. Nonetheless she looks wonderful.

My father must think so, too. He takes her hand and kisses her forehead. They rarely show affection around us, and it is nice to see them act this way. The only thing missing is Taylor and Abigail; if they were with us, the night would be complete.

"I forgot to give you something," my mother says. "This is for you."

She takes my hand and places something cold and metal in it.

Her hands feel warm and sweaty against mine, and I wonder

why she is so nervous. Maybe she knows we shouldn't be having a celebration for something like this. Or maybe she is afraid of seeing President Esther again. Maybe it is neither of those things, and she feels uncomfortable in these fancy clothes that we aren't used to wearing—because I have to say I feel the same.

"Open your hand," she says.

My hand is clenched tightly around the object, as if I'm holding a small bug and I don't want it to get away. I relax my fist to find the cold metal object is a charm on a silver chain. The charm is a beautiful silver dove, and the dove is holding an object in its mouth that looks to me like seeds. The small seeds are colored in green, yellow, and blue.

"A dove can symbolize peace, love, and hope," my mother says. "The seeds the dove eats are yellow for joy, green for growth and harmony, and blue for calmness."

She moves my chin up to meet her eyes.

"Legend has it, the more of these colorful seeds the dove eats the more of these things we will have," she says with a smile. "Legend also says, the reason you only see a speck of the color blue is because the dove has already eaten most of it and its tucked away in his stomach."

No matter where my mother is, she always sounds like a schoolteacher. She always has some lesson to teach us. That was before her job was eliminated. It is nice to hear that spark in her voice again.

"Where did you get this legend from?" I ask, smiling.

"My mother handed this down to me, and now I can hand it down to you."

"What about Taylor?" My lips quiver thinking about my sister.

"I gave her a special bracelet when she turned eighteen, but this necklace was always meant for you."

"Can we go now," my brother rudely says, as a demand instead of a question.

"We don't want to be late," my father adds.

My mother puts the chain around my neck. The metal feels cold against my skin. I wrap my old, black jacket around me, and it pales in comparison to my fancy dress. But the wind is strong, and I feel more comfortable with it on. My mother grabs her jacket as well, while my brother and father remain jacketless.

I expect us to start our stride down to the bus terminal. My eyes widen when I see, and hear, one of President Esther's long, black, four-door cars screeching around the corner. It stops right in front of our house.

*

I've never been in a car before. I mostly travel by foot, except for the bus I used to take to school. The bus was bumpy and unsteady, while this ride is smooth like a baby's bottom. The bus sat up high, and made a loud mowing sound. President Esther's car is quiet; the engine is almost unnoticeable.

Everything that was once dark and gloomy has turned brighter because we've reached the downtown area where my father works. I see a large tan-colored building; it is the main hospital where he goes every day. Now that school is out, I have no reason to come down here. It is livelier than our area of town. There are streetlights, which make the sky look bright at night; unlike where we live, where there seems to be no light at all. The streets are wide and smooth here, and there are no gravel or dirt roads.

President Esther makes sure the part of town she frequents looks better. Even the air smells clean like lemons. This is what I imagine Territory U to look like, only better. A few doors down from the main hospital is the large brown brick school where my mother used to work and where I went to school. It is the only dim building on the street because it is closed now. I heard rumors that it may be torn down.

My family is unusually quiet. My mother sits beside me glaring out of the opposite window. I can't see her eyes, so I don't know if they're glistening or saddened. Across from me sits my father and brother. My father dabs beads of sweat from his forehead with a tissue, as if he is nervous about what the night's events will bring. My brother is pulling on his black suit tie. It is probably bothering him because he is not used to wearing one. He reminds me of the fun loving brother I'm used to being around, and I can almost forget he is training to be a guard.

When we were younger, Father sometimes sent T and me to the store for groceries. T would buy everything on the list but somehow still manage to have a few coins left over to buy one piece of candy. He would race me from one end of the marketplace to the other, and whoever won got the candy. I was around ten at the time, and back then, he would always beat me; but he gave me the candy anyway.

I face the opposite window this time, and see the brick two-story, maple-colored city council building. I know we're getting closer.

"We're here," my brother announces, as if he is a five-year-old, excited to be on a field trip.

The mansion is painted white and takes up most of the block. It looks like a castle, where a king and queen would live, in a fairy-tale book. There is a long, white fence in front that covers the entire area. A large, golden gate is just beyond the fence. Guards stand in front of it and issue security passes that let you in and out. Only those who are invited are let in. The grounds are beautifully kept, and the grass is greener than broccoli. There are an array of red, pink and yellow flowers out front. I have no idea how they keep the flowers from wilting when the weather is cold outside. But I'm sure President Esther pays someone handsomely to do that.

I've heard she divides her time between here and Territory U. She doesn't trust anyone else to be in charge of us, so she likes to be here to watch over the underlings herself. If her mansion here looks like a castle, what must her mansion in Territory U—surrounded by all of her important friends—look like? It is probably bigger and more extravagant than this one.

As the car sits in front of the mansion, my stomach feels queasy. One of the guards, dressed in all black, opens the car door for us, and nods as a sign of respect. My brother jumps out first. He almost looks excited to be here. He says a few words and then shakes the guard's hand. They whisper something to each other, and my brother's chest rises as he chuckles. It sickens me to see how at home he is here.

The guard takes my hand and helps me out of the car. Then, he helps my mother and father. I shiver, not from the cold air, but from the whole experience. We aren't even inside yet, and I already feel overwhelmed. I think my mother senses my worry because she takes my hand. I walk with her and my father inside.

Someone stands in the foyer and takes our jackets. Once my jacket is lifted from my shoulders, I feel naked, instantly wanting it back. I need it for comfort, and to hide in. I don't feel like I belong here. The air is light. Jasmine perfume fills the hallway. The same guard that puts our jackets away walks us down the hallway. He is tall and thin and looks to be in his thirties. He has brown hair and a brown thin mustache. His politeness astounds me. The only men I'm used to are my father and brother.

"Excuse me," the tall guard says. "You're Emma Whisperer, aren't you?"

"Y-yes, I-I am," I say.

I've suddenly developed a stutter because he knows my name.

"Well, you have a nice time." He nods his head. "After all, this is your party," he says, winking one of his gray eyes at me.

His stare makes me shudder. I'm glad when he turns to talk to my parents.

"You can take your assigned seats in the ballroom. President Esther wants dinner to start promptly at seven," he announces.

My parents turn and walk into the ballroom, and like a lost child, I follow them. I haven't seen T since we arrived. He thinks he is one of them since he already knows his way around.

The scent of jasmine continues into the ballroom, and the queasiness in my stomach remains. I find my name on one of the tables near the front. My mother, my father, T and I are seated at a table together. There is even a place card for Taylor right next to my seat. If asked, we are to say she is home sick.

I look around the room at all the people. It is unlike anything I have ever seen in my entire life. The walls are as blue as the deep sea. The room is quite large and very bright; there is a humongous chandelier in the middle of the ceiling. The chandelier is made of crystals that look like teardrops. I know this because my mom would show me pictures of crystal earrings in magazines, and it looks just like them.

My mother has tons of old magazines from before our world was divided. Mother told me, before she was born, there were new books and magazines published daily; but now nothing new is published here. Every book or magazine I read is filled with old news because it was published decades ago. Our school also used old, outdated textbooks. Why should President Esther buy us new textbooks when the school would be closing anyway? I've heard the upper territories have new books and magazines; it must be nice.

My mother told me that in 2030 there was an internal war over farming land in Craigluy. The elected officials wanted to take land away from some of the citizens that owned it. The people decided to fight for what was theirs. It tore everything apart, and life as people knew it changed. Many lives were lost.

The nation of Craigluy is in between California and Arizona, near Blythe, along the Colorado River. A lot of people moved to those places after the war was over. But others decided to stay here and rebuild because this was the only home they knew. As the years went by, the weather shifted and it wasn't hot here all the time. Craigluy, and the nearby areas, started to receive colder weather— and now the seasons are all messed up.

Mother wasn't born until 2045, but she heard stories from her parents. Grandmother told her there used to be television shows and radio music and plenty of food to eat. But after the war, they had to start over. They planted and grew their food. They rebuilt their hospitals and schools. They sewed their own clothes from bamboo and rayon and wood, and used chemical resources, like nylon and polyester.

Craigluy was never the same after that, and it became even worse once Esther divided it. A lot of people wished they had left the area and fled when they had the chance, but it was too late once Esther took over. She made it so there would be no way out.

I see about fifty round tables, with satin white tablecloths over them, scattered around the room. The flatware is gold. And, there are purple flower arrangements in the middle of each table. A few feet from where we sit, there is a long table and podium. I'm guessing President Esther will be seated there. I shudder to think of her being so close to me. The thought of meeting her sends a tremor up my spine.

On the opposite side of the room, I see a large dance floor with musicians playing soft orchestra music. The president must have loaned them out from Territory U because I've never seen anything like that here before. We don't have fancy dances or formal dinners. I see couples conversing, and others swaying on the dance floor as if it is a natural thing.

I shift in my chair, not because my dress is too tight or I don't know how to act around important people. Being here, in a place I'm not used to, and around people I'm not used to, makes my throat tight. No one here looks familiar to me. Where are all the people I know?

"How is everyone enjoying their evening?"

I hear a crackly voice. President Esther is at our table. Her hair lands on her shoulders. It's silver like the necklace my mother gave me. Her eyes are a piercing blue and even sharper than they appear when she is on the box. Up close, they make her look like a vicious dog protecting its owners. She wears a long, silver gown that eerily matches her hair. She has long silver earrings that dangle and clank when she moves her head from side to side. Her lipstick is blood red, and her fingernails are coated black.

"It's so nice seeing you again," she continues. "It has been a long time, hasn't it?" Her skinny eyebrow rises.

My mother's voice quivers, as though she is afraid to speak. "Y-yes it h-has."

"It seems like a lifetime ago," my father chimes in.

"I trust all is well with your family." President Esther's smile is wicked. She glances around the table. "I hear good things about your boy, Theodore."

Her smile widens and all of her teeth show. They're white and glisten like snow. "I feel he'll be a welcome addition to my staff."

"I'm sure he will," my father says, then clears his throat. "He is a good listener and a fast learner."

My father sounds like he is reading off attributes for a decent job opportunity instead of a crime-filled one. Yes, he'll be a good addition to a staff of killers and bullies. My skin crawls listening to their conversation, and I want to slide under the table or become invisible. A thickness is in my throat. I find it hard to swallow watching President Esther talk to my parents as if they are normal people and they talk back as if she isn't the leader of our world.

"So, how are you this evening, Emma?" she says, turning to me with wide eyes.

This is the moment I've been dreading, and my knee shakes under the table.

"I'm fine," I say, with a frown because I don't know how to respond.

"Now that your brother will become a guard, what do you want to be?" she asks.

Her eyes capture mine.

"She is looking for a job down in the marketplace," my father quickly says, before I can answer.

It's as if he's afraid of what I might say.

"Well, I hope you have more to say during your speech." She ignores my father and glares back at me.

The sound of her voice sends chills up my spine, and I only catch the tail end of what she says.

"Speech," I repeat, because I don't understand.

"Yes, dear." Her eyes slant this time. "I expect you to give a speech about how grateful you are to be the last eighteen-year-old and all. It will be broadcasted for all to see on their boxes."

"B-but I didn't know anything about a speech," I say, with a stutter.

"That is why I'm telling you now." The corner of her mouth turns up. She stares at me like a mongrel stares at a bone because it is his last meal.

"I don't think I can give—"

My mother cuts me off. "It'll be fine, Emma." Her eyes are caring.

"Dinner will be served soon," Esther says. "But once it is over, I would like for you to come and see me in my chambers, so we can discuss what you will say. A guard will bring you up to my room. Now enjoy your meal." She gives a wide smile. "I want everyone to eat up."

My leg jolts as she walks away.

"By the way." She turns around. "I see someone is missing." She stares at Taylor's name on her placement card. "Joan, where is your eldest daughter?" Her eyes shift.

"She is sick," I blurt out, so mother doesn't have to.

"There now, I knew you could speak up," President Esther says, with a smirk. "Let's hope you do that during your speech tonight."

Her heels click on the hardwood floors as she walks away.

"Sorry, Mother."

"No worries," Mother says, placing her hand over mine on the table. "You did fine covering for your sister. And I'm sorry about her catching you off guard about the speech. If we had known about it, you know we would have warned you."

"Yes, we would have," Father chimes in. "But you'll do fine with that, too."

I give a half-smile. It is nice they have such faith in me. Hopefully, I'll do them proud.

T makes his way to the table, and dinner service starts. Men dressed in black pants and black ties along with white shirts bring the courses to the tables. The food is extravagant, and I don't know what half of it is. The waiter explains the different courses to each table.

The first course is cheese and crackers along with a fruit platter. There is a variety of cheeses, unlike any I've seen before. I'm used to the cheese the government hands out when President Esther is in a good mood and thinks she is doing us a favor. Some slices of cheese tastes sweet and others taste tangy and creamy. It is all quite good. I find myself crunching loudly on the crackers. I sound like a squirrel gnawing on a nut, so I chew quieter.

The French onion soup is delicious, and my stomach growls from satisfaction. The salad is a field of greens that are small but elegant. It reminds me of the tiny portions we had to eat when my father or mother brought home less money. There is a special dressing, the waiter calls it a vinaigrette with olive oil, to go over it. It is delicious. I can't believe people eat this way every day.

I'm stuffed, but I still gluttonously down the rosemary chicken as if I haven't eaten in weeks because I may never eat like this again. I glance at my mother and father and they look as stuffed as I am. Theodore has a satisfied look on his face, too. He probably knows he'll eat like this all of the time now that he is one of the president's henchmen.

The waiter takes the plates from our table and sets down ice cream. He corrects me and calls it sorbet. It is orange and tastes sweet, but it is lighter than ice cream. Everything is enjoyable, but I still have a queasiness in my stomach. Why should we have a meal we don't deserve while Taylor and baby Abigail have none? I push my bowl away. I don't want any more sorbet. My face feels flushed, and I'm embarrassed for even being here.

I glance around and finally see some familiar faces. There are a few people here that my dad works with at the hospital. I also see a few of the people my mom used to work with. I see Lily, the girl I know Theodore likes. She is sitting at a table over in the corner with her family. The Wessel family and their daughters, Leslie and Sara, are sitting near the back. At the table next to them is the Horton family with their son, Cameron. Maybe I'll corner Sara later and ask what they did to be picked to move on to Territory M.

A young, light-skin guy with dark hair sits next to the Horton's table. I catch him staring at me at the same time I'm looking at him. He doesn't look away. And I feel goose bumps rise on my arm. I don't know why his stare bothers me so. Maybe I have food on my face, but I feel around my chin and nothing is there. His gaze is still on me. Out of all the beautiful people here to look at why would he choose me? I gulp down a sip of water, hoping it will calm me. I feel like an art piece on display. My heart races, and I stand to get out of his view.

My purse feels awkward hanging off my shoulder, so I place it in Taylor's seat. I walk into the hallway and see Sara standing outside the women's bathroom. Her blue gown is long and her blonde hair is up in a bun. It is strange seeing everyone in such bright colors.

"Hi Sara," I say, throwing up my hand. She looks puzzled, so I continue. "I know you don't know me but—"

"I know who you are," she says, cutting me off. "You're the reason for this party."

Her snappy tone catches me off guard. I don't know how I could have offended someone I don't even know. The door to the bathroom opens and I hear the roar of a toilet flushing.

"If we're done here, I was on my way inside." She glances at the bathroom door.

"Have I done something to you?" My throat tightens.

"No." She shakes her head. "But you've never tried to speak to me before. So, I have a feeling you want to ask me how my family is able to move ahead to Territory M."

"Well, yes. I do," I say, fumbling over my words.

"You know you can get in trouble for asking me." Her eyes are cold. "And, I can get in trouble for answering you. My family could lose our privileges and not get to go, but that doesn't seem to bother you."

"I don't want your family to lose their privileges. That is not my intention." My mouth feels dry. "I thought—"

"Emma," I hear my brother calling my name, before I can finish my sentence.

"Sorry she bothered you," he says, grabbing my elbow and pulling me to the side.

This is the second time he has grabbed my elbow in the last few weeks, and I don't care for his behavior.

"Do not speak for me," I shout, while pulling away from him. I lower my voice when I see guards glancing over at us. "What are you doing here anyway?"

"Are you crazy?" His brown eyes glare at me. "I had a feeling where you were going when you left the table, and I was right. You can't go around asking unwanted questions or our whole family will be punished for it. Is that what you want? For us to suffer?"

"Of course not." There is a bubble in my chest because every time I do what I think is right, it ends up hurting my family.

"You two should get back to your tables," a green-eyed, red-haired guard says. "The president is about to speak."

I follow T to the table. I have a weird feeling in the pit of my stomach as though someone is staring at me. I glance over and see the same dark-haired guy gazing in my direction.

CHAPTER SEVEN

"I TRUST EVERYONE ENJOYED their meals," President Esther says.

She stands at the podium. My brother and I take our seats. My parents glower at me as if they know what I've been up to.

"If you notice," she continues. "I wanted the meal to have a French theme. It is one of my favorite meals. I'm sure most of you—except for the few friends I've invited from Territory U—have never eaten it before. Since this is a celebration, I want my guests from Territory L to try something new."

The room is eerily quiet, as if people are afraid to sneeze, for fear it would interrupt her precious speech.

"I want all of you to enjoy your evening. We'll have more music and dancing."

She waves her hand over to the area where the musicians are sitting.

"We'll end the night with an eagerly anticipated speech by our guest of honor, Ms. Emma Whisperer. I trust you will thoroughly enjoy what she has to say, as I will."

I squirm in my chair like a child because I don't want to make a speech. Isn't it enough that I showed up to this dreadful event when I know how stupid and unnecessary it is? I don't know why she is making such a big deal of it.

"Emma, Emma."

I hear my father calling my name. My mother touches the top of my hand, and my eyes broadened.

"Snap out of it." My brother growls at me. "They're here to take you upstairs."

I look up to see two guards, wearing black uniforms, standing next to our table. They're both tall. One has blond hair with gray eyes. The other has red hair and green eyes; he is the same one who demanded I return to my seat earlier. I don't know why there needs to be two. Do they think I'll make a run for it, like a prisoner on death row?

"We need to take you upstairs now, Ms. Whisperer," the gray-eyed one says.

"The president will meet you there," the other one chimes in.

"It'll be okay, Emma," my mother says, with soft eyes, as if I need nurturing.

"We'll be right here when you get back," my father adds.

"Don't do anything stupid." My brother smirks.

I remain quiet and stand. I follow the two guards out of the ballroom and down the hall to a series of elevators. Guards seem to be everywhere, and my jaw twitches. I can hear the orchestra has started playing music again in the ballroom. I wonder if my mother and father will dance. I've never seen them dance before, and it would be nice. I'm trying to distract myself because my knees are wobbling, and there is a pit in my stomach. I don't want to be in some unknown room, alone, with the president.

There are three, silver-colored elevators that have black signage above them. The one on the right says Guard. The one in the middle says President, and the one on the left says Commoner. The guard hits the button for the elevator on the right. The guard's elevator dings and the doors swoosh open. The redheaded guard waves his hand so I'll step in first. Then, he and the other guard step in after me. The air in the elevator is dry, and it smells like smoke. I frown with disgust. The redheaded guard pushes the button for the second floor. The elevator roars upward.

"You hit the wrong floor," the blond one says.

"I thought President Esther wanted to see her in the conference room." His green eyes go dull.

"No, I specifically heard her say take her to her private chambers on the fifth floor." The blond one's eyes narrow.

"Fine then." The redheaded one seems annoyed as he pushes the button. He uses force as if he is punching in someone's eye.

The elevator rips open on the second floor and after a few seconds closes. I hear metal grinding as we move upward again. The elevator dings and stops at the fifth floor. The doors swing open, and we all stand there.

"You can get off now," the redhead says. He glares at me as if he wants to shove me in my back. "We can't go any farther."

"Why?" I ask.

"We're not allowed on this floor."

A hammer beats down on my chest. "Then why am I allowed?"

"We don't ask questions. We only do as we're told. And we're not allowed to step foot into the president's living quarters, unless she specifically asks us to. Her orders are to make sure you get to her quarters safely, and then we are to leave." The redhead is doing all the talking. "Now, would you kindly get off, so we can get back downstairs to our posts?"

"Yes, sorry." My mouth is parched. I wish I was downstairs drinking something cold with my parents.

I step off the elevator and my eyes shift to my surroundings. I'm standing in a big, bright hallway where the walls are burgundy and the air smells like vanilla. There are big, white double doors in front of me, and I can only presume the president's quarters are on the other side. There is a doorbell on the wall. When I hit it, soft music plays. The music sounds like the orchestra music from downstairs, only shorter. No one answers, so I turn the gold colored doorknob and the doors swish and open.

The room is unlike anything I've seen before. It is the same feeling I had downstairs. I step in to what looks to be the living room.

The walls are tan, like a camel's fur. This one room is bigger than my whole house. There is a tan sofa in the center of the room that matches the walls perfectly. The sofa is circular, and there is a glass table sitting in the middle of it. Three steps lead down to the sofa, and above the sofa is a crystal chandelier that reminds me of the one in the ballroom.

The white-and-green pillows on the sofa look soft, like my niece's skin. There is a spiral staircase, which leads up to her quarters. I assume her private kitchen and bedroom are up there, too. Farther back in the room is a long, black bar, and tall bar chairs sit in front of it.

There are long, square windows with no blinds or shades. The windows are tinted and remind me of the windows on the car that came to pick us up. The air is light and floral scented. Pictures sit on a long, brown table; and I walk closer to look at them. Maybe they'll give me a clue into the Esther my mother used to know.

Before I can look at the pictures, I notice the desk has a drawer with one silver knob. I'm curious as to what is inside. My hand shakes as I pull the drawer open, but I keep pulling anyway. I see a series of maps.

The first map is of Craigluy. Craigluy is oval-shaped and reminds me of the human brain. The top right half is Territory U. The top left half is Territory M. The entire bottom half is Territory L, my territory. My territory is the biggest because the poor outnumber everyone else.

The map next to it is of Territory M only. There are words marked in red ink on the different zones of the territory. I see a mainstream market, a trainee station and a newbie camp. Centermost, a school and, midpoint, a burial ground. I don't care to look at the map for my territory, so I move on to Territory U.

Territory U's zones are marked with the Gentry Theater and an elite library. I see affluent housing. I don't know what any of this means, so I close the drawer with a *thud* and move on to the photos.

There are five crystal frames, like the chandelier. One shows

President Esther in a blue dress, smiling. Her smile is nice, almost friendly-like, instead of wicked. Another photo shows an outside shot, and it looks like it is her wedding day. She looks much younger. She has on a white dress and is holding a flower bouquet. A third photo shows her dressed in black with dozens of people around her. It could be her inauguration day. The fourth photo is of Esther kissing a man. I can only assume it is her husband, Henry. I've never seen him before, but he is dark-skin like my mother. They look happy, and I can't help but wonder what happened to him.

My hands shake picking up the fifth and final frame. The picture is ripped in half. The top half is gone and the bottom half shows a blue background. I can't see what, or who, it used to be. Why would she keep a damaged picture in a frame? I feel a cold chill rush over me and my shoulders shake.

"I didn't mean to keep you waiting."

President Esther is behind me. I drop the frame. It clanks against the floor and shatters. Tiny shards land everywhere. I lean down to pick them up.

"Leave it. I'll have someone clean it up later." Her bold blue eyes stare at me.

"Sorry, I shouldn't have touched your things."

"It is fine, Emma, you're curious and there is nothing wrong with that. It shows you're eager to learn, which I encourage. Now sit." She waves her hand toward the sofa. "Here are your index cards, dear."

"What are these for?" My mouth goes dry.

"That is what you'll say in your speech tonight." She crosses her legs. I see silver high heels under her dress. "It is not word-for-word but summarized. I'm sure you'll get the gist of what you need to say."

I see a lot of mumbo jumbo about being honored and it is a privilege. There is something about being happy I was spared, so I can make something of my life. My chest beats unsteadily because I don't believe any of the things she wants me to say. How can I speak a lie?

"Now that your index cards are prepared, you won't have to worry about what you will say."

She clasps her hands together. Her nails are long and thick. The black polish looks darker than in the ballroom, and now reminds me of the sky at night.

"What makes you think I'm worried?"

"If you're not worried…" She pauses and her eyes harden. "Why is your knee shaking?"

I hadn't noticed, but she is right. My knee is betraying me, bouncing up and down. It is making me appear weak, and I can't show fear in front of her. I place my hand on it to stop it from shaking.

"Why was I spared?" I ask, quietly.

"You may ask." She leans forward. "But that doesn't mean I will answer."

She lets out a scary laugh that sounds like a bird chirping. "But seriously." Her eyes enlarge. "If your parents told you that we were friends, then you should already know the answer. So, there is no need for me to explain. You should go now." She stands. "I'm sure you want to get a few dances in before your speech."

I stand but my feet won't move, as if they're glued to the floor.

"Is something wrong, dear?" She glares at me like an evil witch in a children's story.

"Don't the guards have to take me back down? I didn't think I was allowed to take the elevator alone."

"I'm sure you'll be fine. Use the commoner's elevator and go straight down to the first floor." Her eyes lower.

I step into the hallway, and get on the commoner's elevator. I'm surprised the elevator for the commoners even comes to her floor. Why would she want to mingle with commoners? Maybe her servants have to use it to bring her things. The doors swoosh closed, and I stand with the cards trembling in my hands. I accidently hit the button for the wrong floor. The third floor button is right above the first floor. I correct my error by quickly jamming my finger into the first floor button. The elevator hums going down. When the doors swish back open, I'm on the third floor. I know I shouldn't, but I'm curious; so, instead of waiting for the doors to zip closed so I can continue riding down, I step off the elevator. My mother said I was an inquisitive child; but my father said I was just nosy. I suppose I haven't changed.

My stomach cringes because the floor is dark and smells musty. The hallway is long, yet I keep walking down it. I see several doors but the rooms look dark so I walk past them. The last door on the right has light seeping under it, and I wonder why. My hand spasms as I reach for the knob. I have an uneasy heaviness in my chest, as if I'm turning the knob to my death; but I keep turning anyway.

The room is large and dark and the walls are black. There is a big screen on the wall. It reminds me of our information boxes, only this screen is longer and wider. I walk closer and see one single chair in the middle of the room. It is brown and wooden and reminds me of an electric chair, the kind I have seen in my history books in school. Looking at it makes my knees tremble. There are chains that go from the chair to brown leather handcuffs. They're thick in size. If someone is chained there, I don't see them getting out.

"What are you doing in here?"

My shoulders jump. I turn to find the tall guard with the red hair and green eyes staring at me.

"Just because you're the *chosen one*, you think you can go wherever you want, do whatever you want. You don't belong here." He growls at me as if I'm a bug that he wants to squash.

"What does that mean?" My tone is shaky.

I feel a mountain of anxiety deep down.

He is coming straight for me. I walk backwards and bump into the wall. My fingers grip the cards so tightly not even a crowbar could loosen them.

"You think you're special," he continues with his rant.

He pokes his long, skinny finger into my clavicle. His chest is touching mine. I can feel the gun in his holster pressing up against my hip. His breath is hot, and it makes the hairs on the back of my neck stand.

"I don't know what you're talking about," I say.

I feel my pulse quicken. I'm trying to push him off me, but he is too heavy.

"Rich, what are you doing? Get off her!" I hear a guy's voice. "Do you know who she is?"

"Yes, I know."

The guy who I now know as Rich turns his head to talk to the person behind him. But he is still leaning into my chest so hard that I can't breathe.

"I suggest you move away from her, unless you want me to tell President Esther what you're doing."

Rich walks away from me and moves toward the door.

"Thank you," I say, after Rich leaves the room.

Once my heart stops pounding through my chest, I realize it is the dark-haired boy who stared at me as though he knew me in the ballroom.

"Thanks for the save," I say again, adjusting my dress. The bodice has twisted a little from the commotion.

"You know, he is right. You shouldn't be in here." He frowns.

"I was invited to the president's quarters," I say, as if it is something to be proud of even though I know it is not.

"This doesn't look like the president's quarters to me." His mouth turns up and his amber eyes slant.

"I made a wrong turn." I shrug.

"A wrong turn," he says, with a chuckle in his voice. "You would have to make a lot of wrong turns to end up all the way down here." He moves closer to me. "President Esther wouldn't like you being in here."

"Then maybe they should have locked the door."

He grins. "I don't think you're as tough as you pretend."

I feel myself blush. "You don't even know me."

His tuxedo is not buttoned. He has a muscular build, and I

can see ripples through his white shirt. I've never been this close to a boy, except for T—which doesn't count—and Rich. But that unfortunate incident with Rich made my stomach queasy. Now that queasiness is gone and my stomach feels warm like coals on a fire.

"You're right about that," he says.

I can feel his hot breath on my neck, and I shiver. He is medium height, and I don't have to look far up for my eyes to reach his.

"I don't know you," he continues. "But I get a sense about people, and I get a sense about you."

"Instead of talking about me, why don't we talk about you?" My chest stiffens. I don't like people assuming how I feel.

"President Esther wouldn't like you roaming around either," I say, in a rough tone. "Shouldn't you be downstairs with the other guests?"

"So, you think I'm a guest." He grins. "I'm not a guest. I'm a guard in training. That is why I'm allowed up here."

"But you look too young to be a guard. And you have on—"

"A tuxedo," he says, cutting me off.

"Yes," I say.

"Your brother has on a tuxedo, too, because he is in training. He wasn't allowed to wear his uniform since he doesn't have his silver buttons, yet. Well, it is the same for me."

So, he is the other young trainee.

"We better get out of here."

"What is this place?" I ask, looking around.

"I don't know."

"You're lying."

"They don't share everything with the trainees, so I honestly don't know. Why do you care so much?"

"It looks like somewhere you'd come to be tortured. Why would the president have a room like this in her mansion?"

"You shouldn't concern yourself with such things. That is what got you in trouble with Rich." He turns toward the door.

"Wait," I say.

He seems annoyed. "What is it this time?"

"Why did that guard, Rich, treat me that way? It's as if he hates me." I frown. "I don't even know him."

"From what I've heard, a lot of the guards here don't care for you because you were saved while their loved ones weren't."

"Why is that my fault?" My throat tenses. "I was a baby. I didn't even know what was going on."

"I didn't say it was your fault. But when they look at you, they think of their baby brother or sister that didn't make it. You have to understand," he says, with emotion in his voice. "Most of these guys are in their late twenties, so they were around ten or eleven during that time. They saw their siblings being taken away to be killed. So, they resent you for that. They resent the fact that the cutoff point stopped with you."

"But that's not fair," I say, biting my lip.

"You should know better than anyone that life is not fair."

"Why should I know better than anyone else?" There is a roaring in my chest, much like a lion. "What does that mean?"

"We better get downstairs," he says, ignoring my last question.

*

I enter the ballroom and see the dancing has come to a stop. The boy with the amber eyes slithers away like a snake, as if he doesn't want anyone to see us together. I stand in the back of the room and wonder if my parents danced together. I missed it all, and now all I see is President Esther's glare on me as she stands at the podium. My legs vibrate, and my heels wobble underneath my long dress. I don't have time to gather my thoughts, or talk to my parents because she announces me.

"You're all here to witness this historic moment. We even have the information system on so the people at home, who weren't lucky enough to be invited, can partake," President Esther says.

Her smile shows all of her white teeth.

"The last child in our territory has turned eighteen, and I feel there is reason to celebrate this milestone, since there will never be another one. Now, no child will go hungry, or be sick, here ever again because no more children exist."

The room is quiet as though we're in the school library. I watch as her chest expands as if what she has just said is something to be proud of.

"Let's hope she does something worthwhile with her life, so we can all be proud that she is here. Now, let's all give a warm welcome to the youngest person in Territory L."

She stretches her arm out to point in my direction.

"Ms. Emma Whisperer."

My feet feel as if they're stuck in quicksand. I can't move. I brush the gold sequins on my dress. My hands are trembling so much that I need to do something with them.

"Emma."

I hear my name again and this time it is sterner. But I still can't move because the quicksand seems thicker and deeper. My parents look sympathetic while my brother frowns as if I'm embarrassing him. There is whispering behind me and blank stares in front of me. I hear the slapping of people's hands as they clap for me. I force myself to put one shaky foot in front of the other and walk toward the podium.

President Esther wraps her slender hands around me and gives me a quick hug. I can feel her bones poking through the skin in her back. A cold tremor goes up my spine as her long fingernails touch my arms. I feel like I'm in a horrible nightmare, and I gasp for air to wake up. But this is not a dream; I'm wide awake.

So, here I stand, in front of two hundred invited guests, and they all have their eyes glued on me. They're all waiting with eager anticipation for me to say something profound in my speech. My father stares at me with his serious face, but when I hesitate to speak his eyes become somber. Then there is my mother, sitting next to him, with a half-smile that at its best is weak. My brother's face is motionless. I can't help thinking this whole event is a waste of time.

No one really wants to be here, but they're all afraid of the woman throwing the party.

President Esther is standing behind me, and I hear her footsteps as she walks closer to me. I feel the hotness of her breath, making the hairs on the back of my neck stand at attention.

"You can start anytime now, dear," she whispers.

I open my mouth but still cannot speak. My older sister, Taylor, should be here. But she is in hiding, and my family has to lie and cower in fear about her whereabouts. And then, there is the baby, Abigail, who can never show her face or she will be killed. The more I think about things the madder I get.

Fire is coming from my ears, and my hands tremble. President Esther's cards are burning a hole in my clenched fist. I rub the silver dove chain that hangs from my neck, to make sure it is still there. It was only given to me a few hours earlier, but it gives me comfort. I glance in my mother's direction again. Her forced smile is still weak, and her posture is bent.

"Hello people of Territory L, and any other Territories that are here or watching."

I push myself to speak.

"You already know my name is Emma—Emma Whisperer."

I feel acid rising in my throat, almost choking me, but I have to continue.

"I'm here today because I'm the last eighteen-year-old in the territory, and I'm…" I pause and take in a breath. "I'm grateful for this party, grateful that I'm here, and grateful that my life wasn't cut short like so many others."

I glance at my parents again. I love them so, but I can't be like them and follow the rules. I can't lie about what I believe in to make others happy. I can't, and I won't. I crumble the cards in my compressed fist as if I'm crumbling up dirt from the ground.

"I should begin again." My voice shakes. "What I should have said was that I'm the last eighteen-year-old there will ever be here. It is wrong, and it is sad, and it shouldn't be this way." I swallow hard.

I hear gasps from the audience. I'm fully prepared for the president's guards—or the president herself—to stop me, but she lets me continue.

"I don't feel comfortable up here. This isn't a proper reason for a celebration. Deep down in our hearts, I think we all know that. President Esther is sinful, and she forces her convoluted ideas onto us," I say.

I'm trying to use big words to pretend I'm not intimidated by her stance behind me.

Like a bear growling at its prey, she mumbles in my ear; but doesn't physically stop me, so I continue to speak. My knees buckle underneath me as I gather myself and press on.

"No one should live in fear. Our world of Craigluy was once united, but now, because of the efforts of one woman, we are divided into three territories. It doesn't make sense to me," I say, shaking my head. "And I'm sure it doesn't make sense to you either. Why should the poor not mingle with the rich? Just because one person's income isn't as much as another's, does that mean they shouldn't be friends? Are we not good enough, or smart enough, to be friends with someone from Territory U?"

I'm feeling stronger now, so I clear my throat and continue.

"We may have less education than those in Territory U but that doesn't mean we're not capable. And if some of us want to seek higher education, why shouldn't we be allowed to? Why should the rich get treated with respect, while we don't?"

My parents' eyes expand, and my throat shrinks, but my voice doesn't.

"I may be young, but I do know, no one should be allowed to take away our rights to have a family. Having children should not be judged by how much money we make. We may have less income but we will love our children just as much or even more than the upper class."

I close my eyes and wait for the guards to grab me. It doesn't happen, so I continue.

"The law is stupid and unnecessary, and it should be changed. President Esther insists her laws are protecting children from violence. But how can that be true, when her violence is killing them? Her laws are the biggest instigator of violence. She should spend her time making sure our streets are safe for children, instead of banishing them. The gates should be opened and all territories of Craigluy should be reunited into one. The president has the power to do all of this and more. If you agree with me, stand and show your support."

I hear a loud uproar in the room, like a tiger's growl. My heart expands. It is the sound of applause. Everyone stands and my eyes water.

"Emma, your speech is over," President Esther says.

Her eyes are cold like ice. If they could they would shoot daggers at me.

I move aside to let her have the podium. My once steady legs turn to jelly.

"We have just endured the ramblings of an eighteen-year-old child. If any of you take anything she has said to heart and decide to protest, you will be jailed for a minimum of thirty days. If you continue on with this nonsense, you will be moved down to the prison where you will serve a maximum sentence of my choosing."

Like a lion walking onto a street full of people, the room falls quiet and everyone takes their seats.

"We, as grown individuals, know why my laws are necessary. I know your applause was for the young lady's courage and not because you agree with what she has said."

So now that she is angry, I'm no longer Emma, I'm young lady. There is a gnawing ache in the pit of my stomach, and my blood pressure rises like water in a tea pot. Now she wants to pretend that we're stupid and we don't know what our applause was for.

"Don't stand there, Emma," she says, glancing over at me. "You're a smart girl. You should know this is your cue to leave." Her eyes narrow.

In my own head, my footsteps sound loud like an elephant's. All eyes are on me as I walk to my parents' table. My parents' stares are drab, and I don't bother to look at T. I can't stomach the expression that must be on his face.

"I had hoped to end this event on a high note, but now that is ruined." President Esther shakes her head with disgust. "You can all leave now. My guards will give you your coats and show you to the door."

I hear whispering around me, but I can't make out what anyone is saying. The earlier applause meant they were all pleased with what I had said. Now that the applause are gone, I can't make out what anyone is feeling. Along with my parents' subdued expressions, I see disappointment in their eyes.

"Mother," I say, glancing at her. "Father," I say, looking over at him. "Please don't…"

I can't continue because I feel a weird presence behind me. Someone grabs me from behind. I turn to see Rich, the guard I encountered earlier. His arm is tightly pressed around my waist.

"What are you doing?" my father demands. His face is harder than I've ever seen it before.

"Let my child go," my mother says. Her eyes are big and her voice is strong.

"I'm sorry, ma'am, but I can't do that. I have strict orders from the president," Rich says, with a hint of delight in his voice.

His arm is pressing into the sequins around my waist, and I can't breathe.

"He is right, Mother," Theodore chimes in. At least he doesn't sound delighted about my predicament like Rich does. "She went against the laws—"

"Yes, and she has to be punished," President Esther adds, finishing T's sentence. "Mike, where are the handcuffs?"

The blond guard from the elevator walks to one side of me, and hands Rich the handcuffs. I hear the click of them closing around my wrists. I feel the cold metal around my skin. My insides quiver.

"Esther, please," my father says.

He uses her first name, eerily reminding me that they once used to be friends.

"I'm sorry, friendship only goes so far." Her mouth creases at the corners. "Once you disobey me, there has to be consequences for your actions."

"You are hereby under arrest, for a minimum of thirty days, for causing a disturbance and disobeying the protest law. You caused commotion and confusion among the territory. You tried to get others to break laws and protest with you. Because of this added wrongdoing, your sentence could be extended beyond the thirty days. If you do not show repentance for your sins in this allowed time, it will be up to the president to do as she sees fit regarding your case. This means you could be let go, or you could be reprimanded to the prison for a longer sentence. Do you understand?"

Rich's voice is loud, and his words echo in my ear.

I don't respond. I feel like someone is standing on my chest, and I can't breathe.

"I said, do you understand?"

He shakes the handcuffs, and like a bird swaying back and forth in a dangling cage, my whole body moves with them.

"Yes," I say, nodding. "I understand."

I feel like I should say some meaningful words to my family; but I have none, so I remain quiet.

CHAPTER EIGHT

I'M TAKEN DOWN TO the jail. It is crazy to me that the jail is located in the president's mansion. It's on the basement level. You can also gain access to it through an outside door. If you go farther down, you run into the underground tunnel. Once you're in the underground tunnel, if you go about a half a mile more, you reach the prisons. That is where inmates with longer sentences, or life sentences, are housed. Stories of how big and unusual her mansion is circles around town, and now I get to see it for myself.

The walls are dark and gloomy. The air is damp, and the odor is musty. My parents and T are gone now, and so is President Esther. I'm glad Mike is here with me and I'm not alone with Rich. His eyes are fixated on me, like a dog glares at an unknown cat. I feel like he wants to kill me. My heart bounces in my chest like a ball. I don't scare easily; but ever since the encounter in the death room, my jaw twitches when I'm around him.

Both men are quiet. All I hear are the sounds of my high heels on the hard floors. I see six jail cells. Mike points to one of them. Rich smiles as he unlocks my handcuffs. Then, he shoves me inside and closes the squeaky metal bars behind me.

The handcuffs had only been on for a few minutes, but I rub my wrists because they feel raw as if it had been hours.

"This is your new home, *chosen one*." Rich winks. "I hope you enjoy it."

I hate that he keeps calling me *chosen one*. I don't understand, or welcome, that title. I watch him walk away, and then I shakily turn around to assess my surroundings. My chest constricts as I look at the bars around me. It is as if I'm in a small freezer. My cell is the last one on the end. There is a brick wall on one side of me, and a set of metal bars on the other. At least I can see inside the cell next to mine and the one across from mine. They're all unoccupied now; but if someone comes later, I'll have some company. I see six square, box-shaped cells on my side as well as the opposite side.

I've heard the prison, which is used for inmates with longer stays, have toilets right inside the cells. But there is no toilet where I am. I can be glad about that. If I'm taken to a real bathroom, it will give me a break from this place for a few minutes, which is better than no break at all.

The stench is horrible. It smells like a dead animal, and I want a clothespin to hold my nostrils together. There is one cot with a dirty mattress on it. I don't want to sit on it; but I suppose it is better than sitting on the cold, hard floor. My heart races in my chest, as if I'm in a marathon, as I slowly sit down. I can't calm down and my leg jerks. I glance around the cell again and wonder who used it before me.

"*Chosen one.*"

Rich's voice makes my shoulders jump.

"If I had it my way, I would make you sleep in that fancy dress of yours, but forces beyond my control want you to change into more appropriate attire."

He runs his hand through his red hair and stares at me with a grin.

I look down at my gold heels and see a hairy brown spider crawling on the dark ground. I look everywhere but where Rich is. Spiders make my skin crawl, but I would rather look at it than him.

He puts his hands through the bars and throws me a bundle of clothing and white gym shoes. They land on the floor with a smack. I lean down to pick them up and see four button-down, blue shirts and four pairs of blue pants. There are four pairs of white underwear along with four bras and six pairs of white socks. The clothes feel like polyester. The gym shoes look thin, and I'll probably feel the floors through them. The pants are one size bigger than I need, but I don't care. It will be nice to get out of this tight dress. It'll give me room to breathe and move around.

"If the underwear doesn't fit I can get you a different size." He glares at me like a cat wanting to devour a mouse. "And here are some clothes to sleep in."

He throws another bundle of clothing in between the bars. It thumps, hitting the floor like the first bundle did. There are five oversized white t-shirts. But they look see-through and thin. I don't have any plans on using them.

"Make the most of it," he says, with a growl. "Laundry is done once every two weeks around here, since we supply you with so much to wear. Down in the main prison, they are only supplied with two brown jumpsuits. The main laundry down there gets done once a week."

He glares at me as if I should be happy for the abundance of clothing. He keeps talking as though he thinks I want to hear what he has to say.

"Aren't you going to leave?" I say. "I can't change with you here."

"What you have is nothing new to me. I've seen it all before." His green eyes are dead and cold. "Seeing one naked female body is like seeing them all."

I shiver at his words. He has to be at least six years older than me and twice my size. His arms are thick like tree stumps. I know he doesn't like me. It is quiet down here, and there are no other prisoners. He could easily do whatever he wants to me. I've always been a fast runner, and I know a few moves from tumbling around with my brother. But I don't know if I'm strong enough to fight him off. My body trembles at the way he stares, and my breathing becomes heavier.

"Maybe you should leave and let the lady change alone. President Esther wouldn't like having a rapist on her detail."

"Hey, hey, no one is raping anyone." He holds up his hands. "You have the wrong idea."

He turns to the dark-haired boy who was my savior earlier.

"Fine, I will leave," he barks. "But, I'll be back. You can count on that."

He looks back at me and smirks, showing all his teeth, and then he walks away.

"Thank you," I say. "You have saved me twice tonight."

"Don't thank me." The dark-haired boy walks closer to the bars. "I'm sure you can handle yourself. After all, you're the one who took on President Esther tonight in your speech. No one else has ever done that. Congratulations on standing up to her. I'll leave and let you change now."

I didn't notice it earlier, but his voice is deep, and it sends a chill up my spine.

"Wait," I say. "I don't even know your name. I didn't catch it earlier."

"Because I didn't want you to know it," he says. "But now that I know you're worthy, I can tell you." His eyebrows slant together.

Even though his face is serious, I still find it inviting. I feel I can easily talk to him.

"What does that mean?" I ask, stepping out of my heels. My feet are aching. "What makes me worthy?"

"You can think for yourself. I like that. I'm Eric," he says, putting his hand through the bars. "Nice to meet you."

My stocking feet swish across the cold floors, as I walk over to the bars and extend my hand.

His hand is warm against mine, and I hold the embrace longer than I should. Finally, I pull away, and step back from the bars.

"I should change clothes."

"I'll leave and let you do that." His serious face looks embarrassed. He turns and walks away.

I quickly take off my dress. The air feels cold and damp. I put on the blue shirt and pants I was given. I refuse to sleep in the thin nightshirt, not with all the male guards walking around and not with the cold chill rushing over me. I take the upsweep portion of my hair down and run my fingers through the strands. I lie down on the bed and curl up in a ball. Every creak and screech I hear makes me jump. And, my body frissons.

I wonder if Rich will come back down here tonight. Maybe I should sleep with one eye open—if I can sleep at all. I can't keep worrying about him. I have to think about more pleasant things. But it is dark and grim here, and that request is hard to fulfill when I would rather be at home in my own bed. I want to cry, but I can't show weakness; so, I blink until the tears go away.

*

"How was your night?" my brother asks.

T is standing outside my jail cell wearing his black uniform. Maybe it's my imagination, but it looks as if he has silver buttons on his black jacket. I wipe the sleep from my eyes and wobble to my feet to get a clearer look at him. I use my hands to wipe off the blue clothes I slept in, as if that would take the wrinkles away.

"What time is it?"

"It's almost ten." He glances at his wristwatch. "I'm surprised you could sleep here."

"I'm surprised I could, too. I guess I was more tired than I thought."

"Are you all right?" My brother has concern plastered on his face. It's a different look for him but nice to see.

"I'm fine."

"Don't say it if you're really not."

"No." I shake my head. "I'm really fine," I say, trying to sound convincing.

All the while knowing the thickness in my throat is choking me, and I'm scared of what each new day will bring.

"How are Mother and Father? Are they okay?" I ask, changing the subject.

"I could hear Mother crying all night, and Father was really quiet."

"I'm sorry for hurting them. That wasn't my intent."

"I'm sure they know that."

I like this side of him. The side that is there for me as a big brother, instead of being a jerk to me as he sometimes is.

"I can't believe I have to stay in this dungeon for the next thirty days." I glance around at my surroundings again. "What will happen to Tay—" I stop myself from saying her name aloud.

"It's okay if you say her name." My brother grips his hands around the metal bars. "One thing I know is they don't bug the jail cells or the prison. It's an invasion of privacy to listen in on a prisoner's private conversation. President Esther doesn't allow it."

"I'm glad you have such faith in her word, but I don't." I place my hand around his on the bars. I know we love each other, but we never express it. I touch his hand because it's nice to have family nearby.

"And don't worry about Taylor. I have it covered."

I know he means well, but he doesn't convince me. If I keep thinking about it, my eyes will swell; so, I try dwelling on other things.

"How did you get those?" I ask, removing my hand from his fingers. I point at the two circular, silver buttons on the top left side of his black jacket. "You didn't have them yesterday."

"My trip here wasn't just to see you." He removes his hand from the bars. "The president summoned me and the other young recruit to be here at eight this morning."

"Summoned?"

"Last night she told me and Eric to be here at eight because she thought it was time we received our silver buttons. I'm a full guard now." His chest puffs up proudly. "She wanted to give them to us last night during the ceremony but—"

"I ruined everything and the party ended early."

"Yes, that's correct."

"How can you be proud to be one of her guards?"

"It's a great honor to be a guard so young. She doesn't usually let you be a guard if you're under twenty-one, and even then, you have to start off on the streets as a patrolman and work your way up. So, I'm happy I skipped past that step, and after only a few months of training I'm a guard."

"Yes, we discussed this in the marketplace," I say, raising my eyebrow. "And I now know you lied to me when we were in that very marketplace. You already knew the real reason you were chosen, and that is because she used to be friends with Mother and Father."

"I don't think that's the only reason." T's face is red.

I've probably hurt his feelings and his pride. He wants to think he got in because of what he can do, and not because of who he knows. I shouldn't, but I continue ranting anyway.

"What other reason could there be?" I ask.

"Why are you making a big deal out of it?"

His face is even redder now, like the color of blood. I didn't mean to make him angry.

"Why can't you let me have this?" he asks.

I bite my lip. "I don't think this way of life is going to make you happy."

He doesn't know that I overheard the two guards in the woods calling him weak. And even if President Esther does know my parents, why would she want someone weak to guard her? She could have made him a patrolman—there are thousands of them—and if he screwed that up no one would notice, but this is different.

"I'm sorry, Theodore. I didn't mean to upset you." I bite the inside of my jaw. "What do the buttons mean?" I ask, changing the subject. "I see you have two."

"It depends." He gives a half-smile, as though he is happy to be talking about his new job again. "The more buttons you have the more courage and bravery you've shown. That is according to

President Esther's standards. The maximum you can have is six. The more you have the higher up in the ranks you are."

I don't want it to, but my brain goes back to Rich. He had six silver metal buttons. Of course he would. My leg spasms and my insides convulse.

"What is with the look on your face?"

I realize I'm frowning. "Congratulations, T," I say, even though I'm lying. But I don't want him to think the frown was for him and the amount of buttons he has. "Congrats on your new job."

"Thanks, but I should go now." He glances at his watch. "I wouldn't want to screw up my very first day out of training."

"No, we wouldn't want that."

"You take care, okay?" His eyes turn grim. "I'll be back to visit when I can."

I watch him turn to walk away.

"One more thing, T," I say, loudly. "What do you know about the other young guard? I think you said his name is Eric."

I pretend as if I haven't already met Eric.

"Not much." He shrugs. "He seems nice but way too serious. Why do you ask?"

"No reason." I place a strand of hair behind my ear.

I glance down and see another brown spider like the one from yesterday. The jail seems to be riddled with them. I step on it. It splats and I see its insides spread across the floor. I shudder, because I fear the same thing will happen to me and my brother, the longer we're around here.

*

I hear footsteps coming near my cell, and I pray it's not Rich. My chest feels lighter once I see who it is. It's a tall, dark-skin young man I've never seen before.

"I'm Samuel," he says, walking up to the bars.

He has light brown eyes, brown hair, and his face is kind. He looks to be in his middle twenties like most of the other guards. His black uniform has five silver, circular buttons, and I now know what five buttons mean. There is a gun sticking out of a holster on his hip, and another black, smaller device on his opposite hip, along with a small radio.

"I'm one of the guards watching over you today. I'll be walking you down to the bathroom, so you can wash up and brush your teeth. And then, I'll bring you back here, so you can have breakfast."

I remain quiet, so he continues.

"I realize it's twelve o'clock and breakfast is normally served at nine, but there was some commotion upstairs."

"What was the commotion?" I ask, not expecting him to answer me, but he seems friendlier than most, and he does.

"A new guard moved in upstairs which means someone else got kicked out."

"I'm not quite sure what you mean."

"Only twenty guards are allowed to live here. That means when new recruits are brought in someone has to leave."

"Who decides which recruits stay, and which ones will go?"

I already know the answer, but I want to appear friendly, and keep the conversation going, that way I can ask the question I really want answered.

"President Esther, of course."

"How does she decide?"

"No one really knows, but everyone tries to do their best work and stay on her good side. Living here as a guard pays more than being on the outside. And she seems to favor the ones who are always here, by her side. Their families get better treatment and they get more perks."

"May I ask which recruit was chosen to live here?"

That's what I really wanted to know.

"If you're asking because of your brother…" His eyebrow rises. "He wasn't chosen. The other recruit, Eric, was."

That was like a stab to my heart, since I know how badly Theodore wanted to live here. And it would have been nice having him close by, during my thirty day incarceration. But it's for the best that he stays close by my parents, especially with the Taylor situation going on.

"May I ask you another question?"

"Yes, go ahead."

"Why would President Esther allow a jail cell to be in the basement of her home?"

"I wondered the same thing when I got here. It sounds stupid." He grins. "But it's not. This, of course, is not a regular house; it's a mansion. She likes the prisoners close by so they're easily accessible to her, and she can use them as she sees fit. This way, she can come down to see them whenever she wants."

He stops talking and glances around as if he's divulging secrets he knows he shouldn't.

"Even if they somehow broke out and got past the guards, got on the elevators and made it to the fifth floor, they would still need to get into her quarters. That's not going to happen, unless you have a key to her private door, or she lets you in."

He takes the keys out of his pocket.

"But the prisoners here are in for mild crimes, at best." He raises his eyebrow at me. "You know what I mean."

"Yes, I know." I nod, because he is talking about me.

"Now the prison is a different story. That's where the lifers are. Prisoners for life in case you didn't know what that meant." His eyes shift.

I did know—well, I could figure it out—but I keep quiet and let him continue.

"You have to go through the underground tunnel, which is about a mile or more away from here. The prisoners there have committed more treacherous crimes, so it is heavily guarded. No one is escaping from there." He shakes his head, and continues talking. "She really believes in what she is doing. She has different values then most—"

"Yes, that's why she thinks it is all right to kill children, if their parents are poor." I frown, cutting him off.

"She justifies it by saying they can't take care of them, so the child will be better off dead," he says.

"Do you agree with her?"

"We shouldn't discuss what I believe."

He lowers his eyes, and I can't tell if he agrees with her or not.

"Anyway," he continues. "I'm supposed to tell all inmates that their privacy will not be invaded here in her mansion. There are no listening devices or security cameras around here."

I already heard about the bugging devices from T, but not the cameras, so my ears perk up, standing at attention.

"The only cameras you'll find are in the hallway leading to her quarters—for safety reasons, of course—as well as in the tunnel leading down to the prisons."

"Are there cameras outside?" I ask, wondering if she, or someone, watched my family and me get out of the black car.

"Yes, at the front door and the back, but that is only to see who is coming and going from the house." He glances down, then back up. "We better go now, so you can get washed up."

Maybe he realizes he has said too much.

The keys dangle in his hand, and the metal door opens with a screech. I've only been here one night, but it feels like a lifetime. The stale air is the same inside the bars as it is in the hallway, but I still feel lighter walking out of them.

"Sorry, I have to do this." He takes out the handcuffs. "But it's protocol, whenever a prisoner leaves their cell."

He snaps the metal handcuffs around my wrists, and they feel cold to the touch. We walk down a long, dark hallway. I see a few other guards, wearing black gear, standing around. There are two desks that the guards must take turns sitting at when it's their turn to watch the cells. Now that I know what the silver buttons stand for, I'm inclined to look at them more intently. The stale air gets cooler as we head down the hallway, since there are no brick walls confining me.

The bathroom isn't far from my cell. It is only a few steps away. Samuel unlocks the handcuffs. I walk inside, and the door creaks behind me as it closes. Now I know what the squeaking noise was all night. It was people going in and out of the bathroom. It is odd to me because I seem to be the only prisoner, but maybe the guards use the same bathroom as I do. The thought makes me cringe.

I walk up to the sink. There is a small, white paper cup, and a toothbrush laid out for me. The brush, whooshing back and forth in my mouth, is heavenly, since it is something I can control. I can control how fast I brush, and how much toothpaste I use. What I cannot control is how long my sentence will be, or what will happen to my family, my siblings.

There is a square, cracked mirror in front of me. I blink while staring at myself. My hair is messy, and my eyes are red. I look like a castaway, lost on an island. My hand shakes as I reach for the white cloth on the sink, but I do my best to wash up with it. Even though it is not a shower, or a bath, it's better than nothing. The cool wetness of the cloth against my dirty skin feels like diving into a swimming pool when the weather is a hundred degrees outside.

There are no windows here. I hoped there would be, so I could see outside.

I hear a rapping at the door and Samuel's voice.

"You done in there?"

"Yes," I say.

Even though I wish I could stay in here forever.

I open the creaking door. Samuel quickly snaps the cuffs back on me, as if I'm planning to escape, and he takes me back to my cell.

"Sorry about the accommodations. The prisoner's bathroom is much larger, and there is a shower unit attached to it. It is out of order right now. That is why you had to use the guard's bathroom. As soon as it is back in working order, you'll be able to take a proper shower. Prisoners are normally given a chance to shower every other day, for five minutes."

He holds up his five fingers.

That was my next question. He must have read my mind. My chest softens, knowing I'll be able to take a shower and use a different, hopefully cleaner, bathroom.

"Samuel, you're needed upstairs."

My insides are queasy; it's Rich's voice.

"You sure about that?" Samuel asks.

"Yes, I'm sure." Rich's eyes narrow, as though he is upset someone questions his authority. "I can take *chosen* back to her cell."

"*Chosen*," Samuel says. "What does that mean?"

"Emma, knows what it means." His eyes angle in my direction. "It's a joke between us. Isn't that right, Emma?"

I remain quiet.

"She's in good hands with me."

Rich waits for Samuel to walk away, then he yanks the handcuffs as if he's pulling a vicious dog's chain. My chest narrows as he leads me back to my cell. All the guards, who were around on my way to the bathroom, have seemed to disappear. The hallway is dark and empty. If I scream now, no one would probably even hear me.

The cell door shrills as Rich opens it. He pushes me inside, as if I'm a feather and it takes no effort to move me around. I land on my cot and hear the scraping of the springs underneath me.

"Maybe we should play a game." His tone is low and wicked. "Prove to me how badly you want out of the handcuffs." He plops down on the cot next to me and caresses my cheek. "I can say one thing about you, you're a pretty little thing."

I'm not used to those words, and I always thought if I heard them, I would feel elated, instead of sick to my stomach.

He twirls his finger around a strand of my hair, and my body tenses from his touch. He moves his finger over my cheek again, and I feel his scorching breath on my skin. The tiny hairs on my neck stand, and I want to vomit. If I can only get out of the handcuffs, maybe I can defend myself.

"You don't want to do this. I'm special to the president." I hate the words as they come out of my mouth. My skin creeps, but I don't know what else to do—or say.

"The president can't save you now," he says, moving closer to me.

He is so close it's as if he's sitting on my lap. My head is lying against the hard cement wall. I choose to believe he won't really hurt me, and he only wants to scare me; but what if I'm wrong? I can't take that chance. He brushes his fingers across my lips. I open my mouth, and like a squirrel biting a nut, I bite down as hard as I can on his finger. His skin tastes salty, and I scowl in disgust.

"You little—"

"What's going on in here?"

I hear Samuel's voice, and I can breathe again. Rich stands and pretends he's getting the keys out of his pocket to take off my handcuffs. They clank together in his hands.

"I'm taking off her handcuffs."

"That's normally done outside the cell." Samuel glowers. "Are you all right, Emma?"

I don't think he trusts or believes Rich's story. I'm sure he can see my body shivering. But instead of telling him what happened, I keep quiet. Rich has six buttons and Samuel only has five. Rich is higher up and holds more weight around here. Maybe if I don't say anything, Rich will be pleased that I'm not a snitch, and he'll leave me alone. I know I'm lying to myself, but that is the only way I can justify not opening my mouth and spilling my guts to Samuel.

"I'm fine." My eyes feel like a faucet being turned on.

"I'm not sure if that's true, but you have a visitor. That's why I was called upstairs."

At least Rich hadn't lied to get me alone, which was my first thought. Samuel really was called away.

"I can remove her handcuffs," Samuel says, brushing Rich aside.

Rich gives me a heated look and walks out of the cell.

"Who's here?" I ask.

Samuel turns the keys. They click, unsnapping the cuffs from my wrists.

"It's your mother. But I know you haven't eaten anything yet. Would you like to eat before I let her visit?"

"No," I say, as I shake my head. "I'm not hungry."

I wipe my eyes with the back of my hands. The food here is probably no more appetizing than what we have at home, and I can't stomach it right now.

*

I just saw Mother yesterday, but she looks even older now. Her hair seems to have more gray strands, and her face looks paler. The circles under her eyes have doubled overnight. Her coat is unbuttoned, and I can see that her pretty green gown has been replaced by a dark brown, knit dress and black, flat shoes.

"I'm surprised to see you here." I want to say that I am happy to see her and I want to go home, but I have to remain strong and saying those words would only make me cry. "I thought part of my punishment was no visitors for the first three days." My leg is still shaking from my encounter with Rich, and my heart is in overdrive.

"I managed to work my way around that." My mother clutches her fingers around the bars. "Are you all right? Have you been eating?"

"Mother, it's only been one night."

Her fingers tremble, and I rub my hand over them.

"Well, it seems like a lifetime." Her voice quivers.

"I'm sorry, for what I did at the party." A tear falls down my cheek.

"Don't be sorry." She reaches her hand through the bars and wipes the tear from my face. "I'm proud of you for standing up for what you believe in, and not shying away as the rest of us did. I wish I had more of you in me." She brushes a strand of hair behind my ear. "I did, when I was younger; but as I got older, things changed.

I learned to go with the flow, for the sake of peace; but you're still young, and you haven't learned that lesson, yet."

"Your eyes don't show pride."

"My eyes are sad because of where you are, not for why you were placed in here."

"Thanks for saying that. I appreciate it."

"Don't forget, Em, I'm always your biggest supporter."

"Unlike Father. I can't help but see he didn't come with you. I know he's ashamed of me."

"Your father needs some time. He's not a rule breaker, like you and me." She rubs my chin.

"I know you're trying to be supportive, but I saw the disappointment on your faces."

"We weren't disappointed in you. We were saddened because we knew what was coming. We knew your fate, for disobeying, would be jail time." She lowers her head. "That was the look on our faces. You know we love you. And your father is not ashamed. We're going to get you out of here before the thirty days are up." My mother's eyes water.

Mother tries to be strong, and I love her for that. I know the reason they need me out of here. Even though T said it would be okay, I don't believe it.

"I'm so sorry, Mother," I say again. My throat is on fire. "I know you need me out of here, so I can take food to Taylor."

My mother's eyes constrict, and she looks around like I did this morning. "Maybe we shouldn't discuss this here."

"It's okay. T said you can talk freely."

"That's good."

"I was foolish," I say, completing my earlier thought. "I wasn't even thinking of who would help Taylor if I was locked up." My voice is shaky. "Father gets out of work too late to go. And I love you, Mother, but you would get rattled if the patrolmen stopped and questioned you."

Looking at Mother now, it's hard to believe she used to be a teacher. Once her parents passed away, she weakened, and the school threatened to fire her because she couldn't keep up with the workload like she used to. They only kept her on because they couldn't find anyone from Territory L qualified to take over her classes, and no one from the upper territories wanted to come and teach here every day, especially since it would mean a pay cut. Since the school was closing soon, they let her stay.

"I know everyone thinks I'm this delicate, little flower. I'm not," my mother says, with a thin smile.

The more I think about it, the more I know my brother only said what he did to appease me. How can he go help Taylor when he is a guard? He has schedules to stick to, and his every move might be challenged.

"All you need to worry about right now is surviving this place." She pats my hand that is wrapped around the bars. "I also wanted to give you this." She holds up my ID card. "You left your purse in the chair last night, and I noticed your card was in it. You may need it."

"Why would I need it in here? They already know who I am."

"I'm not sure, but it's supposed to be on you at all times; so, take it, just in case," she says, handing it to me.

"Mother," I say, gripping the card in my hand. "You said you would tell me everything after the party."

"That was before you ended up in here." She looks down. "But I realize you still have a right to know."

She looks back up, and purses her lips together. "President Esther and I grew up together," she continues. "She was a good woman during those times and was still the same after she married her husband, Henry."

My mother pats my fingers through the bars as if she is settling a small child.

"Henry was president from 2072 to the end of 2075, and he made many mistakes, like the men before him. Once his term was up, there were rumblings that he wouldn't be elected for a second term. Esther decided if her husband wouldn't win that she should run for office. She had many good ideas for our world. We agreed with her, then. So, we helped her campaign—"

"You and Father?" My eyebrow rises. I've never seen my mother speak with such passion.

"Yes, the both of us." She takes in a breath, and continues. "We were ecstatic when she won. So, in 2076, she became the first woman president and the youngest president our world has ever seen. She was a strong woman who brought new ideas and change to our world of Craigluy. During her first term, she managed to keep almost every promise she had made to the people; so, it was inevitable that she would win another term."

My hands tingle listening to the passion in her voice.

"While she was campaigning for her second term, she came up with the idea that if she won again there would be a law put in place that she would remain president until her death—or until she decided to leave office. Her first few years in office had been so wonderful that everyone agreed it was a good idea and the law would be enforced if she won. It may sound crazy to you now. But back then, it sounded like a good idea. Why bring in someone every few years to start over again, when she was doing so well, and we were all happy?"

She clears her throat, and the gleam in her eyes goes away.

"Why did things change so drastically?"

"No one really knows." She shakes her head. "But seven months after she was reelected, she changed. She no longer invited me, or your father, to the mansion for visits, and she stopped taking my calls. The only thing I can think is that maybe the power hardened her. She was thirty-seven when she was reelected, and maybe it was too much for her. I'm not sure." She shrugs. "But I do know her husband, Henry, disappeared, and right after that, many things began to change. Esther lost a lot of weight. Her hair went from golden blonde to silver. She became a different person—"

"Evil," I say, cutting her off.

"Yes, evil," my mother continues. "Esther said there needed

to be division among the different classes of people. Those who made more money shouldn't mingle with those who made less. She decided to divide us into territories. She spread those territories out and built a concrete brick wall around each one, so there would be no way for us to leave. She built an electric fence near the mansion and a gate. She and her guards now decide who they'll open the gate for, and who is allowed to cross into another territory."

She pauses for a minute and takes in a breath. I wait patiently for her to continue.

"The year you were born was the year everything changed. All you know is that Territory L is for the lower class, Territory M is for the middle class, and Territory U—"

"Is for the upper class or the wealthy," I say, finishing her sentence.

"Yes." She nods.

"Why didn't you tell me you were friends with her?"

"Your father and I decided there was no reason for you to know." She clears her throat. "And I suppose, we were embarrassed for helping her get into office. But I said when my children were of the appropriate age, I would tell them. So, I told your brother and sister when they turned eighteen. I told them not to tell you, because I wanted to, when the time was right."

"Weren't you afraid I would hear it from someone else?"

"I knew that was a possibility. But since a lot of the people who knew about it moved on to other territories, I figured there was only a slim chance of you finding out."

We see one of the guards appear, off to the side, which must mean visitation time is over. Mother makes a smacking sound as she puts her hand to her lips to blow me a kiss.

"Why are we stuck here among the lower class when Father is a doctor?" I know she has to go, but I've asked this question before and have never gotten an answer. I'm hoping she'll answer it, now.

"There are different classes of doctors." Her eyes amplify. "Your father is a family doctor, and they don't make as much as ones that specialize. All the ones with specialties live in Territory U."

"But some family doctors do live in Territory U." My chest feels hollow. "Why can't Father?"

I don't want to sound ungrateful for the things we have here, but I know I do.

My mother blinks a few times before answering.

"When Esther divided up the job classes, she picked some family doctors to go and some to stay. The ones who stayed here were paid lower wages. I think the main reason Esther kept us here was because we were no longer friends, and your father and I no longer supported her ways. But your father didn't mind living here because he knew the people here needed help, and he wanted to help them. Not by going back and forth through the gates, but by really being here, full time, to help them. Besides, my parents lived here and we didn't want to leave them."

I couldn't argue against that, especially seeing the pain in her eyes when she spoke about them.

"I love you, and I'll be back," she says, then walks away.

I plop down on the cold cot and sob into my mattress. I have answers to many of my questions now. But it still doesn't help me get out of here. What good was my big speech for justice if it gets my sister and her baby killed in the process? My heart crumbles, as if someone is hitting it repeatedly with a mallet. I'll never forgive myself if something happens to either of them.

CHAPTER NINE

"WHY ARE WE HERE?" I ask Samuel.

We're on the third floor of the mansion. The elevators were slow so we used the stairs at the end of the hallway to get here. Samuel has walked me past the room with what resembles an electric chair and down to another room. After eight days of being confined to a cell, I'm happy to be out. My chest feels lighter, like a feather. But I still don't know where we're going, or why I'm out and about with no handcuffs on. He has on dark gray jogging clothes, and I wish I could wear something else besides this blue ensemble.

Samuel still hasn't answered my question, and my eyes broaden, searching the room. The room is empty right now. It is quite large and looks like some kind of training facility. The walls are dark green and the lights are bright. It smells citrusy. The back of the room has benches to lift weights; and far off, in the corner, are yellow exercise mats. There are mirrors in the front and on the sides, so you can see yourself. The front of the room reminds me of a big dance floor, but I have a weird feeling in my stomach that it is not used for dancing. There is a long, dark green mat next to the area that looks like a dance floor. Over in the far corner, I spot several punching bags. I hear a loud popping sound that makes my shoulders vibrate.

"That's the gun range," Samuel says, seeing the frown on my

face. "It's where you learn to shoot a gun and to handle a stun gun or Taser."

"Taser?" My eyebrow rises.

"Yes. The patrolmen carry guns and the guards carry guns, Tasers or stun guns. Some even carry knives. They use whatever is needed to protect the president."

"What can a Taser or stun gun do?"

I'm not sure why I'm so interested but I am. I've never held any of these weapons, not even a gun, for that matter. I don't agree with violence, or killing, unless it is in self-defense. But like a kid in a Territory U candy store, I'm fascinated.

"A stun gun is an electrical device that uses high voltage to stop an attacker, but you have to use direct body contact. A Taser does about the same, except it can be used from a distance of about fifteen feet. Would you like to walk down and see the gun range?"

"Why am I here?" I ask, again.

"The president wants me to let you out of your cell for a while. She says to show you around the training and workout areas."

"I don't understand." My jaw tightens. "I've only been incarcerated for eight days, so why would she let me out now?"

"You're not out for good, only for a few hours. So, don't make a big deal out of it."

"But it is a big deal." My chest shrinks. "I don't want any special treatment around here. I want to serve my time like any other person would."

"Why are you so bent out of shape?" His light brown eyes are fixated on me.

"Some of the guards already don't like me because of who I am. This will only make it worse."

"You're talking about Rich, aren't you?"

I ignore his question because I hear loud footsteps and voices of guards entering the area. Some go off to the weights and others go over to the punching bags.

"I knew he did something to you the day I found him in your cell. The next time he hurts you—"

"He didn't hurt me," I say, because I don't want to be treated differently than the others. "I can handle myself."

"I'll say it again." He puts his hand on my shoulder. "If he does something to you again, you need to tell someone. Understand?" His eyes are sincere as he nods his head.

"Yes, I understand." I nod back.

"W-why are you so nice to me when a lot of the guards hate me?"

"The guards dislike you for stupid reasons. Besides, I didn't have a younger sibling that was taken away from my family." He scratches the back of his neck. "Even if I did, I wouldn't take it out on you when I know it's not your fault. You cannot control other people's actions."

"Thank you." I give a small smile.

"Besides, you don't have to worry about Rich. He was sent out to Territory M to take care of some business. He'll be gone for a while."

"How long is a while?" My chest compresses.

"At least ten days."

My chest opens and I can breathe again.

"Will you be all right here by yourself? I want to hit the bags for a while." He points over at the punching bags. "I'll take you back to your cell once I'm done. Unless you want to come with me?"

"No, I'll stand out of the way and watch everyone else."

I step back and look over the room. There are guards working out in the large area that I thought looked like a dance floor. They have on black, or dark gray, loose jogging clothes. They look different out of uniform. They are doing a series of high kicks and hand movements. An instructor is up front, guiding them through each movement. The instructor is dark-skin, tall, and muscular; and, he wears gray jogging gear. He asks for two volunteers to go over to the green mat and to go head-to-head with each other.

A tall guy, with black eyes and sandy hair, raises his hand.

"All right, Jason volunteers," the instructor says.

He looks like the tall guy who was training my brother. Another guy raises his hand to volunteer, and he looks like the tall guy's friend who was also training my brother. He is short and stocky, with brown eyes and brown hair.

"Rob, you volunteered last time. I would prefer someone else."

"Will I do?" a deep voice says.

Cold rushes through my chest because I know that voice. I turn to see Eric walking in. I haven't seen, or heard, from him in days. He wears a loose-fitting, black jogging suit much like the others. But his sweatshirt has the sleeves cut off. Some of the other guards working out have their sleeves cut off as well, but I hadn't really noticed until now. I see Eric's muscular arms and it sends a tingle up my spine. It's a feeling I've never felt before, and I can only assume it's inappropriate for me to think this way.

"So, the newest addition to our family would like to play," the instructor says. "Come on up and let's see what you got." He points to the green mat.

I don't know Eric that well, but from what I've seen, I assume he can handle himself. He assumes the same about me.

I watch as the two men square off and crouch down. They size each other up. Jason lunges first. Eric blocks his path with his right arm and pushes him back. Jason grunts like an ape and stumbles onto his feet; but Eric stretches out his left leg and kicks Jason in the side before he can fully hold his stance. Jason falls. Eric jumps on him and pins him down. Eric's right arm perches on Jason's throat, like a bird on a branch. And, from where I am, it looks like Jason is gasping for air.

"Eric wins this one," the instructor announces, as if it is a televised match on the information box. "Who would like to go next?"

I see a lot of guys raise their hands, but I don't notice who is picked because my attention turns to Eric. He is walking toward me. My knees vibrate.

"Y-you s-saw all of that?" His breaths are jagged from the fight.

"Yes, I did." My voice cracks. "I have to say that was the fastest fight I've ever seen."

"H-have you ever seen a fight before?" he asks, while wiping beads of sweat from his forehead with a towel.

"No." I shake my head. "So, I should rephrase that. That was the only fight I've ever seen, and I'm sure there've been faster ones, but I wouldn't know since that is the only one I've seen." I could kick myself because I'm rambling, like a little girl overcome by her first crush.

He gives a narrow smile, as if my rambling is cute. "What are you doing out of your cell?"

He walks over to a table in the corner where there is a refrigerator humming. I follow behind him and watch as he opens it. The cold air feels good on my face. Maybe it will help stop my knee from trembling.

I remember his question and finally answer, "Samuel brought me down here so I could look around. He said the president wanted to give me a break from my cell for a while. Do the patrolmen train here, too?"

"They used to, but that all changed when the number of patrolmen got to be as large as five thousand. Now, they have their own training facility down the street."

"That makes sense." I bite down on my lip, not knowing what else to say.

"So, what do you think of our training facility?" He gulps down half the bottle of water. Then, he crinkles the bottle in his hand while waiting for an answer.

"It is not what I expected." I glance around and see the next two volunteers, going at it on the mat. There are a series of kicks and moans and grunts.

"Exactly what did you expect, then?"

I turn my attention back to him. His sweatshirt is soaked with sweat, as though he has been outside in a rainstorm.

"I don't know." I shrug. "I know you guys have to be able to defend the president and you have to stop any crimes that go on in the streets, but I never dwelled on what your training would look like."

"Well, this is part of it." He gulps more water. "We learn skill and balance as well as strength and endurance. The other part of training is learning how to properly use a gun or knife. The most important part of training is using your hands as a weapon. I'd rather do that than defend myself with a gun. I want to show what I'm made of, not what a weapon can do. I have a rule that I live by. I don't fight to kill, just to maim or disable." His jaw looks tight and he clenches his fist.

"I agree with that logic," I say. "Do you mind if I adopt that rule as well?"

I glance over at Samuel. He is still punching the black bags. I smile a little, inside. I'm enjoying my conversation with Eric and as soon as Samuel comes to get me, I know it'll end.

"Be my guest." He shrugs. "It can be both of ours." His mouth creases. "Our little secret," he mumbles under his breath. "Even though I'm sure you've never been in a fight before."

"No, I haven't." I shrug. "I've never had a reason to." My jaw tenses, since I do have a reason now. I need to defend myself against Rich. He may be in Territory M right now, but what will happen when he gets back? "Fighting has never been my thing. I'm an acceptable runner though."

"What do you mean acceptable?" His eyebrows angle together.

"I consider myself fast."

"Have you ever timed yourself?" His tone is serious.

He's acting as if I stepped on his manhood and said something out of the ordinary. Maybe he considers himself a fast runner, and I have overstepped my bounds.

"No," I say, still wondering what the big deal is, and why he is getting so defensive. "I feel I do all right in that department. My brother and I would have races and I would always win." I lie, knowing the real reason is that I sprint through the woods, taking food to my sister.

"And that's what you're basing this on?"

"Do you think you could show me some moves, sometimes? It would be nice to know how to defend myself," I say, changing the subject.

"I don't see a problem with that," he says, crinkling up the bottle and throwing it at the garbage can. It thumps the side and then falls in. "The next time President Esther lets you out, I will show you a few."

"Why not now?" My voice cracks. Thinking about Rich makes me eager to learn.

"Samuel is coming." He points behind me. "I think it's time for you to go."

He's right. I hear Samuel running toward me, like a stampede of cattle.

"Emma, we should get going," Samuel says.

Sweat is pouring down Samuel's face, and he smells like a skunk after it has used its spray.

"Take care of yourself, Emma," Eric says, and then heads off in the other direction.

*

We stand at the elevator, and I accidently hit the button on the left for the commoner's elevator instead of the guard's. Samuel corrects my error by hitting the guard's button on the right. The commoner's elevator swishes open, and my eyes broaden because my father is standing inside.

My heart feels as light as a balloon floating on air because he is coming to visit me. But my heart quickly deflates like a popped balloon when I realize we're on the third floor and the elevator is on its way up. If he is here to see me, he would be nowhere near the third floor; he would be heading toward the basement.

"Father," I say, stepping inside.

"This is not the correct elevator," Samuel says.

"I'm a commoner, so why can't I use this elevator?"

"Because you're with me, and I'm supposed to use the guard's elevator. These are the rules."

Samuel has put his hand in between the elevator doors, so they can't close.

"The rules are stupid," I snap.

"I'll allow it, this one time." He holds up his finger to my face as if I'm a four-year-old disobeying him. Then, he steps inside and stands beside me.

"What are you doing here?" I glance at my father as the door swooshes closed.

"Emma," he says, then clears his throat.

His face is flushed. He wasn't expecting to see me.

I search his expression and it looks blank. There are deep circles under his eyes. The air in the elevator is cold, or maybe that's the chill coming from my father's stance.

"Are you here to see me?" I ask.

I know he's not, but I want to get some answers out of him.

"Actually, I wasn't." He shakes his head. "I'm on my way up to see President Esther."

There is no guard with him. I suppose, since they used to be good friends, he doesn't need one. Maybe he can come and go as he pleases.

"Why are you going to see her? Is it about getting me out of here?"

Samuel is right behind me, and I hear him clear his throat. The conversation is probably making him uncomfortable.

"No, Emma. There is no way you can be released before your thirty days are up. I trust you're doing what you're told, or your stay will be even longer." His eyes harden.

Mother said he wasn't disappointed or ashamed of me, but the way he looks at me now makes me think differently. My heart pounds in my chest because he is being so cold.

I pull out the red stop button and the elevator screeches to a halt in between floors. My stomach bounces along with it, as if I'm on an out of control bus that quickly stops at a red light. I'm pleased that no alarm sounds. Samuel looks at me and grits his teeth.

"Emma, what are you doing?" Samuel's voice is loud. "Are you crazy?"

"I need to discuss some things with my father. Please."

"This is unorthodox. I'm jeopardizing my job, but I'll step off the elevator for only a few minutes and let you talk alone."

He jams his finger on the red stop button, and like a cooker pressure exploding, the elevator ramps back into action. It dings and stops at its original destination on the fifth floor, but Samuel hits the button for the third floor; and, as quickly as the doors swoosh open, they close again. Once we reach the third floor, he steps off, as promised.

"You have two minutes." He puts up his fingers to indicate two, as if I can't comprehend what he means.

The elevator whizzes closed and stands still.

"Emma, was this really necessary?" My father rubs his hand through his gray hair.

"Mother said you weren't mad at me." My eyes betray me. They're swelling up with tears. "Or disappointed," I add.

"I'm not mad. But I am disappointed; not because you stood up for yourself, but because you know we need you for certain things and now I have to be the one to—"

"Is that why you're here?" I cut him off. Maybe he was caught going to see Taylor.

"No." He shakes his head. "It has nothing to do with that. The president wants to discuss a job opportunity with me."

"You already have a job."

"She's adding a personal doctor to her staff to look out for her. The doctor will be on call and she wants me to do it."

"But she's never needed a personal doctor before." My eyes narrow. "I thought any medical need of hers was taken care of by her wealthy doctor friends in Territory U."

"Well, I suppose that is all changing now." My father's voice is stern. "She wants someone nearby not an entire territory away."

"But this makes no sense." My throat feels scratchy like something is crawling on it. "Why can't she go to the hospital here if she needs someone right away? Why is everything changing?"

"I don't have all the details. That's the reason I'm here, to find out more."

"You can't really be considering this. You can't trust her."

"I'm a grown man, so you don't have to tell me about Esther. I know her better than anyone." He sounds disgruntled by my concern for his well-being.

Before I can question him further, the elevator rustles open and Samuel is standing there.

"Let's go, Emma. Get off the elevator, now."

His mild-mannered temperament is no more, and his eyes look straight through me as if I'm the enemy. I glance back at my father, once more, before exiting.

"Take care of yourself," he mouths. "I love you."

I don't have time to respond. The door rushes closed. The guard elevator rings and hisses open. Samuel grips my elbow in a manner I'm not used to.

"Don't ever put me in that position again," he says.

My eyes stretch open. "I'm sorry. But I needed answers."

"I give you more leeway then most guards only because I like you as a person, and I like that you stand up for yourself. But I should warn you: don't ever compromise my job like that again. I can't afford to lose it, and I will not jeopardize it for you—not a second time."

He is like a dog growling at a cat. I don't know him that well, but I somehow thought we were becoming friends. Maybe I was wrong.

The key clanks in the cell lock and the door clangs behind me. I drop down on my cot and the dust wafts up in the air. I hear Samuel's footsteps stomping away. A few minutes later, I hear footsteps stomping across the floors again.

"Emma, I'm sorry." His eyes are soft. "But you have to remember, I've been assigned to watch you temporarily. If the others hear that I'm showing you favoritism, they won't hesitate to replace me. If that happens, you could end up with one of Rich's flunkies watching you. And there is no telling what he'll tell them to do to you. Try and remember that." The corners of his mouth crease up, slightly, and he walks away.

I lay my head down on my balled-up gold dress that I have turned into a makeshift pillow. The sequins on the dress don't provide much comfort against my bare cheek, so I turn it inside out, but it still doesn't help much. My skin aches for a soft pillow, but it is all I have. I pull my dingy blanket up to my chin.

They never took my belongings from me after I arrived, so I still have my necklace with me. When I leave the cell to wash up, I hide it under my cot, next to my ID card.

I take it out, from time to time, and hold it up to my skin. It continues to give me comfort. Maybe it's because my mother gave it to me, or because of the special meaning it holds. All I know is I feel safer with it near me.

I can tell Samuel is one of the good guys, but I still need to watch my step. I have no friends here. I have to remember that.

CHAPTER TEN

IT FEELS WEIRD BEING back in my cell. Being on the third floor in the training facility made it feel as though I was in another world. It was a world that I felt energetic and vibrant in. It helped to remove my thoughts from how Taylor and Abigail—and my mother—are doing. It has been a few days since my encounter with Samuel. Since then, he's only brought me my meals and taken me to wash up.

I've had no visitors, not even Theodore. I've had plenty of time to be alone with my feelings and thoughts. Thoughts of what happened when my father spoke with the president. Thoughts of why Samuel is being so distant after he apologized. There were even thoughts of Eric and what he has been up to lately.

I push my tray away. I can't stomach any more breakfast. It is cold oatmeal; it tastes like dirt and looks like mud. The air still smells musty here, and it is hard to keep from crying. My body quakes because I'm cold and it is damp. There are still no other inmates. It would be nice to have someone to talk to. I haven't seen the pregnant woman who was taken into custody down at the marketplace. I wonder what became of her, but I don't dare ask. I lower my head in my hands. I want these thirty days to be up, so I can go home. I feel like a rat snake that eats its own skin because my thoughts are eating me alive.

I hear the jingling of keys and the pounding of footsteps. It is probably Samuel coming to get my tray. Maybe he won't be so distant this time, and we can have a conversation.

My face feels lighter. Eric is standing there with his hands embracing the bars. He has on a black zippered jacket and black jogging pants. I'm surprised to see him out of uniform, but my heart expands because he looks nice.

"I never got to say sorry about your brother. I know he wanted to live in the mansion. He expressed it to several of the guys."

"Thanks." I frown.

I know it's shallow, but I smooth out the wrinkles in my blue shirt and oversized pants.

"Why are you acting like you lost your best friend?" His eyes are glued to mine. "You should be happy your sentence is half over."

"Maybe it's because you said you would train me, and I haven't seen you in days," I say quietly.

That's not the only reason for my quietness, but he doesn't need to know that.

"If you remember right, I said the next time President Esther lets you out. I haven't seen you out of your cell recently, so how am I supposed to train you? I can't do it from in here."

His gaze is hard, and I tingle.

"The one and only time I was out to do anything eventful is because Samuel said the president wanted me to see the workout and training areas."

"That's not what I heard."

"What did you hear?" I ask, stepping closer to the bars.

"I heard the president questioned Samuel on how you were doing, and he said you would do much better if you could get out, from time to time, and look around."

My knee vibrates. "Why would he do that?"

"Maybe he felt sorry, seeing you locked up in here." He takes a silver key out of his pocket and dangles it in front of me. "You haven't been out for a while, and Samuel thought you might like to get out and stretch your legs."

"I don't understand why he wouldn't take me up."

"I don't know." He shrugs. "And I don't ask questions when things don't concern me."

"Out of all the guards, why would he ask you?" I bite down on my lip.

"Once again, I will reiterate, I didn't ask him a lot of questions. He saw me talking to you in the training facility, so maybe he thinks I'm the only guard you feel comfortable around, or maybe I'm the only one you know. Either way, it's none of my affair."

"Why did you agree to his request?"

His eyebrow rises. "Why does it matter who takes you upstairs? You did say you wanted me to show you some moves. Now, do you want to get out of your cell or not?"

"Yes, I do." I don't want him to change his mind, so I decide to keep quiet, for now.

"Let's go, then." He puts the key in the lock. "And what you need to be asking yourself is why the president would agree to let you out of your cell to watch the training sessions. She only lets people out for three reasons: to go to the bathroom, to take a shower, or to stretch their legs outside in the fenced in area. She never lets anyone up to the training facilities to observe or to work out."

The cell squeals open, and I can finally breathe because the bars aren't surrounding me. I see guards in black uniforms staring at me as we head for the elevator. Maybe they think I don't have a right to be out of my cell. And maybe Eric is right, and I should wonder why I've been allowed out and others haven't.

*

"We'll start with breathing. Proper breathing is important in fighting because you want to be able to move and duck, as well as block and kick, without running out of breath. Paying attention to your breathing also helps improve your focus and stamina," Eric says.

He walks over to a yellow mat. The zipper on his jacket screeches as he undoes it. He tears his jacket off. I hear keys clanking together in his pocket as his jacket hits the floor. I see the gray, sleeveless t-shirt that was hiding underneath. I also see the leanness of his chest, and the ripples in his arms, just as I did the other day. The material seems to grip his muscular chest.

"Do you have something else I can train in? These are my last pair of clean clothes, and I don't want to get them sweaty." I remove my gaze from him and glance down at my blue ensemble.

"You're supposed to sleep in the white t-shirt they give you." He looks me up and down.

"I don't feel comfortable in it." My stomach feels warm under his glare.

"The only female clothes we have are like the ones you already have on." He puts his left leg out, and bends his knee, downward, to stretch. "We don't have female training clothes here. But once we're done, I can get you some clean blue digs to wear."

"Thanks," I say, pushing the sleeves of my shirt up above my elbows. "Why is that?"

"Why is what?" he answers, a question for a question.

"Why are there no female guards?" I continue.

"Female guards," he says, repeating my words. His mouth crinkles up. "That's not heard of around here. President Esther would never allow it."

"Why?"

"Because women are weak, mentally and physically. They can't handle the job."

"Is that what you believe or what the president believes?" My jaw tightens. I hope he doesn't believe that.

"That's what most of the guys around here believe. As far as what the president believes, I don't know." He shrugs and cocks his head to the side. "I've heard rumors that she'd never allow a female guard."

"You still haven't told me what you believe." My voice cracks.

"You're small and, from observing you, you're quick-witted. I believe you could fly under the radar undetected. So no, I don't agree with the others." He puts his right leg out and bends his knee to stretch. "I would never knock a female. I think they have their own set of skills and strengths. And, if you're as fast as you say you are, after I teach you some of the training moves, you might become a force to be reckoned with." He stands and gives a small smile.

It is nice to hear him say that. And, it's nice to see him smile; his face is always so serious.

"How come you never smile?" I ask, but maybe I shouldn't.

"There's not much to smile about here. Besides, laughter and smiling shows weakness. I don't want to appear weak, or let my guard down, at least not around here. Now, can we get started before this place gets too crowded? Once the others arrive, they'll be in the way, and we won't be able to get much done."

"Fine, I'm ready."

I stand next to him on the mat and follow his instructions.

"As I said earlier, you have to learn how to pay attention to your breathing. When you're going up against someone, you have to breathe in as you prepare to make your kick."

He stretches out his leg to show me an example.

"Then, you exhale forcefully, grunt, or scream each time you kick someone or you get kicked. Take deep, steady breaths when your opponent is out of reach. Do you follow me so far?" His eyes are wide.

"I think so. But I can get it faster, if I do it instead of watching it."

"It's good that you're eager to learn. But let me explain a few more things, first." He walks in front of me. "So, first off, I want you to get in your stance, on your guard, in your fighting pose."

He bends his knees and squats, a little, as if he is squatting down to lift up a heavy weight.

"Go ahead, get in your stance," he says, staring at me.

I squat down and get ready for what he says next.

"If you're right-handed, like I am, then take a big step forward with your left leg. Then, let your right leg naturally point out to the side. Make a fist with each hand and raise your arms so they are bent at the elbows. Your right fist should be near your waist, while your left fist should be raised higher and more forward. Keep your arms raised at all times, so you can be prepared to attack or to block."

I do exactly what he says and wait for further instructions. His voice is calm, and his face is tense. Watching him makes my heart beat louder than the music that played during the ball.

"As you're getting your right leg ready for the kick, you should bend it so the back of your calf is almost touching your thigh. Point your knee out to the side and lean your upper body in the opposite direction, so you can balance yourself. You don't want to tip over because you're not balanced."

I picture myself tipping over and Rich taking that as his opportunity to pound me in half. I'm not concentrating on my body, and I find myself falling over. I wobble, like a ball, and try to steady myself again.

"You're doing exactly what I told you not to!" Eric's eyebrows slope together. He sounds annoyed.

"I'm sorry," I say.

I regain my composure and put my left leg out front and my right leg to the side. I bend my elbows and make fists again, keeping the right one closer to my waist. I bend back my right leg, so it almost touches my thigh, and I try to hold steady there. I lean my upper body in the opposite direction. I feel like a bottle on a ledge that sways until it finally steadies itself. My stomach tenses as I try to stabilize myself and wait for instructions.

"Pivot on your foot and then move your body so your right leg snaps toward your target. Extend your leg in a..."

He keeps talking, but the muscles in my stomach ache because it is hard holding this stance while he belts out instructions. So, I put both feet on the ground. Now that he is done explaining, I can start over. I follow all of his instructions and extend my right leg out to kick him; but before I reach his chest, he grabs my foot with his hand, I fall back, and smack down hard on the mat. The pain in my back feels as though someone is kicking me, repeatedly, and the pain in my head feels as if I'm being stabbed. I blink several times because my vision is blurry. I sway as I try to sit up. The room is spinning. I groan like an old person who is having trouble getting out of bed.

"Why did you do that?" I scream, as if I'm eight years old and the boy I like takes my ice cream.

"That's what happens when you don't follow my instructions." He shows no remorse.

"But I did." I brush myself off.

I try to stop my lip from quivering. But now, my stomach is in knots, like a rope tied to an anchor.

"No, you didn't. First of all, you didn't use any force behind your kick. You didn't shout or grunt. And, you didn't breathe in while preparing to kick. Most importantly, your kick was too slow. For someone who said she can move fast, you sure didn't show it here. I was able to grip your foot so easily because of how slowly you kicked me."

"Fine then." My ears burn. "Let's try it again."

I take my stance, like before. I hold up my arms. And this time, like a mother watching her newborn take its first breaths, I watch my breathing. I grit my teeth and dig deep down into my throat.

"Oomph," I say, grunting.

My right leg snaps toward him and, like a tiger seeking out its prey, I decide to go for his stomach. It is closer to me than his chest. Maybe he won't expect it since I didn't go there the first time. I kick with more force this time, and I feel the breeze from my leg swooshing up in the air. The ball of my foot lands on his stomach. It doesn't move him, but he gives me a thin smile.

"There you go," he says. "That was better." He rubs his hands together as if he is rubbing two sticks to start a fire. "Let's try it again. Come at me." He waves his fingers.

I grit my teeth again, and I see red, as I kick him with all my force. This time, he wobbles back, a little. I'm not sure if he did it for my benefit, or not; but gratitude flows in my chest.

"Good. Let's keep going," he says.

"All right," I say.

I like this more and more. I know we just started, but I feel stronger, less weak.

We keep going over this drill several more times. I'm out of breath, and I start to sweat.

"That's enough for today."

"I-I want to keep going," I say, even though I'm tired.

"No, you don't want to overdo it your first time."

He walks to the table on the side of the room and goes to the refrigerator. It buzzes as he opens it. He throws me a water bottle and it crumples in my hands.

"I want to let you in on a little secret." He holds the cold bottle up to his forehead, as if it is a cool breeze on a warm day.

"What is that?" The bottle clicks as I open it, and I gulp down as much as I can.

"When you kick me, it's not really hurting me. I move back, a little, so you think you're doing something. That way you can gain confidence."

"Well, thanks for the confidence booster. But now that the secret is out of the bag, my confidence level is going way down." I lower my hand to the floor to emphasize my point.

His abs are rock hard and his arms are like steel, so why would I be able to move him?

"As I said earlier, you can be a force, if you really apply what you learn and take this seriously."

"How," I say, shrugging. "If I wasn't even hurting you."

"The key to your success when you're going up against larger opponents is to kick them fast, where it will hurt the most." He wipes the sweat from his forehead. "If someone is really trying to hurt you, then you have to kick them where they least expect it."

"Such as…" My eyes search his.

"In the groin area or in the face." He moves closer toward me. "If they appear weak, as though they've never been in a fight before, then go for the stomach or chest. But if they're a strong opponent, then they could grab your foot like I did and really hurt you. So, with a stronger opponent, you need to kick them hard and fast in their face. Try and break their nose or their facial bones."

"How will I know if they're a strong or weak opponent?"

"You size them up." He looks me up and down. "You're smart. I'm sure you can handle it."

His finger brushes my chin and my shoulders frisson.

"The first time we saw each other at the party..." I hesitate because I shouldn't ask.

"Yeah, what about it?"

He turns and throws his water bottle in the garbage. It swooshes in the can, like a ball hitting its target. His face is firm as he turns to look back at me.

"During the party, you were staring at me." My voice cracks. "And I want to know why." My throat is dry, so I take another sip of water and gulp hard.

"If you must know, I thought you were pretty, like someone I might want to get to know."

His compliment is nice, but it's hard for me to believe I'm pretty. I know I'm only average. His gaze is hard and strong. My hands prickle.

"That's why I came looking for you. I wondered why you were upstairs for so long. When I came up, I found you in that room with Rich."

"So, you were worried about me?" My throat recoils.

"I wouldn't say worried." He shrugs. "I didn't know you well enough to be worried about you."

His voice drifts off, as he walks over to the mat to retrieve his jacket.

"Let's say I was a bit nosy about what was taking so long. We should get out of here now. A training session will be starting soon," he says, brushing past me.

I don't see any guards coming in to train. The room is so empty, I could probably hear my echo if I yelled. But my line of questioning seems to make him uncomfortable, so I let it go and follow him out of the room.

CHAPTER ELEVEN

"Better. Now, let's try it again," Eric says. He has on his gray jogging outfit again.

We have been at this for over a week, and I have to admit, I'm enjoying it. I wish I could wear normal workout clothes like the others, instead of this heavy blue uniform. Even so, coming here has become the highlight of my day. Not just getting out of my cell and getting some activity, but getting to know Eric. If we miss a day I will be disappointed.

We normally come early, to train before the other guards arrive; but today, we start late. The noise in the room is a little distracting. There are guys over at the punching bags, grunting and groaning. There are other guys over on the green mat, following an instructor through a series of moves. The room smells like musk mixed together with sweat. Eric and I are on the yellow mats, which has become our usual spot. I say *our* spot, as if we are a couple and this is the spot we always occupy for our dates. The thought makes me quake, and I find it hard to concentrate on my target.

"Em," he yells. "You're not paying attention."

"Sorry. I'm ready."

I start wearing my hair in a braid during our training, so it won't fall in my eyes. I need to be in control, at all times. Since we've been practicing, I have been getting faster. My confidence level is high.

I could go for the groin or the face like he taught me, but I have a few tricks up my sleeve that Eric doesn't know about. I would like to show him, but I don't want to hurt him.

If he was a real opponent, someone who was a threat to me, I would go for his eyes. If I could move fast enough, kick an opponent hard enough in the groin, and daze them, then I could finish it off by poking their eyes. My opponent would be blinded and that would give me a good chance to get away. When I'm in my cell at night, I think of ways to injure my opponent. I think Eric would be proud of my ambition.

I breathe in and take my stance. I move fast. My right leg goes to the side, and I kick as hard and as high as I can. The ball of my foot lands squarely on his left shoulder. He stumbles back, and I don't believe he is acting because he moans and almost falls over.

"You've never gone for the shoulder before. That's good." He rubs his arm.

"There are a few other places I could go as well, but I don't want to hurt you."

"Really?"

"Yes, really." I smile.

"Well, I don't want to hurt you either, but maybe we should change that."

All of a sudden, he kicks back, which he has never done before. I feel the ball of his right foot hit my waist and I fall to the ground. I hold onto my side and groan out in agony.

"You left yourself wide open."

My side feels as if I'm being stabbed with tiny little needles. My eyes water, and I look up at him.

"W-why did you d-do that?" My breaths are jagged and it is hard to speak.

"When you were giving me all that trash talk, I realized I've been showing you how to hurt someone. But you need to know what it feels like to get hit. How to take it like a fighter and get right back up."

"I don't think I like this part." Tears stream down my face, and I wipe them with the back of my hands.

Guards are all over, and I don't want them to see me crying.

"You're supposed to keep your stance and your arms up, at all times." He kneels down beside me.

"I thought that was what I was doing?"

I'm still lying on my back as though a train mowed me down. My chest is tight as if a tiny person is standing on it.

"Now you see that you weren't." He grips my hand and pulls me back up toward him. "Whisper, you have to get as good as you give."

"What?" I ask. My legs twitch as I stand.

"It means you want to destroy me, but you have to be able to take the pain as well."

"That's not what I mean." I groan and brush my hand through my mangled hair. "Why did you call me Whisper?"

"Because you're getting fast. You're like a deadly weapon." He brushes a strand of hair that I didn't catch from my eye. "You're like someone who sneaks up on you. They appear quiet and weak, like a whisper. But once they've pounced, you see that they're really a deadly weapon. And, your last name is Whisperer." He cocks his head to the side. "So, it's a good fit."

His hand moves to my waist, and I feel a tickle go up my spine along with the pain.

"Now that you're quick on your feet, we need to move on to your response to pain when you're hit."

"I don't think I like that part." I bite my lip. I know I've already said that; but I really mean it, so I repeat myself.

"I realize that," he says, continuing to rub my side. "But it comes with the territory, and it is something you need to learn and be prepared for. That's enough for today."

I see tiny beads of sweat across his brow.

"No," I say, as I glance around. "I want to be as tough as anyone in this place, so I would like to move on to the punching bags. Maybe that will help me to gain some upper strength."

"Are you sure?" His face scrunches up, and it seems he is concerned for my well-being.

"Maybe we can start on that tomorrow." He hands me a towel.

"No, I want to start on it today." I wipe the moisture from my forehead.

"Okay, but you need to start slow, so you don't over exert, or hurt, yourself."

"I think it's a little too late for that last part," I say, touching my side. "Why did you get so mad at me the first day I saw you here?" I ask, while walking over to the bags. "When I said I was a fast runner?"

My side aches—like the needles jabbing it are going at a high rate of speed—and I continue to rub it. Maybe the punching bags aren't such a good idea for today, but I have to learn to work through the pain.

He gives me a blank stare, and I think he wishes I hadn't brought up the subject.

He hesitates, and then finally speaks, "It angers me when people say things and aren't able to back them up."

"So you thought I was lying?" I frown.

"I'm sorry, if you felt my anger was directed toward you." He stands behind one of the black bags. "I've had a lot of people in my life make promises and not back them up."

"I didn't mean to bring up a sore subject."

Maybe he's speaking of his family. But the pained look on his face tells me I shouldn't pry anymore. I've seen him angry, and I don't care to see that side of him again.

My throat thickens, staring at the bag in front of me. I feel a little intimidated by its size and weight. From across the room, this didn't look hard; but now that I'm standing in front of it, I'm not sure if I can hold my own. Besides that, I smell like a cow in a field of hay on a hot day. I should take a shower.

"We don't use gloves, or hand wraps, here. We use our bare fists because it strengthens the bones, muscles and tissues of our hands.

I'll hold on to the back of the bag to keep it steady." He bends his knees, a little, to hold his posture. "Follow my instructions."

"Okay," I say. The thickness in my throat now feels like burning.

"I want you to punch the bag with a flat fist. Close your hand. The top row of knuckles and the fingers below should make contact with the heavy bag at the same time. Try to keep your hands loose while you're in your defensive stance. Tighten your fist just before you strike the bag."

I do as he says and punch the bag with all my might; but it doesn't move.

"That was good." His eyes expand. "Now, I noticed your wrist was slanted. I want you to make sure you keep your hand, wrist and forearm all in a straight line each time you make contact with the bag. You want your arm, shoulder and wrist along with the hand to be tight before you make impact. They should work as one unit. Understand?"

I nod. "Yes, I understand."

"Also, try and keep your balance, so ground your feet. Make sure to punch, don't push. And, don't forget to breathe."

There are so many instructions that my head spins. And, my side still throbs as if my appendix has burst.

"Punch quickly and then pull your hand away just as fast. Don't worry so much about power but on how accurately you hit the bag. Hit the bag three or four times, rapidly."

"Okay," I say, taking in a breath.

I have a tendency not to breathe when we're training, so I want to make sure I don't forget that. I take my stand, breathe, and ball up my knuckles. It is harder than I thought to keep my entire arm in the same plane. I do my best, and then punch the bag as if I'm punching my opponent in their face. I notice that when I follow his instructions exactly, the bag wobbles a little.

"Good. Keep going, two more times," Eric says.

"Okay," I say.

I grunt from the pit of my throat and punch the bag again, as hard as I can. I keep this up for what feels like hours, but Eric claims it has only been ten minutes.

"That's enough for today." He stands from the bag. "The skin on your knuckles is broken. We don't want you to fracture them, because then we would have to send you over to the hospital, which is a hassle."

I was in the moment, and hadn't noticed, but he's right; my skin is broken. I don't see any blood, so that's a good thing.

"I should get you back down to your cell." He grabs my hand and rubs the broken skin.

The loud yells in the room are silenced because I'm so focused on him. My eyes cling to his and my knee trembles.

"Whisper," he says, with soft eyes.

This is only the second time he has called me that, but it sends a warm rush up my spine.

"I know you started all this to defend yourself against Rich, but your thirty days are almost up, and he hasn't even been around."

He lets my hand go and gives me a towel, breaking the moment between us.

We walk through the training area, and I hear whooping and hollering from every corner. Even so, I can't take my gaze off him and what he is saying.

"Why do you keep this up, if you'll be leaving soon?"

I may be reading more into this, but his eyes look sad, and I think he doesn't want me to leave.

"Now that we started this, I realize I like knowing how to defend myself. Even when I leave this place and go home, it will be good to know how to handle myself in any situation."

And, I like spending time with you, I think.

But, of course, I can't say that out loud.

CHAPTER TWELVE

IT FEELS GOOD BEING out of those sweaty clothes. Now that I'm back in my cell, I've changed into another blue uniform. I lie here, nursing my side. It hurts more than I was willing to admit to Eric. Maybe I should've let him put ice on it, like he wanted. I could've used the ice on my knuckles, too; but now, I'll have to bear the pain.

I don't know what time it is, but my internal clock tells me dinnertime should be soon. What will it be tonight: cold spaghetti or burnt meatloaf? I shouldn't complain; the food here is better than the beans back home, and it comes regularly. It is not like at home, where we sometimes have one or two meals a day instead of three.

My mother was usually out of work for four months out of the year, when school was on break. Yes, Father worked; but since he is a doctor in the lower-class territory, he doesn't make much. We had to watch every penny.

Now that Mother's job is gone for good, things are that way again, unless T can contribute his paycheck. I know he wants to help out, but I don't think he will make as much as he hopes. President Esther is not trustworthy. And, if she doesn't like you, I believe she will garnish your wages.

I hear keys clanking together. I fully expect it to be another guard, bringing my meal, since Samuel doesn't come anymore. But along with the keys, I hear crying. I can tell it is from a female. My shoulders jolt because I hear a commotion. A guard yells at her to quiet down. I don't like this kind of uproar; it unnerves me and makes my skin crawl.

"Pipe down. I don't want to hear all that whining in here."

I see the short, husky guard with the brown hair standing next to the tall guard with the piercing black eyes. I haven't seen them since that day in the training facility. Looking at them now makes my stomach wince. They're the ones who said my brother was weak. If I remember correctly, the two jerks are Jason and Rob.

Jason, the tall guard, has a grip on the girl's arm.

"I said pipe down," he yells.

"Aren't you lucky?" says Rob, the short one, while looking at me. "You finally have some company."

I grit my teeth as I watch him unlatch the squeaky cell next to mine. He shoves the girl inside. She lands on her cot with a *thump.*

"Good workout there, Jason," Rob says.

"Thanks," Jason says. "But I was just doing my job." His chest puffs up. "Taking out one who disobeys is what we do." He chuckles as if he has done a good deed. "Now, let's get out of here and get a drink."

Rob slaps Jason on his back as if they are best buddies going to a party.

I turn my attention away from them, and I stare at the girl crying in her cell. Her shoulders are hunched over, and she shakes. Her dark hair falls in her eyes. I recognize her. Cassandra Thompson is the granddaughter of Mr. Thompson, the pawn shop owner. We're not really friends. But I know she is Taylor's age because they went to school together.

"Are you all right?" I ask, leaning on the bars in between our cells.

"N-not really." She wipes her hair from her green eyes and looks at me.

"What happened? Why are you here?" My fingers twitch holding the bars, in fear of her answer.

Her eyes stretch, and she glances around.

"It's safe to talk here," I say.

She shakily stands and tugs on her gray sweater, pulling it over the top of her pants. She looks thinner and frailer than I remember. Her light-skin face is sunken in, and it makes my throat stiffen.

"You're E-Emma." Her voice quivers. "Emma Whisperer."

"Yes, that's me." I glance down and then back up. I'm not sure if she thinks that is a good or bad thing.

"Y-you're Taylor's little sister. I s-saw you make that speech over the information box." She sniffs and wipes her face.

"Why are you here?" I ask, again.

She slides down to the floor as though all the strength has left her body. I sit down as well. She speaks softly and I want to be close to hear what she says.

"I made a mistake, an awful mistake." She shakes her head. Tears engulf her face, like a typhoon.

"I'm pregnant."

"That's not a mistake." I'm close enough that I can rub her hand through the bars. "Don't ever see it that way."

I feel my own eyes tearing because this reminds me of the conversation I had with my sister.

"The president sees it that way, and so do a lot of the people here."

"That doesn't matter. All that matters is what you believe." I blink away a tear. "May I ask what happened?"

It takes her a while, but I see the heavy motion of her chest going in and out, slowing down. Her tears lessen and she looks back at me.

"I was attracted to a guy, Garret, in school," she says, then pauses and closes her eyes. "I'm an only child, so I was lonely. After graduation, we started dating. He wanted to marry me, but my parents said I was too young. They said I needed to focus on more important things—such as finding a job, and being a good citizen— so we could make it to Territory M."

She blinks.

"But I was in love with him, and he said he loved me." Her voice trembles along with her hands.

My stomach is woozy because I've never been in love with a boy. I don't know how it would feel to care so much about one person. I love my family, but I suspect the love for a boy is quite different. I rub her hand and it is as cold as ice. I don't know what to say to comfort her, so I remain quiet.

"Even though my parents were against it, we still saw each other, in secret. We would go to his house while his parents were at work. One thing led to another, and we did things." She glances down. "But we always used protection. They give it out free for that purpose, so why wouldn't we?"

She looks back up at me. She stares at me as if I'm judging her, but I'm not. I'm waiting for her to finish what she has to say.

"I'm not stupid. I understand the laws. I know what happens if you end up pregnant. But we used protection, every time." She takes in a big breath and her eyes water again. "B-but the protection didn't work, one time, and now I'm having a baby."

She twists her hands together. It remains quiet for a while, and I hear some of the guards talking, around the corner.

"How far along are you?" I ask, breaking the silence.

"Four months." She blinks.

"How did you end up here? How did they find out?"

"My parents turned me in."

My ears ring. Maybe I didn't hear her correctly. What parent would do that to their child?

"I was so shocked, at first," she continues. "It was hard processing everything. Garret wanted to run off together. But there is nowhere to run, there is nowhere to hide here. And even if we were able to find some place to hold up in once the baby is born..."

Tears stream down her face like it's coming from a hose.

"There is no way to keep it a secret. You need baby clothes and baby food." She shakes her head. "The baby is going to grow and need schooling. I guess I could homeschool the child, but I still think a child should go outside, every so often, and see the sunlight or get some fresh air."

My thoughts go to Taylor and baby Abigail. My chest locks up.

"I told Garret that we couldn't run off and that I was going to tell my parents because it was the right thing to do. But he said if I did, I was jeopardizing the baby because it would be taken away and killed. He wanted us to try and sneak past the gates into Territory M. And then, if somehow we made it there—which we wouldn't— he wanted us to try and get to Territory U where his aunt and uncle are." She scratches the top of her head. "He was living in a dream world. There was no way we could make it all the way to Territory U without getting caught. But he said once we were there, his aunt and uncle could help us raise the baby."

It is quiet again, and the silence is eating me up like a rat snake, again. I want—no, I need—her to finish her story.

"I told him the whole idea was crazy; but he said if I told my parents, I would be killing our child and he would be done with me. I didn't see any other way out." Her tears puddle on the floor. "I was two months along when I told them. My dad was furious and wanted to turn me in, but my mom wanted more time to figure out another solution. My dad said I was putting my entire family in jeopardy. All their dreams of moving on to Territory M were now destroyed. Everything was my fault because I was promiscuous."

"None of this is your fault. The same thing can happen to a grown, married woman. The laws are stupid and out of order." I feel a fire in my belly, as if two matches are rubbing together under my skin.

"My parents started fighting all the time over the situation. I felt as though I had no other choice. So, I tried to abort the pregnancy."

"I don't understand." I blink.

I heard what she said but I don't fully understand what she means. The law states no abortions are allowed. If you get yourself into a predicament, you're responsible to carry the baby to term.

Once you deliver at the hospital, you have to watch as the

guards take the baby away to some unknown place, and the baby is killed. It is part of the punishment for committing the crime, along with being jailed for thirty days, or longer.

"I didn't want my parents to be jailed for keeping my secret. And, I didn't want a baby to be born just to be killed. I figured I was only three months along, and I could terminate it myself." Her eyes are red and puffy.

"How could you do that?" Heaviness lies on my chest as she speaks.

"I starved myself. When my family was at the dinner table, I would chew and spit into a napkin. If I did swallow, later on I would make myself throw up, hoping the baby wouldn't get any nourishment. I wanted the baby to die before it was big enough to know what was going on."

She rubs her eyes.

"I know, I'm a horrible person." Her shoulders wobble. "P-please, don't think less of me."

"I don't think less of you. It takes guts to go through what you have—"

"Don't say that," she says, cutting me off. "I'm not brave. I'm a coward. My mother wondered why I was becoming so skinny. She said I was only skin and bones and told my father. He put two and two together and realized what I was doing." She wipes her nose with the back of her hand. "My father tried to make me eat something, but I refused. He said enough was enough because he'd already been having trouble helping my grandfather pay bills at the pawn shop. My father was fed up with everything. He told one of the patrolmen walking down our street one night. The patrolmen informed the guards. And, the next day, they came and put handcuffs on me. That is how I ended up here. I'm sure they took Garret in, too, after my father told them who the baby's father is."

"I'm sorry," I say quietly. My stomach is in knots, and I don't know how to help her.

"All I can think of is my mother's distraught face when they took me away. My parents are good people, and they don't deserve what I put them through." She looks down. "And, neither does this little one. All of the trouble I went through was for nothing." She rubs her belly. "This little one will suffer." Her tears flow again.

Darkness emerges over me. I know it is wrong, but I wish I was alone again in my cell. I no longer want to make conversation because it reminds me too much of my sister and the baby. The more she speaks about her unfortunate circumstances, the more anguish wells up in the barriers of my chest. Tears are caught in my throat. The walls close in on me, and I'm suffocating.

I wish Eric would come and take me for another training session, so I can blow off some steam. But we've already completed our training for today, and there won't be another one until tomorrow.

"All right. Lights out, you two." It's Samuel's voice. "Here are your clothes."

He balls them up and throws them through the bars at Cassandra. They hit the floor with a *whack*.

"You can change now," he says, walking away.

A heavy hand lies on my chest; he barely looks at me.

"What does that mean?" Cassandra sways as she stands.

"They cut the lights off at nine. They usually come around and tell you to change into your night clothes because the lights will be going off in ten minutes. That's your chance to tell them if you need to go to the bathroom before going to sleep."

"Do we change in here?" Her bloodshot eyes blink.

"Yes," I say. Knowing what she is getting at, I continue. "The lights come on at eight and go off at nine. They come around and bang on the bars for you to get up in the morning. You have ten minutes to get dressed. Then, they come and take you down to the bathroom and the showers. Once you take a shower, you put back on the very clothes you just took off." I stand. "In case you're slow changing, they yell 'all decent' when they come around the corner, to make sure they're not catching you in a compromising position. If you're changing, you yell back 'still changing' and they'll come back in a few minutes. The same thing happens at night. They announce lights out so you can change, and then ten minutes later, they come around to make sure you're changed and on your cot."

"I don't think that's ethical."

"Nothing here is." I shrug. "But there are no female guards, so it's what we have to deal with."

"Why can't we change in the bathroom, or where we take our showers, so they don't walk in on us?"

"They say it's too much trouble for us to carry our clothes to the bathroom and bring our night clothes back once we've changed out of them. And, they say it takes up too much time."

Her voice shakes. "Trouble for whom?"

"I think that's what they tell us. Some of them are perverts and want to catch us changing. I don't worry about it. I don't change into night clothes, anyway. I normally wear my blue uniform to bed. I feel more comfortable in it. Since I only change into fresh clothes every few days, I don't really worry about them walking in on me. But you should change before he comes back," I say, wanting the conversation to end.

I smack down on my cot and dust puffs up in the air. All I can think about are my parents and how they would never turn Taylor in. Even if it meant they would get caught and go to jail, they still wouldn't do it.

I hear Cassandra's cot scrape as she lands down on it. My ears sting as she cries again; I want to cry as well. Maybe she is right and all our efforts for Taylor and Abigail are a waste. Maybe she had the right idea, trying to abort her baby. Maybe it's for the best. I don't like the thoughts I'm having. I can't let wicked views like that creep in. My stomach cramps.

I don't like this feeling of vulnerability. It makes me weak. I wipe a tear from my cheek. Everything she said reminds me that my family hasn't visited me since the first day, after the party. My insides ache, wondering how they are and why they haven't come here. I close my eyes and picture my parents having dinner—probably some sort of beans—without me. My mother makes small conversation like everything is grand, and my father nods at everything she says. Taylor and Abigail might have no food at all. And then, there is T. How is he? I don't know how any of them are because I'm stuck in here.

*

Morning comes quicker than I'd like. I sit on my cot wearing a fresh, clean uniform; but it's still baggy and blue. Nothing has changed, except for the fact that I have a new roommate. There is a twinge of guilt in my chest. I feel sorry for her, and don't know how to help.

I watch as Samuel stands in his black uniform and dangles the keys to open her cell. Cassandra is coming back from using the bathroom. Her gym shoes squawk as she stumbles back to her cot. She looks different from the girl I saw last night. She now resembles me—an inmate in a blue oversized uniform. I remove my gaze from her and stare at the corner of my cell, where a brown spider has made herself at home again. She has built a web, and I see tiny babies crawling around. All I want to do is step on them and crunch them one by one. But they deserve a life, just like Abigail and the baby Cassandra is carrying.

Ever since Cassandra arrived, my thoughts are all over the place. I feel like a passenger on a runaway train. I don't like feeling this way.

My cell door opens, and it sounds like chalk on a blackboard. Samuel's eyes burn into mine, as if he doesn't trust me. He places a tray of cold eggs and burnt bacon along with a glass of juice the color of carrots on my cot. I continue watching him as the bars of Cassandra's cell swooshes open, and he places the same meal in front of her.

All I hear for a while is the sound of crunching bacon and gulping orange juice. The smell of eggs linger in the air.

"Aren't y-you scared in here?" Cassandra's voice quivers.

"I was, at first." The bacon cracks as I snap it in half. "It was intimidating being around so many boys, or men, I should say." I shrug. "But I tried telling myself I'm only here for thirty days, and it will be over before I know it. And I realized, if what I've heard is true, and I was saved because my parents used to be friends with the president, then I don't think she wants me harmed." I gulp down some juice. "I don't think anyone would defy her, except for one of her top guards—Rich," I say, then clear my throat.

It feels as though a piece of bacon is stuck even though I know it's not.

"He has this hatred for me and some of the other guards follow him." My hand shivers thinking about it. "So, I am afraid of him."

"If he is one of her top guards, why would he go against her?" Cassandra asks.

She puts a dime-sized portion of eggs on her spoon. This leads me to believe she is still keeping up with her starvation tactic.

I try to ignore it and answer her question.

"Even though he's one of her right-hand men…" I clear my throat again. "I think he would defy her, if he felt it was necessary. I believe his hate for me is strong enough that he would go against her."

"I hope that doesn't happen. I also hope most guards will be as kind to me as they are to you, but I don't see that happening. I'm not afforded the luxury of having friends in high places."

Her fork clanks against her plate. "Is there anything I should know?" She wipes her green eyes. "Anything I should look out for or be aware of?" she asks. She places her tray on the floor and it squeals as she pushes it away with her foot.

"Not really." I shrug. "Lights go out at nine and come on at eight—but I already told you that. If you do what they ask, you should be okay."

"How are the guards around here?" Her eyes widen. "That Rich guy sounds like a mean one. But how are the others?"

"It depends. I guess you have to know which guards to watch your step around and which are a little more flexible."

"How will I know that?"

"You just do." I shrug. My throat tightens. I don't have all the answers. I still don't know if Eric is a good guy or what Samuel's deal is. I think they're good people, but what if I'm wrong?

"Do they let you out sometimes, or are you confined to your cell?"

"This is pretty much it," I say. I put a spoonful of cold scrambled eggs in my mouth, chew and swallow. "How is it on the outside?"

Talking about the guards makes my stomach uneasy, and telling her that they let me go up to the training center makes it queasier. If she found that out, she would think I was receiving special treatment because of my parents again; so, it's best if I change the subject.

"Nothing has changed." Cassandra stands. She walks closer to the bars that separate our cells. "The patrolmen police the area and arrest people doing wrong. And, if they get a tip that someone's pregnant and hiding it, they report it to the guards. The guards investigate any tips."

"Has anyone tried to escape Territory L, lately?" I remove my tray from my lap.

I stand and walk closer to her. There are often reports during the president's Monday night announcements on those who have tried, and failed, to escape the territory.

"Wouldn't you know more on that than I would?"

"I don't get to see the Monday night speeches in here. I haven't seen one since I arrived."

"But don't you see all the comings and goings?" Cassandra shifts her weight. "I mean, if someone is brought in and jailed, wouldn't you see them?"

"Not necessarily." I bite down on my lip. "I'm on the female side. I've been told that the male jail cells are on the opposite side of the bathrooms. So, if a male is brought in, I wouldn't know about it. I only see the females. And since I've been here, you are the first female to arrive."

First offenders caught trying to escape the territory get a light sentence and are remanded to jail. If you are caught a second time, you get a longer sentence down in the prison.

"What do you think will happen to me?" Cassandra asks, as she sits back down on her cot.

"I'm not sure." My grip around the bars tightens. "I guess you will stay here until you are ready to deliver. That way they can make sure you eat. Then, when it is time for you to give birth, they will take you over to the hospital. But that's my theory. I really don't know for sure."

I stare down at her plate. Two pieces of bacon sit there and most of her eggs haven't been touched. I only saw her take two small sips of juice.

"This little love fest is over," Samuel says. His voice is loud, and it echoes along the walls of the jail. "I'm breaking this up." His keys clank as they dangle from his fingers.

Cassandra's cell door opens. His steps are loud as he stomps inside.

"Get on your feet," he says, with a serious face.

His voice reminds me of the day in the elevator when he scolded me.

"D-did I do s-something wrong?" Cassandra's voice shakes.

"You're being moved."

"Why is she being moved?" I ask. My heart drops. "She just got here."

"It's none of your concern." His eyes harden as they look in my direction.

My body shudders at his cold gawking. This is the most interaction I've had with him since the day in the elevator. I have to find out what's going on. She reminds me of Taylor, and I need to look out for her.

"She's my friend, so it is my concern," I say, with a strong voice even though my knees jiggle. "Now, why are you moving her when she has done nothing wrong?"

"Maybe it's your fault?"

"What does that mean?"

"Maybe you two talk too much, and the guards around here don't like all that chatter." He turns away from me and looks at Cassandra. "She is going to be here for a long time, and she needs to learn to be quiet. She can't do that living in the cell next to yours. So, I have strict orders to move her down to the end, so you two won't be in contact with each other. Now let's go."

Cassandra stands. Her frail body is weak, so she falls down with a *thump*, back onto her cot.

"I said, let's go."

Samuel grasps her by the elbow and pulls her to her feet. He grabs the clothing on her cot with his other hand, and quickly leads her out of the cell. I watch as he leads her down the hallway. I thought there were only six cells on each side, but he walks farther than my eyes can see. There must be more cells that I don't know about. He walks back and slams her old cell door closed. It bangs, and I jump.

"Samuel," I say, as he walks past me. "What's wrong with you?"

"Nothing is wrong with me." He stops. "I'm only doing my job and following orders."

"But you're not acting like yourself." I walk up closer to the bars, facing him.

"You don't even know me." He shrugs. "Maybe this is my normal self."

"If this is really you, then I don't like you. You're acting like Rich."

His frozen stare softens, and his eyes show that my words have hurt him. He turns and walks away from me without saying anything else.

CHAPTER THIRTEEN

"YOU READY TO GO?" Eric stands in front of my cell with his workout gear on. His jacket is unzipped, and I can see a white t-shirt underneath.

"I'm not in the mood to train today." I shift on the cot.

"Why? What happened?" One eyebrow goes higher than the other.

"They brought in a new female inmate."

"I heard." He clutches onto the bars. "Word gets around fast when they arrest someone new, especially when it's a female."

"Do you get a lot of female inmates in here?" I ask, wondering about the woman from the marketplace.

"It depends." He shrugs. "It varies from month to month or from week to week. Sometimes, we get females in here for disorderly conduct, like stealing, but mostly we get—"

"Pregnant females," I say, while standing. My ears are on fire, as if darts are shooting me in my temples.

"Yes." He nods. "We get older females, younger females. Some married, others not married. Not long ago, we had a married female who was pregnant. She miscarried in her cell, due to the stress. President Esther released her early because of what happened."

"Don't you think a female should be able to do what she wants with her body?" I walk closer to the bars. "Poor or rich, she should be allowed to have a child?"

"Whoa...whoa." He holds up his hands. "When did I become the enemy?"

I don't mean to take out my aggression on him. But now that I know what happened to the woman, and now that Cassandra has been moved, I feel like a train has steamrolled over me. I don't know how to make it stop.

"Does this have anything to do with the new inmate? Is she a friend of yours?"

"No, but she is a friend of my sister." I blink.

"You never really speak about your sister." His eyes lift to mine. "Why is that?"

"I've changed my mind. I want to train now."

I might as well be under water because I feel like I'm suffocating. I need for this subject to be dropped.

*

"Are you sure you want to hit the bags? Your hand still looks raw from yesterday."

He takes my hand and brushes my knuckles. His hand feels warm against mine. I feel some of the tightness in my chest loosen. His eyes glisten. I could remain locked in this moment forever, if I didn't have the urge to hit something.

"I think you need to lay off the bags." He rubs my hand again. "At least for today."

"Fine, then," I say, pulling my hand away. "Then, maybe we could spar again. If that's okay with you?"

"It's fine with me." He walks over to one of the yellow mats.

The training room is quiet and empty. Our usual time to train has become one o'clock; but today, since it took me a while to get going, we don't start until after two. There is a training session, with an instructor, around ten, and also one at four. Eric said one o'clock is lunchtime, so it is always a good time to have the place to ourselves. Even though we got a late start, we should be done before the others arrive.

Eric takes off his hoodie, as usual, and turns to me.

"Are you ready?" He cocks his head to the side.

"Yes." I nod.

I squint, take my stance, and watch my breathing. I decide to try something that I saw the instructor do the first time I was allowed to come here. Instead of putting my right leg out to the side, I raise it in front of me. I lean away from the kick, so my body weight is balanced. I pivot on my standing foot, grunt as loud as I can, then quickly extend my right leg forward, kicking him in the leg. He doubles back and almost falls to the floor. I like this form of kicking. It seems quicker and is more powerful. I know he was expecting me to go for the groin, or the face, but I really don't want to hurt him. Now that I'm moving around, I notice my side is still tender from yesterday.

"New move," he says, wobbling back to his stance. "I like it." He gives a small smile.

"This time I will come at you, so we can work on your pain levels again. That is, unless your side hurts too much."

"No, I'm fine," I say.

My side still aches but I can get through this. I take my stance. His right leg goes to my left side, and then he quickly snaps it forward. I panic because he's going for the side that already hurts. My heart races. Instead of blocking his kick with my arm, I step back to get out of the path of his foot. That is a bad idea because his foot kicks me in my left buttock. I sway. I lose my balance, fall backwards and land off the mat. My back whacks on the hard floor. I close my eyes. The pain now goes from my side to my back. My chest feels as if I swallowed fire, and I can't suck in any air.

"Whisper, I'm sorry. I thought you would block that." I feel him hovering over me. His breath is hot on my face, and his torso is pressing against mine. "Are you okay?"

He slides his hand over my cheek. I open my eyes, and he's so close to me that my body trembles. I stare at him; he stares back. It doesn't feel awkward or uncomfortable; it does feel nice and warm. My insides are jumping all over, yet I'm enjoying our closeness. I've never felt this way around anyone before. I want him to kiss me. It will be my first kiss, and it will make all the pain I feel right now worth it. His gaze is still strong as he caresses my cheek, but instead of kissing me he rolls off.

"That's enough training for today," he says, grunting as he sits up on his knees.

I slowly take deep breaths and maneuver myself onto my knees as well. His chest seems to rise and fall with mine.

"Good workout." His voice cracks. "Once again, I'm sorry. If you're in too much pain, I can sign you out and have a guard take you over to the hospital." He stands.

"No, I don't need the hospital," I say, in between jagged breaths.

I wipe my nose with the back of my hand. It feels as if it is bleeding, but when I glance at my hand there's no blood, only moisture from my upper lip. There's sweat pouring from every pore in my body, and I'm sure I smell like an animal that has just played in muddy water. I stand, and he throws a towel at me. It wafts in my face.

"Well, if you're okay, then you should cleanup." He walks over to the refrigerator.

I wipe the sweat off my face, and slowly make my way to where he is. From the pain in my side and back, I have now developed a limp. I am favoring my right side. He takes two bottles from the refrigerator and leaves one on the table for me. He clicks open one of the bottles of water and guzzles it down. I grab my bottle and the coolness feels good on my fingertips. Instead of drinking it, I place it under my shirt and use it to nurse my side. The coolness feels like a cold shower on a hot day. It's hard to believe we're standing here silent, when we were so close a minute ago. He gulps down his water as if nothing has happened. My head aches from trying to figure him out.

"Why do you work for her?" I ask, throwing my towel across my shoulder. I crinkle the bottle up against my side.

"What?" he asks.

"I know you heard me," I say, with strength in my voice. I'm trying to pretend my side and back aren't still throbbing.

"I did." He walks away from me and back to the mat to retrieve his jacket. "I was just surprised. No one ever asks me that. No one cares about the answer, not around here." He shakes his head.

"Well, I care."

"This guard job pays well. And, living in the mansion, there are perks. Nice facilities, good food whenever you want it."

"Now you sound like my brother." I throw my towel back in his face. "And, that's not a real answer."

"What would you consider a real answer?" His eyebrow rises. He throws the towel, and it hits the floor with a smack.

"The truth would be nice."

"I don't know what you want me to say." He walks toward me. "I mean, I don't have any sappy answer for you, like I'm here to make money so my family can have a good life. So, I guess I can't give you the answers you're looking for." His voice rises.

"Where is your family? I've never heard you speak of them."

I can tell by the look on his face that I've come across another topic he doesn't want to discuss. Even though I remain silent, his face turns red.

"That's none of your business. If I wanted to talk about them, I would. I'm done for today."

He crinkles up his bottle and throws it across the room. It misses the garbage can, and leftover water splatters on my arm.

It seems he is always either furious with me or happy with me. A minute ago, our faces were so close we could have kissed; and now, it's like he can't stand the sight of me. His moods are so hot and cold. I don't know how to read him. Granted, earlier I didn't want to talk about my sister; but in no way did I explode like that.

He left me all alone. It's not a big deal. I can find my way back to my cell. But I'm not supposed to be left alone without a guard. Maybe this is my opportunity to go exploring; maybe this is a good thing.

It's much later than I thought. I hear the commotion of guards walking into the room. They sound like a herd of cattle as they make their way over to the green mat where another training session is starting. I also see guards going over to the punching bags. My eyes widen because one of those guards is Samuel. It is good the guards are keeping up their normal routines, that way I can search the mansion without anyone noticing me.

I ride the commoner's elevator down to the first floor. I sneak around and enter the dining room. I haven't been here since the night of the party. The walls are still bright yellow, the color of the sun. Funny how our homes have to be dark, while the president's home can be any color she desires.

The air smells fruity, like berries. A stronger smell is coming from the kitchen. I bend my knees and lower myself down to the beige carpet. I stay low in case someone comes. I moan, feeling the pain in my side. It still feels like I'm being stabbed with a knife. At least the pain in my back has lessened.

There is a swinging door, so you can go back and forth from the kitchen to the dining room. I hear voices coming from the kitchen, and the smell of some kind of meat—maybe chicken. I crawl up to the door. There is a gap between the door and the wall, which leaves enough room so I can hear what they're saying.

"I'm sorry. I don't have any more information for you."

It's Rich's voice. He's back from Territory M. Maybe searching the mansion wasn't such a good idea after all. If he catches me, he'll probably kill me or, at least, do me bodily harm. But I need to hear what he is saying and who he is talking to.

"I don't think it is being handled properly." Rich's voice continues. "And, it shows a sign of weakness. They're even getting squeamish over the newbie camp being there."

"You think you can do better?"

I know that crackly bone chilling voice is President Esther's. A cold spark goes up my spine.

"I'm next in command," Rich says. "Why shouldn't I be allowed to run Territory M, if the one in charge cannot?"

"I'm not convinced you could do any better."

"The way I see it, the people in Territory M are practically running themselves," Rich says, angrily.

"It's my call and, for now, I'm leaving it the way it is."

"I think you're making a big mistake."

"Are you defying my orders?" she says, curtly.

"No, ma'am," he says, clearing his throat. "I mean, President Esther."

"Then do as I ask. I'm done with this discussion. We have more pressing matters to talk about."

My ears are burning, and I'm ready to hear what is so pressing. I lean closer to the opening in between the door. I feel something grip my arm and yank me up. My first reaction is to scream, but a hand covers my mouth. Samuel stands in front of me. My heart pounds as if it will burst out of my chest.

"Are you crazy?" he mouths to me. His one hand grips my arm while his other hand is tightly placed over my mouth. "Do not say a word until we get down to your cell," he mumbles, taking his hand down from my mouth.

He jerks my arm as if he is yanking an out of control dog. He pulls me all the way to the elevator. The elevator dings, the doors swish open, and he shoves me inside. My leg shakes and I want to speak, but he told me to remain quiet. From the hard look on his face, I know he means it.

"What is wrong with you?" he yells, pushing me into my cell. "You could have been caught." The cell door bangs as he slams it closed. "What were you thinking?"

"I was—"

"You weren't thinking!" he yells, before I can finish my sentence.

"Is everything okay in here?" A blond, blue-eyed guard dressed in black comes around the corner.

"Yes," Samuel says, turning to him. "Everything's fine."

"Just making sure." The guard throws up his hands and walks away.

"If you would've let me finish, I was going to say, I was looking around and I heard someone talking. I had no idea it was Rich and the president."

"And after you found out who it was, why didn't you walk away?"

"I wanted to hear what they were saying."

"If you were caught, do you know what could've happened? Your sentence could've been increased or something worse. Do you even care?"

"Yes, I care," I say, biting down on my lip.

"Well, you don't act like it."

"How did you know where I was, anyway?"

"I saw you arguing with Eric in the training room, and I saw him take off." He rubs his hand over his forehead. "I had a feeling, since he left you alone, you wouldn't go back to your cell. So, I came after you." He paces back and forth in front of my cell. "Good thing I did because look where I found you."

"What concern is it of yours?" I move closer to the bars that separate us. "I mean, for weeks now, you haven't been cordial to me. I thought you hated me because I could have gotten you fired. So why do you care if I got caught?"

"Because I care about you." He scratches the back of his neck. "And I don't want to see any harm come your way."

His eyes cling to mine.

I'm silent and my throat thickens. What does he mean by care? Does he care about me like a brother cares for his sister? He has to be at least five years older than me, so I know it can't be in a romantic way.

"I'm not sure what you mean." I swallow hard. "If you care about me so much, then why have you been treating me so badly?"

"I used to have a little sister." He blinks. "She was smart and attractive, like you."

My face feels hot.

"What happened to her?" The tension in my chest seems to match his. "You said 'used to'."

He is silent and his eyes look sad.

"You don't have to tell me. I'm sorry if I've overstepped."

"You didn't." He shakes his head. "Her name was Elizabeth. She was two years younger than me. She would have been twenty-one this year."

He clasps the bars tightly, as if they're holding him up, as if without them he would fall. He keeps saying "was" and "would have been" and I feel a pang in my stomach.

"She met some boy in school. I don't know how since boys and girls weren't allowed to share classes. Maybe they met in the hallway. It's not important. What is important is that she fell in love and dated him behind our parents' backs. She begged me not to tell them. Once they found out, they wanted her to get married; so, she did as they asked. When she was twenty, she got pregnant, accidentally." He wipes his hand over his mouth. "She ended up in here because she broke the laws. But she wasn't scared. She was strong, like you." His eyes water.

"I'm sorry."

"Anyway, they took her over to the hospital when the baby was due, but she died during childbirth. The irony is the baby lived, only to be taken away and killed. So, we don't have my sister anymore or her baby." He rubs his temples with his fingers.

I don't know how to make him feel better, but his story makes my insides slink.

"At least, if we still had the baby, we would have a piece of her with us; but we don't even have that. My parents were crushed." He wipes the tears from his eyes. "My mother passed away soon after that, and my father has become weak and feeble. He can't work or take care of himself, anymore; so, I had to put him in a home for the elderly. Those places are really expensive, and that's why I work here now. This job pays better than most. It helps me pay for his care and for what I need to live."

"That's the reason you got so mad at me in the elevator?"

"Yes, as I said before, I can't afford to lose this job. And, I stayed away from you because you're strong-willed, like my sister. You remind me so much of her that the memories of her came flooding back, and it hurts."

His eyebrows hang low. I know it's from tiredness over what he's been through. I feel as if a rope is being squeezed around my waist. He is not looking at me in a big brother or mentor type of way. The goose bumps going up my arms tell me it's more. I could be wrong, but it's not important right now. The room starts to spin. Light-headed, I groan and double over. The aching in my side has returned. It has been there all the time, but suddenly, the pain feels more pervasive.

"Are you all right?"

"I'm fine."

"You don't look fine. You look pale."

"I hurt my side yesterday while training, and it's still a little sore." I put my hand under my shirt and rub.

"Why didn't you go to the hospital?"

"Eric wanted to take me, but I didn't want to go."

"You really should. I'll sign you out and take you over, right now."

"You don't have to do that. Besides, I want to take a shower and change clothes."

I'm sweaty and my clothes are sticking to me like cotton candy sticks to your hands. I smell like my brother's feet when he wears the same socks for days.

"Why don't I walk you down to the showers, and then you can change?" The key clanks in the lock as he turns it. "I will sign you out afterwards, and we can go have that side looked at."

"You don't have to check with someone first?" I ask.

I haven't been outside the mansion since I got here. I'm not really sure how this all works.

"No, my assignment most days is to look after you, even though I know I sort of handed that duty over to Eric. I'm supposed to be in charge of you today, as well. So, I don't have to check with anyone. I'm allowed to take prisoners over to the hospital. If something happens to you on the outside, it will be my head because you're my responsibility."

I give a weak smile, while trying to mask the pain. "So, don't try and run away."

He nods. "Yes, something like that."

CHAPTER FOURTEEN

EVERYTHING LOOKS DIFFERENT ON the outside. The air smells fresh like daisies, and the normally gray sky appears blue. Maybe it's because I haven't been outside in a while, and now I can exhale. I'm sitting next to Samuel as we ride on a white prison bus.

The bus is not that big; it has five rows. There are two seats on each side of the aisle. It reminds me of the days when I rode the bus to school, only this bus has bars on the windows; the school bus didn't.

Samuel let me sit by the window while he sits next to me on the aisle. Samuel and I are the only passengers, besides the dark-skinned, brown-haired bus driver. The sun is partially out today. It feels good, bearing down on my skin.

I have on a clean uniform that smells like bleach and soap. My hands tingle against the cold metal handcuffs. I haven't worn them in a while. They feel foreign against my skin.

About a half mile down the street, we pass the maple-colored city council building. As we hit bumps in the road, the bus bounces up and down, and my stomach bounces along with it. The mansion is not far from the hospital. It is only about two miles away, on the opposite side of the street.

"Thanks again for letting me sit here," I say. "It's nice to be able to look out."

"You don't have to keep thanking me. I owe you for treating you badly." His eyes are sincere.

"It wasn't your fault. I need to learn to listen sometimes, instead of being so bullheaded. My father always said that when I wouldn't fall in line."

"Your father is wrong. You're perfect the way you are." He brushes a strand of hair behind my ear.

After I had taken a shower and changed clothes, I unbraided my hair. The look he gives me says that he likes my hair this way, and maybe he sees me as more than a little sister. It makes me shiver.

"And, by the way, you had your reasons for treating me the way you did." I shove my shoulder into his. "Your sister was on your mind and so were all your responsibilities. I know I said it earlier, but I'm sorry about her."

"Thank you." He turns away from me and looks ahead.

"Okay, you two. We're here," the driver announces.

I see the school my mom used to work at, and then, there is the hospital. It's six stories high, which is not that big. I have heard that Territory M and Territory U have much bigger hospitals.

"You ready?" Samuel asks. My handcuffs jingle as he pulls on them.

"Yes," I say, standing.

The air inside the hospital is thick and smells like medicine. It reminds me of the cough syrup my mother would give me when I was little. It grossed me out then just like it grosses me out now. I see nurses in tan scrubs and doctors in long gray lab coats. My father looks like one of them when he leaves for work every morning.

I follow Samuel into the emergency ward. The walls are a dim dark brown, like the rest of our world.

"The prisoner needs to see a doctor," Samuel says to a nurse behind a long, white counter.

"What is the prisoner's name?" the gray-haired nurse asks. Her name tag reads Mary.

"Emma Whisperer," Samuel says to Mary.

My shoulders cringe, hearing the word prisoner. I never thought I would hear that word in the same sentence with my name.

"Have her sign in, right here." She points at a pad. "And, sign your name next to hers."

We do as we're told. I notice his last name is Wilkins.

"Now, what seems to be the problem?"

"She hurt her side," Samuel says. "I called this in before we got here, so you should already have this information."

"Yes, I do." She nods. "But I still have to ask. You two can take a seat, and we'll be right with you."

I squirm, like a child, in my seat. Everything is strange here. There is no laughter, no crying, just silence. I only see a few people sitting here. An older man—who looks to be in his sixties—with sandy hair and gray eyebrows, sits near the back. An older-looking woman, with dark hair and light eyes, sits across from us. There are no children. No matter how many times I say to myself this is our world, and this is the law, it baffles me that no children exist.

I see a young woman, a little older than me, come out from the back area. She is dark-skin with short, brown hair. She wears a black dress. Her dark eyes glare at me as if she is staring into my soul. Her glower makes me shiver. She mouths the words 'thank you' and turns to leave the waiting area.

"What was that?" I whisper to Samuel. "Why would she thank me?"

"The people here are proud of you, Emma. The young women around your age want to be like you, some of the guys, too. You stood up and they feel like they should as well. But they don't know how."

I don't know why it is such a big deal. I only spoke my mind, but I'm glad that people are supportive of me. If it helps them to go up against Esther, then I know I did the right thing.

"You can go in back now," the gray-haired nurse says. "They're ready for you."

My body tenses. Samuel leads me into a large, dark room. He

tells me to sit down on a table that has a white sheet spread across it and to wait for the doctor to come in. The air is cold and smells like room cleaner.

"I'll be right outside the door," Samuel says.

"Can you take the handcuffs off?" I ask.

"Only if the injured area was on your wrists. Since your injury is on your side, I'm not allowed to take them off. They can clearly see what they need to with the handcuffs on."

"I understand."

The door smacks closed. I sit and wait. The handcuffs are only on my wrist, but they feel like a third hand when I have to drag them around. They remind me that I'm an inmate, and I feel stifled, at times.

I hear the door whoosh open. My jaw drops because my father walks in with a gray lab coat on. I know he is a doctor here, but I had no idea I would be allowed to see him. The uneasiness in my chest goes away.

"Hello, Emma," my father says with a stiff look on his face. He shows no emotion. I can't tell if he is happy to see me, or not. "The paperwork says you hurt your left side."

"Yes. I did." The uneasiness in my chest returns because he is all business. He doesn't look pleased to see me.

"Lift up the side of your shirt and show me where it hurts."

I show him.

"Is it tender here?" He presses lightly on my skin.

I flinch from the pain. "Yes." I nod.

"It looks to me like your ribs are sprained."

"What does that mean?" I ask, hoping it's nothing serious.

"One of your ligaments attached to your ribs is not in its normal position. I can give you some aspirin to take with you." He writes on his pad. "I would also suggest that when you get back to your new living quarters you put a cold pack on your ribs, several times during the day, twenty minutes at a time. Once the pain lessens, then you should use a heating pad for twenty minutes. That will help loosen the muscles, and the pain should eventually go away. I'm sure the guards at the jail can give you those things." His eyes lower to my hands. "I can also give you some ointment for the broken skin on your knuckles."

"You say new living quarters, like I want to be there, like I'm enjoying my time there." I grit my teeth. I brush past all the instructions he has just given me.

"Don't be cross with me, young lady."

"I'm not being cross. It would be nice if you could show some sign that you miss me. I was happy to see you walk in here, but you don't look happy to see me, at all." My eyes are watery.

"You know your father loves you." The door whacks closed and my mother stands there in tan scrubs. "He told me that he spoke to you on the elevator, and he told you those very words," she continues talking as she walks toward me. "He doesn't show a lot of emotion."

She speaks to me as if my father isn't standing right in front of me. She acts as if he can't speak for himself. I let the subject go. Now, I'm more intrigued with her.

"Mother, why are you here?" I squirm on the table. "Do you work here now?"

"Yes," she says.

She rubs my cheek and it reminds me of when I was a child and she would do that to calm me.

"I haven't been myself ever since the school closed, ever since they took you away from me." Her watery eyes match mine. "Your father thought it would be good for me to get out into the workforce again, and he found me something here. I'm a volunteer, so I help out wherever they need me."

"How did you know I was here?" I blurt out. Like the anxiety to see what is saved in a house burning down, I'm anxious to hear their answer.

"We need to tell you something." She ignores my question. Her eyes are serious. "We thought, since you were the last child that survived, Esther may seek you out one day, to make an example out of you. I've known her for a long time, and I know how her mind works."

My mother pulls on the fabric around her neck, as if the conversation is choking her.

"That's why we thought, if your brother worked for her, she would already have one of our children in her corner, and she may leave you alone. So, we asked her to make Theodore a guard. When I heard about the party, I knew she still wanted to use you, somehow. I need you to be careful around her. She comes from a rich family. She is a very powerful woman," she says.

Yet again, another secret, I think, while rolling my eyes.

"Does T know why he is a guard? Because he didn't, before."

"Yes, your father and I spoke with him, recently. Theodore would visit you more, but the president has him doing assignments outside of the mansion. Probably on purpose, so he can't come to see you."

"I don't know why I was never told any of this, before." I feel like bricks are bearing down on my chest. I'm always kept in the dark.

"None of that matters now," my father says.

"Your father is right. Our main focus right now is you. Are you all right?"

"Mother, I'm fine."

"How did you hurt yourself?"

"I hurt it in training."

"Training?" My mother's eyes go dull. "Why would you be training?"

"The guards train daily to keep their skills active."

"That still doesn't explain why you do?"

"It helps me get out of my cell for a while." My shoes smack on the floor as I hop down from the table. My father is done examining me, and he is watching our interaction. "And, it gives me something to do."

I inspect her face. I hope she is satisfied with my answer. It is partly the truth. She doesn't need to know the real reason I started training was that I'm afraid of Rich.

"What does this training involve?"

"Does it really matter?" I'm not trying to be curt, but I don't want her to know what I've learned and that I've enjoyed learning it. "Why haven't you come to visit me?" I ask, trying to change the subject. "I mean, since that first time."

"The president informed us that we couldn't come to visit you, anymore," my mother says.

"But every prisoner has a right to have visitors," I say, with annoyance in my voice.

"Most of the laws here change as the president sees fit. You know that, Emma," my father says.

"Yes, I know that." I swallow hard. "But it's ridiculous. Why do we keep letting her make up these insane rules that we follow? If we all stick together, we could overthrow her."

"It's that attitude that landed you where you are right now." My father frowns.

"And you hate it, don't you?" I grit my teeth. "You hate that I embarrassed you, like I did. You want me to follow along and be a good little girl like your other children. I mean, T is a guard that makes the family proud, but what about Taylor?"

"Emma, please." Mother's dull eyes go dimmer.

"I don't understand why I'm the embarrassment of the family for trying to do what is right. But when Taylor announced she was pregnant, you weren't mad at her, or embarrassed by her. She went against the laws and you chose to hide her. If I had gone against the laws, you never would have hidden me. You would have thrown me to the wolves. Is it because Taylor looks like Father, and I don't look like either one of you?"

"That's enough out of you, young lady." My father's face is stern. "You shouldn't speak about your sister where someone could hear you."

"Is everything okay in here?" The door whooshes open and Samuel stands on the other side. "I heard shouting."

"Yes, everything's fine," my father announces.

"I'm ready to go back to my cell now." I look at Samuel. "We're done here."

"Emma," my mother says, softly.

"I love you, Mother, but I think we've said all we need to." I turn to walk away.

"Emma, I need you to know something." Mother grabs my hand. "Your skin color has nothing to do with any of this."

She leans in and hugs me. The hug is tight and she feels warm, but it still doesn't make things any better.

*

"Don't be so hard on him." Samuel leans into my shoulder with his. "Your father's a good guy and it's evident that he loves you. I think he has a hard time showing it."

The bus hits a bump and my stomach feels unsettled. The bus screeches to a halt at a stoplight and my nausea gets worse.

"What would you know about my father?" I ask, staring down at my handcuffs.

"I've known your father for a while now."

I look up at him and his eyes sadden.

"I told you about my sister and how she died in childbirth."

"Yes."

"Well, when she went into labor at the jail, and they brought her over to the hospital, your father was there that day. He helped me and my family out a lot."

"But my father doesn't specialize. He's a family doctor, not an ob-gyn. He's not even a surgeon, so that would be going against the rules."

"I know that, but it took a while for a specialist to come from Territory U. You would think they would have someone from Territory U remain here when they know a female is almost ready to deliver, but they don't. The travel time alone could cost a pregnant woman her life, if the doctor doesn't make it here in time. And the emergency surgeons from Territory M that take turns staying here aren't allowed to perform surgeries on pregnant females or to deliver their babies."

"Maybe that's why they do it," I say. "They don't want babies here, so if a pregnant woman and her baby die while waiting for the surgeon to arrive, they get their wish."

"You're probably right." He nods and continues. "So, while she was in labor, your father looked after her and made sure she was okay. He informed us, if the specialist didn't arrive by delivery time, he would deliver the baby. He said, even if he didn't specialize in that area, he knew how and he would gladly take charge."

My thoughts go to Taylor. Father had said the same thing about her delivery. He would deliver her baby, when the time came; he did.

"Since it's against the law for a doctor to practice outside their area of medicine, your father could have been jailed."

My father was willing to take a risk for what he believed in. He is not as weak as I tend to think, sometimes.

"After the specialist arrived, my sister lost her life, and the baby was taken away, your father was there for my family. He came by to check on my mother when she fell ill. He is a good guy, but I know you know that."

It is evident that my father loves my siblings by the way he hides Taylor; unlike Cassandra's family, who actually did throw her to the wolves. And, I also know in my heart, he loves me because he does tell me, every once in a while. I now feel sorry for that crack about my skin color, back at the hospital.

I can't understand why he is so hard on me, at times. And, I can't understand why they keep secrets. At least I finally know why T was made a guard. My side throbs, not from the pain where Eric kicked me, but from the guilt. In all my theatrics at the hospital, I forgot to ask how Taylor and Abigail were doing, or if my father got that second job with President Esther.

"You all right?" Samuel asks. "You're awfully quiet."

"Did you arrange all of this?"

"I thought it would do you some good to see your family." He smiles. "When I called ahead and told them we were coming, I asked if your father was working today. They told me he was, and I asked if he could be the one to take care of you. I had no idea your mother would be there, but I'm glad she was."

"Thank you." I smile.

"You're welcome."

He brushes his fingers across my hand. They feel warm across my knuckles. The complete opposite of the cold surging off the metal handcuffs around my wrists. I've learned so much in this one visit with my family, and it's all because Samuel arranged this. I think I can call him a friend now. My stomach settles down, like a boat on a smooth river, knowing I have one.

CHAPTER FIFTEEN

"I'm sorry about what happened yesterday," Eric says.

He's standing in front of my cell with a grim look on his face. He has on his guard uniform with the silver buttons and a gun on his hip in a holster.

"It's fine," I say. I place my lunch tray on the floor, and it squeals as I push it to the side. I stand.

"No, it's not. I shouldn't have gotten so angry." He lays his head onto the bars and stares at me. His eyes lift to mines. "I know I've flown off the handle with you a couple of times. I don't mean to. I don't have much experience with women." He shrugs. "I know they like to talk about their feelings, which I'm not used to."

"Sometimes, it's good to get things out and not to keep them bottled up."

"Yes, and sometimes, it's good to let things lie." He looks down and back up. "Anyway, the other day, when you were bragging that you were a fast runner, I got upset because I don't like people to say things if they can't back them up."

"I don't think we should be discussing this." I clench my jaw.

"Why not?"

"I don't want to get into another uncomfortable conversation."

"We won't." He glares at me, but it isn't mean, only serious.

"I don't believe things people say anymore, until I see it with my own eyes."

"It's hard for you to trust?"

He remains quiet and scratches the back of his neck.

"Why do you always have a wall up?" I ask, knowing I probably shouldn't. "You only give me bits and pieces, and then you close up."

"Letting my guard down is what leads to me getting hurt. I refuse to let that happen again." He grips the bars, as if he is seizing the handlebars of a bike during a strong wind and he doesn't want to tip over.

"I'm sorry." I sense he doesn't talk about his feelings often, and when he does, he feels vulnerable and quickly halts the conversation. "I shouldn't have asked you that."

"No, it's fine." His eyes soften. "Women like you catch me off guard."

"What makes you say that?" I bite the inside of my jaw.

"My mother, she wasn't strong like you."

"Wasn't?" It feels like a small fur ball is in the back of my throat. I hope she's not dead.

"I guess I should rephrase that. She isn't like you. She is weak. She would let my father abuse her, and she would just take it." He blinks a few times. "I'm not saying she should have fought back, but she could have at least told somebody or left him." He shakes his head, glancing at the floor. "I begged her to tell the patrolmen, and she said she would. But when they came to our house, she didn't. She always changed her story and made excuses for my father."

"Wasn't there anybody that could help her or you?"

"I was an only child. I was too little to help at the time." His eyes were still. "Once I was older, I fought back. But one time, I fought back so hard I almost killed him. My mother told me I was wrong, and she took his side. After that, I left that house and never returned. I haven't seen, or heard from them, since."

"Don't you wonder how they are?"

"Why should I? After what they did to me, I don't need them." His face is red. "I'm fine on my own."

There's anger in his voice, and I feel foolish for asking the question. But I can't imagine not seeing, or speaking to, my parents ever again. I'm sure I'd feel differently, if I'd been through what he has.

"I didn't mean to upset you." Heat mounts in my eyes. I see tension rising in his chest.

"I'm not upset. It's just that you're the first person I've told and…" His speech trails off.

"Thank you for opening up to me. I know you didn't have to." I take over the conversation, since he's lost his voice. "If you want to talk more, I'm always here. Well," I shrug. "For at least the next twelve days."

"Don't you mean ten?" He smiles; although it's weak, it's still there.

"Just wanted to see if you're paying attention," I say, before groaning.

I clutch my side. I feel a small pain, like a bug is biting me. I walk back to my cot and pick up my ice pack. I shove it down my pants, so it lies next to my side. I slept with one all night, and this morning Samuel brought me a new one. The pack feels cold against my bare skin.

"I see your side is still bothering you." He looks me up and down. "That's why I came by in regular clothes. I knew you wouldn't feel much like training. You should rest your side for a few days, like the doctor said."

"How do you know what the doctor said?"

"Samuel told me. He said we should put off training, for a while."

"Until I recuperate." I groan again, pushing the pack more into my skin. "I don't want to lose my newfound skills. Pretty soon, I will be good enough to beat you."

"Now wait a minute." He holds up his hands. "Slow it down, a little. You're doing well, but don't get ahead of yourself. I think the nickname Whisper has caused you to lose all sense of reality."

"No, I'm still in my right mind," I say. I grin like baby Abigail when you tickle her stomach.

"Seriously, though." His eyes find mine. "Is your side all right?"

"It's fine, or it will be." My fingers sting, holding the pack.

"What about your hand?"

"They gave me some ointment to use."

"Why did you let Samuel take you?" His chest rises and falls like the words were hard to say. "I mean, I asked to take you to the hospital and you refused. Why would you let Samuel take you, instead of me?"

"You didn't say you would take me." The look on his face makes my cheeks hot, as if someone is holding a match next to them. "You said you would sign me out and a guard could take me."

"Well, I meant me." His eyes burn into mine and my knees feel like jelly beneath me. "If this happens again, I'll take you."

"I hope it doesn't happen again." I bite my lip. "But if it does I'll make sure you're the one."

"Good to hear," he says, and turns to walk away.

It may be my imagination, but if I didn't know better, I'd think he's jealous. But there's nothing to be jealous about. Samuel's like a big brother to me. That's if I didn't already have one.

*

"On your feet."

I hear a loud voice. My heart jumps. It sounds like Rich.

There are no windows here, but my internal clock tells me it is bedtime. I was waiting for the lights off in ten minutes call. Instead, I see him standing in front of my cell. He looks the same yet scarier, and his green eyes peer at me. His hair looks as bright as a ripe cherry. My hands shake.

"I'm not going to say it again. You've been summoned to see the president."

"But it's almost time for lights out." My voice quivers.

"I don't care what time it is. I gave you an order."

I stand and my knee twitches. The ice pack, lying on my side, falls and crashes to the floor. My cell door opens with a squeal, and Rich steps inside. He is dressed in his uniform, and he smells of musk and liquor. I didn't think guards could drink while on duty, but what do I know.

"Let's go," he says, clutching my arm.

Once I'm out of my cell, he snaps the handcuffs on. The coldness straddles my wrists. Like a dog on a leash, he leads and I follow. My stomach is in knots. I don't know what to expect once we reach the president's quarters. But, we don't go to the fifth floor; the elevator dings on the second floor. He pulls on my handcuffs and yanks me off the elevator. My gym shoes scuff against the hardwood floors as we walk down the long hallway. We end up at the conference room.

The room is bright red. There is a large window. I see a few remnants of sunlight, peering through the blinds. There is a long, brown table that looks like it is made of marble. There are four chairs on each side and one large chair at the end where President Esther sits. She has on a dark blue pants suit and a white shirt. Her silver hair is pulled back into a bun, and her lipstick is bloodred.

"Sit down, Emma," she says, pointing to the chair next to her. "I thought we could have a chat."

I plunk down, but not next to her. I sit a few seats away.

"You're cautious, I like that." Her mouth curls up.

Rich still stands in the room. He's glaring at me, like a fire breathing dragon. I shiver.

"Thank you, Rich." President Esther looks at him. "That will be all."

"Are you sure you don't need me to stay?"

"No, I'll be fine."

"But, I think I should." He steps closer. His eyes narrow.

"I said I'll be fine, Richard." She uses his full first name. "You can go now."

"As you wish," he says, with a lion-like growl.

I never knew his full first name was Richard, but I'm glad she told him to leave. He seems like he would challenge her, at every turn. I wonder why she keeps him around. He looks like a cold-hearted killer, so maybe she needs his talents. I pray, once he leaves the room, my knee will stop wiggling. He roughly exits, stomping like a drunken man whose liquor has been cut off. The door bangs as he slams it behind him.

"Sorry about that." Her piercing blue eyes gape at me. "He goes overboard, sometimes."

My chest bubbles up. I want to express my feelings. I feel like a lawyer, talking to a jury, back in my mother's days, when the accused had a chance at a trial. I should tell her how he has treated me; but when I open my mouth to speak, nothing comes out.

"I want you to come closer." She taps her finger on the table.

I notice her long fingernails are painted silver to match her hair. An eerie shockwave goes up my spine. I stand and move to the chair next to hers.

"Now we can speak without yelling." She smiles and her perfect teeth shine. "Your time with us is almost over, and I am wondering how your stay has been."

She says stay, as if I'm an out of town guest from another territory, and she is afraid of what I'll say about the place when I leave.

"You only have about ten days left. I thought we could get more acquainted, before your time is up. Are there any questions you have for me?" Her brow rises.

I lean back in my chair. "I don't think so."

"Oh, come on now, Emma. I'm sure there is something you want to know." She crosses her legs under the table. "About me or this place. You can ask me anything."

She taps her fingernails again, and it sounds like the pitter-patter of bird's claws on the ledge of my bedroom window.

"There is something." My throat constricts. "How did you decide who would attend the party, and who wouldn't?" I shift in my chair. "I mean, I thought you only associated with those from Territory U, and I noticed people from my territory were there."

"I thought it would be nice for you to have some of your peers there."

"Peers, meaning poor people, like my family?"

"You don't know what poor is, child. Poor is when you don't have a roof over your head. Poor is when you don't have any food to eat. Poor is when you don't have a bathroom to do your business in, and you have to make a hole in the cold, hard ground. You have food every day. Yes, it may be food you don't desire, like beans and rice, yet you have food on your plate every night."

She speaks as if she was once poor, but having talked to my parents, I know better.

"So, out of all of your peers that were invited, you are probably wealthier than they are."

"How would you know what poor is?" I clear my throat. "I've heard your family was rich."

"Just because my father wasn't poor, doesn't mean I don't know what they go through or how they live. Yes, my father had money, but my mother didn't. My parents were never married. When I stayed with my mother, I saw things—horrible things. The details on how they got together are not important, but I will say, they didn't stay together and I was shuffled back and forth between the two of them."

The room is quiet for a few minutes before she continues.

"My mother took out her anger on me. She said it was my fault that my father wouldn't marry her, and it was my fault she was poor. She beat me, and made me beg and steal, for money. Sometimes, I wished I had never been born. That is how I know poor people shouldn't have children. They don't know how to take care of them. I was saved, when my rich father let me come and stay with him."

The look on her face shows pain, and for a minute, I don't recognize her. She almost seems human.

"Enough about that." Her mouth twists up. "You're a smart girl, so I'm sure you have more questions."

"Most presidents have a council to advise them; so, why is it you have no one, why are you the one who gets to make all of the decisions?"

"Good question."

She smiles, as if she is my teacher, and I have just aced my exam.

"My husband had a council, back in the days when he was president, but there was always confusion. He and the council were always butting heads and things never were done in an efficient manner. When I took over, it was decided that the president should make all of the decisions. If there is no one to contest my ruling, it makes things easier. The people agreed. That is why I'm here today."

"But they decided on that ruling, back when people thought you were doing a good job. If we took a vote today, I don't think most would see it that way, not anymore. What do you think?"

"There it is." Her eyes are bright. "There is that feisty attitude you displayed on the podium. Go ahead, ask me something else."

"Why aren't people tried for crimes? Decades ago, when people committed a crime, they were tried before a judge and a jury of their peers. But here, now, you decide everything. You decide everyone's fates." My heart rhythm is erratic.

"Well," she says, raising her eyebrow. "That question was already asked and answered."

"No," I say. "I believe this question is a bit different."

"There is no need for people to be tried in a court of law. If everyone knows the rules, and knows the outcome they'll receive when a law is broken, then they already know they'll be punished accordingly."

"But what if someone is in jail for murder, and they really didn't do it? There is no lawyer, or jury, to help them out."

"That is why I decide. I give the people a minimum of thirty days in jail, and during that time, I decide if they're guilty or not. If they are, then I sentence them to the prison for the set time that I feel is necessary. It is up to me to make the decision. It is faster and easier that way."

"But that makes no sense." I stand. My throat is burning. "The decision shouldn't always be up to you."

"Emma, if you think I can't be impartial, or fair, then you're wrong. There have been times when I have had the guilty party brought to me at the city council building. The patrolmen bring me their findings, and I carefully go over everything with my guards. I review some cases, over and over again, with my guards, until we make a final decision. There have been times when a person's sentence was lessened, or a person presumed guilty was found not guilty. I can be fair."

She stands and walks over to the back of the room where a round, glass table holds a pitcher of water. It sounds like a running river as she pours the water into two glasses. She walks toward me. The glass clanks as she places it on the table in front of me. I can't help but notice she smells sweet, like daffodils.

"Now sit." She scowls at me. "I think you need to cool down. Have some water. I feel it is best if we move on to a different subject."

I sit and gulp down some water. I hadn't realized it until now, but the conversation is making me thirsty.

"Would you like something to eat? I can have tea and cookies brought in."

"No, I'm not hungry." I shake my head.

"Well, I am. Helen," she calls out.

I see a woman wearing a long gray polyester dress and a white apron walk into the room. I can only assume it is her maid. She has gray hair and bags under her dark eyes. I've never seen her before. I realize now that the guards can't attend to her every desire. She needs people to cook and to clean for her. Since most of my time is spent in the jail and the training room, I've never seen any of her workers.

Helen pushes the president's water glass to the side. In its place, she puts down a silver tea kettle on the table. A silver tray clinks down as well with cookies on it.

"Will there be anything else, ma'am?" Helen asks.

"No, that will be all. Thank you."

The door bangs behind her.

"Now, where were we?" She takes a small bite, no bigger than a pumpkin seed, out of one of the cookies.

The cookie is yellow, and it looks and smells like lemons. I watch as she quietly sips some of her tea. The way she eats reminds me of a squirrel crunching on a nut.

"Do you have any more questions for me?"

"Why won't you let my family visit?" I ask, and then gulp down more water.

"I asked them to stay away because they make you weak." Her eyes hone in on mine. "And, I need you to remain strong, like you are. That leads me to the main reason I wanted us to meet. I know you've been working out in the training room." She leans forward. "Or should I say, training?"

"Yes." I swallow hard. My knee bobbles like it did earlier when Rich was in the room. "Is that a problem? I was told you approved it."

"No, there is no problem. In fact, I have eyes and ears everywhere. I know you're good. From what I hear, you are extremely worthy. I know Eric has been training you. He has only been here a short time, but I hear he has become a decent guard. He is strong and shows the potential to move ahead, like you do."

The kettle clanks against her cup as she pours more tea.

I feel a jab on my side, like a beaver is gnawing on it. The pain is not from the earlier training incident. It is because I don't understand what she means by me having potential and moving ahead.

"I have a proposition for you." She leans forward even more, and I can feel her hot breath on my face. "I will suspend your sentence, if you move into the mansion, permanently, and train to be a guard."

"Why would I do that? My sentence is almost over, and then I will go home." I feel butterflies in my stomach.

"If you remember, I explained to you that I can extend sentences for longer than thirty days." Her eyes narrow. "I can extend sentences for as long as I want or remand you to prison."

"Why would you do that when I've done nothing wrong?" The butterflies now feel like they are eating the lining of my stomach.

"You were out of your cell. Prisoners are not supposed to be out of their cells."

"But you approved me being out of my cell."

"None of that matters. If I say I didn't, and that you took it upon yourself to talk a few of the guards into letting you out, the people will believe me. And, I trust my guards will not go against me."

"Samuel and Eric know the truth."

"Do you really want to put them in the middle of this? You may think they care about you, but I know they'll side with the one who pays them, the one who can fire them."

I feel my palms sweating because she is right. Even if I do believe they'll side with me, I don't want to drag them into a situation I don't want to be in myself. It is not fair to them.

"Why are you doing this?" I feel a hammering in my chest, as if I've been struck several times with a mallet. "Why would you want me to be a guard?"

"I have no female guards. You would be the first. I feel it will be good for the territory to see another female in a power position. It will be good to see a female progressing in this manner. Since you've been training, and I know you can handle yourself, I believe it should be you."

My mouth feels dry, as if I'm on a deserted island with no fresh water and no way off. My hands shake as I reach for my glass of water. I gulp the rest down. I place the glass down with a bang. I'm surprised it doesn't shatter.

"I'm waiting for an answer." Her eyes are fixated on me.

"I thought you didn't want young guards because they can't be trusted. I'm only eighteen, which would make me younger than anyone else." My voice shakes.

"I normally don't like younger guards, but your brother is doing well—and so is Eric."

She takes another bite of her cookie. She looks at me like she is a bald eagle ready to pounce on a fish. I feel like the fish she is ready to devour.

"I trust you'll do quite well."

I remain soundless. I want this conversation to end so I can go back to my cell. I want to pinch myself because I must be in a nightmare, and I need to wake up.

"Besides, Emma, what will you do on the outside? What kind of job is out there for you? Will you go work on the farms or work at the clothing store or in the pawn shop? You know it as well as I do, those jobs are beneath you."

"I thought, if my family made it to Territory M, that I could go to college. I could become a doctor like my father."

"Well, that is never going to happen. Your father is needed here."

"There are hundreds of other family doctors that can work here. Why can't my family move ahead?"

"Your family will never move ahead, but you can." She stands. "You remember that. Our time is up. Guard," she yells out.

The door swings open, and Jason, the tall guard who trained my brother, walks in. The anxiety in my stomach uncurls, a little, since Rich is not standing there. I know I can't deal with him, at the moment.

"I will give you two days to make your decision. Then, I will send for you." Her lips purse together. "I trust your answer will be to my liking. By the way, Jason," she says, glancing back toward me. "There is no need to place the handcuffs on her. She knows why. Soon enough, she'll be one of us." She sneers.

I take it she thinks I don't need the handcuffs anymore because I will be joining the fold. The entire way back to my cell, I feel like I'm having an out of body experience. How can this happen? I've done everything that was asked of me. I'd rather spend the rest of my life behind these jail walls than stoop so low as to work for her. I'll find a way out of this. I have to.

CHAPTER SIXTEEN

"Did something happen?" I hear Eric's low voice echoing through my hollow cell.

My head feels as if a weight is holding it down. I can't lift it to look at him. I'm sitting on my cot in my uniform, trying to picture myself in a black guard ensemble. How many silver buttons will I acquire?

"Whisper, what happened?" I hear him again.

I stare down at my gym shoes firmly planted on the floor. They'll be gone soon; I'll be plastered in black boots like the others. The cell smells like apples and cinnamon. My breakfast tray from earlier is sitting on the floor with cold oatmeal and bacon on the plate. My stomach was queasy. I couldn't eat it. Staring at it now makes me want to throw it against the wall.

"What's wrong?" he asks. I hear him tapping the metal bars with his fingers.

My chest feels as if a fire is burning on top of it, but I manage to turn and look at him.

"What makes you think something is wrong?"

"You're sitting here, looking like you lost your only friend." His eyebrows slope together. "Besides, word came down from the president that you're not to leave your cell until further notice."

"I'm surprised I can still have visitors," I say, standing.

I step over the tray and walk closer to him.

"I know she sent for you. What happened during your meeting?"

I know I just saw him yesterday, but it looks like some stubble has grown around his chin. My eyes broaden. It fits him nicely. I don't know why I'm dwelling on stubble. Maybe I'm trying to amuse myself, so I can forget the decision that is in front of me.

"The president had a proposition for me," I say, and then pause because I don't know how to continue.

"Well, what was it?" His stare is hard like he is tired of waiting for my slow responses to his questions.

"S-she wants me to become a guard—the f-first f-female guard." I feel like hands are clawing at my throat as the words struggle to get out. "I-I will be used as an example of what women can a-accomplish. She feels it will be good for the territory." Saying the words aloud makes me cringe.

He scratches the back of his neck and glances down at the floor. He is eerily silent. All I hear are the sounds of some guards, around the corner, roughhousing. It has become usual banter around here and I don't flinch hearing it, anymore.

He looks back at me with a glint in his eyes. "I think this could be a good thing."

"What do you mean?" My throat is dry, as if I haven't had water in weeks. "How is any of this a good thing? I was to be released in about a week and now…" The air feels thick and my breaths feel jagged. "She says if I don't do this, she will lie and tell everyone I didn't have permission to be out of my cell. That way she can have an excuse for extending my stay. She says that only the guards know the truth, and they wouldn't dare go against her."

"You know that I would. I'm not afraid of her." A light in his eyes flickers. "I would do anything for you." He reaches his hand through the bars and rubs his knuckles against my cheek.

A small tingle goes up the small of my back. I didn't really know if he would back me up or not, but I hoped so. Now that I know he would, I can call him a friend—maybe more than a friend.

"I know that," I say. "But I would never put you in that position." I wrap my fingers around his hand on my cheek. It feels warm and, somehow, it feels right. "How could this be a good thing? You never answered my question."

"We could use this to our advantage." He removes his hand from mine.

A tall guard with black hair comes around the corner. He walks past us with a tray of food. I see something orange that looks and smells like carrots. I also see some kind of brown meat. It's probably dried up meat loaf since that is usually on the lunch menu around here.

His boots click along the floor as he continues his stride down the hall. He's probably taking food to Cassandra. I don't see much of her now that they moved her. Every now and then, I see someone taking her to wash up. And, I see them taking her trays of food. They must have instructed her not to make eye contact with me because every time they walk her through she never looks my way.

"See that's what I'm talking about." His voice is lower than before, as if he doesn't want the guard to hear what we're saying. "If you were a guard, you could try to help Cassandra."

"I don't follow?" I bite my lip so hard that I would swear I feel blood coming from it. "How can I help anyone?"

"The people here believe in you, and they believe in your cause. Don't you remember the faces of the people who listened to your speech?"

"All I saw were blank stares."

"No, you saw more than that." His jaw tightens. "The people from our territory were proud of what you did by standing up for yourself and standing up for them. I've heard rumblings that the ones at home watching on their boxes agreed with your cause. They agree with what you stand for, but they're old and set in their ways. They're afraid to get involved or go up against her. I even believe, somewhere deep down inside, your parents were proud, too."

He glances down at the floor as we hear the shallow footsteps of the guard walking back past us.

He is right though, my mother did say she was proud of me; but my father was a different matter.

"If you were a guard," he continues. "That would give you probable cause to visit Cassandra, and she wouldn't feel so alone down here. It would lead you to places you could never go before." His amber eyes glisten like I've never seen before. "Maybe, since the president seems to like you, that would give you the opportunity to rustle some feathers and get some changes made around here."

I feel as though a lightbulb is above my head. My palms moisten and blood rushes to my ears.

"I believe I could do more good if I could get out of here. What she's doing is wrong. Good or bad, right or wrong, we have the right to make our own decisions. No one should control us."

"I agree." His eyes are glued to mine.

"What if there was a way we could both get out of here and open the territory gates so we could all be one again? I mean, what if Craigluy was one, whole territory again? No more division of classes. And, babies could be born here again." The more I talk, the more my heart beats loudly within my chest. "What if we could go to college, no matter how poor or rich we are? What if all families could prosper, and everyone could have better jobs?"

"Now you sound like the girl on the podium the day of the party." He smiles.

It wasn't a faint smile or a half-smile; this time, he smiled with all his teeth showing. And, I knew he agreed with everything I was saying.

"But how do you propose we make that happen?" He tugs at the collar on his jacket.

"If I was a guard, it would be easier for me to leave. And, if we could somehow make it to Territory M, maybe we could find whoever is in charge and they could help us against Esther."

"That may work." He cocks his head to the side. "If she respects them enough to give them the power over one of the territories, maybe she will listen to them and break down the barriers."

"I don't think Esther will listen to anyone. She seems too bull-headed for that; but I did overhear a conversation, a few days ago, when I went exploring."

"The day I left you alone in the training facility?" His eyes soften.

"Yes, that was the day."

"I'm sorry about that."

"You don't have to keep apologizing," I say. My heart races. I'm eager to get back to the subject. "Anyway, I overheard a conversation between Rich and the president. He was saying he wants to take charge of Territory M because it's not run properly. He said the person who runs it is weak and passive. Esther wouldn't hear of it. She told him no. Do you know who's in charge over there?"

"I have no idea." He shrugs. "Everything's kept a secret."

"If they're weak enough—and not money hungry and filled with power, like Esther—maybe they'll give us a chance to speak. If they listen to us, and agree her rules are wrong, then maybe they'll agree the walls should come down. Maybe they have enough power to help us fight Esther. We could use their weakness to our advantage."

"We have to figure out how to get into Territory M without people knowing."

"Yes, I haven't thought that far ahead, but like you said, it will be easier if I'm a guard. We already know there's no going over the walls. They're too high—"

"Or the electric fence," Eric says, cutting me off.

"We'll deal with the details later," I say, trying to sound strong, even though fear bubbles up inside me.

"So, it's decided? You're going to accept her offer?"

"Yes, I will." A shudder goes up my spine, as if I've stepped into a small room that will lock behind me with no way out.

"One more thing," Eric says, looking me straight in my eyes. "I know you consider Samuel a friend, but I don't think you should tell him about this."

"He's been good to me." I blink. "And, I trust him."

"Well, I don't," he snaps back. "I feel the less people that know what we're planning, the better."

"I guess you're right," I say.

But in my heart, I know I can trust Samuel. After all, he did take me to see my parents. He's a good guy, and once Eric realizes it, we can let Samuel in on our plan. We may need all the help we can get, so we shouldn't count Samuel out.

"We're planning this alliance together, and I don't even know your last name." My heart races, wildly, like a train off its metal tracks.

"It's Wall. Eric Wall," he says, placing his hand through the bars to shake mine. "And, my favorite color is blue." He winks at me. "Do you know enough about me now, or is there something else you need to know before we start this journey together?"

"No, I think that's all for now." I laugh, a little, inside. His last name is Wall. Maybe that is why he has a habit of putting up walls. I'm hoping, now that we have this alliance, I won't see the walls again.

The laughter inside me fades as quickly as it surfaced. I feel angry worms eating away at my insides. Even though I have my own agenda, I'll be a guard soon. The thought of being one of them sickens me.

CHAPTER SEVENTEEN

"The president wants to see you now," Samuel says. The key to my cell clanks in the lock and the door shrills open.

It's ten in the morning. One guard has taken me to wash up; another guard has handed me a cold tray of breakfast. Now, a guard stands to take me to meet my fate. At least it's Samuel, not Rich. I haven't seen, or heard from, Rich since I was summoned to see the president a few days prior.

"Sorry," he says, glancing at the tray in my lap. "You haven't had a chance to eat, yet."

"I didn't want it anyway." I look at him and then back at my tray.

The eggs are yellow, like a banana, and runny. There are two strips of burnt bacon along with them. The entire cell smells like burning wood. I scrunch my nose up, in disgust. I barely slept last night, and I wipe my eyes, knowing the redness I saw in the mirror this morning is still there. The tray swishes across my cot as I push it aside. I stand, and my hands burn as I straighten out my blue uniform, knowing it may be the last time I wear it. I never liked it, anyway; but I always thought I would be trading it in for a drab garment from my closet at home, not a black guard uniform.

"I'm ready," I say, in a whisper. "Let's just go." I brush past him.

"Wait a minute." He grips my hand in his hand; his palms are sweaty.

"I know something's going on. A lot of the guards have been whispering. Rumor has it you'll be the first female guard, as well as the youngest. Is any of that true?"

"I can't speak about it, right now." I pull my hand away and lower my eyes to the floor.

"Please, tell me it's not true." He raises my chin and our gazes meet.

The little hairs on the back of my neck stand. I have the same feeling as before, the feeling that he sees me as more than a little sister.

"This is no place for you." He touches my cheek.

His hand feels warm, but I turn my face in the other direction, as if I heard someone calling my name.

"We should go." I turn and walk ahead of him.

He is now silent, but I hear the soles of his black boots scuffing against the floors. I also hear the guards whispering, like gossiping schoolgirls, as we walk past them to the elevator. I search some of their faces and some smile at me while others frown. Some glare at me, as if I'm a target and they're shooting daggers at my face. I can't stomach the stares anymore, so I lower my head until we reach the elevators.

The elevator ride is unnervingly quiet. All I hear is the sound of shallow breaths coming from my mouth. Samuel moves closer to me, and I feel the fabric of his jacket against the fabric of my shirt. I jump as the elevator rings at the fifth floor, and my heart pounds as we step into the hallway of Esther's quarters.

Samuel jams his finger into the button as if he is frustrated with me. The doorbell outside her quarters echoes throughout the hallway. Instead of the orchestra music I heard last time, I now hear what reminds me of birds chirping.

"Come in, the door is open."

The sound of Esther's voice makes my leg wobble.

"Thank you, Samuel. That will be all." She nods his way.

The door bangs behind me, and I stand there glued to the spot, like a statue.

"You may come closer." Her eyes angle in my direction. "You know I don't bite."

She stares at me like an animal stalking its prey. I don't know how much truth is in the words she just spoke.

"I'm glad you decided to take my offer."

The president is glaring at me with those bold blue eyes that make tremors go up my spine. I see lines under her eyes, so maybe the stress of the job is getting to her. She sits on her circular sofa with a manila folder in her skinny, pale hands. She has on a bright, light blue dress that offsets all the tan in the room.

"How would you know what I've decided, if I haven't told you yet?" I try to sound tough, even though my knees vibrate and my body aches to sit down.

"Take a seat beside me." Her very words mimic the thoughts that were in my head. She pats the spot beside her.

"No, thank you." I shake my head. "I'd rather sit here."

I sit across from her.

"That's fine. Let's start, shall we." There is a crinkling sound as she takes out a paper from the manila folder. "We have a lot to do in the next few days, if we want to make the announcement on Monday evening."

"Announcement?" I repeat, as my eyes stretch wider than ever before.

"Yes, the announcement that you'll be the first and youngest female guard."

"Why does this have to be such a big thing?" I shift on the sofa. "Why can't this be done in a quiet manner? Besides, I thought I could tell my family first, before any of this is made official."

"There is no time for that." She crosses her legs. "The announcement will be made as soon as possible. They'll hear it over the information box like everyone else."

"I don't think that's fair." I feel the acid in my belly rising as I talk to her.

"You'll learn as one of my own that life isn't fair." She glances down at the papers on her lap. "You'll be fitted for a uniform, like the others. And, when you stand at the podium on Monday night, you will say what is written on the papers here."

Her frail body leans over, and I swear I hear her bones crack, like a branch snapping off a tree.

I take the papers from her, and my chest constricts while reading the words plastered on them.

"There is no way I can say this. In fact, I will never say these words."

"Never say never, dear." Her eyes squint, and they appear hard like rocks.

"Why can't I just quietly become a guard, like the others did? Why must I make a speech?"

She snatches the papers from my hands, and a cool breeze hits my face. It is not as cold as her stare, but it almost matches it.

"This is a new day in Territory L. Becoming the first female guard is an important accomplishment, and it should be acknowledged. Becoming one of my guards requires you read this speech. I would like for you to read it word-for-word, this time. I'm sure you understand how important that is. We'll let this go, for now, since we have more pressing matters to attend to—such as, where you'll be staying."

Anxiety curls up in my stomach. I'm so used to the bars surrounding me that I never thought of where my new living arrangement would be.

"You can't very well stay where the men stay. I'm having two of the guards, living on the west corner of the fourth floor, move. That way, you will have a private room to yourself. You'll have your own bathroom and shower, as well."

"I don't want someone to move to make accommodations for me. That isn't fair."

"They'll get along fine with the new arrangements. You'll move in before the ceremony. If anyone has a problem with it, they'll answer to me. Now, it is time for your fitting. I hired Penelope. She is the best seamstress in Territory U. She is down in the conference room, awaiting further instructions."

She stands, and I watch her heels clack as she walks to the door. It creaks open just enough for her to stick her head through.

"Samuel, go and fetch Penelope. We're ready for her now."

She then turns and walks back to me at a snail's pace.

The next few minutes are filled with silence. I take in a much needed breath. My esophagus burns, like someone has slit my throat. The smell of stale coffee is in the air, but I don't see a coffeepot anywhere. I'm trying to dwell on anything but where I am and what I'm doing. I don't want to make eye contact with Esther, unless I have to.

The door whizzes open, and I see Samuel and the seamstress walk in. I take it President Esther didn't lock the door because she didn't want to get up to let them in. She looks comfy and cozy, sitting there scanning over her papers, like everything is right with our world.

"Hello, Esther," a medium-sized woman says.

She has gray eyes and blonde hair, and she looks much younger than I expected. She wears a yellow pants suit along with white high-heeled shoes. It is nice to see bright, sunny clothing, for a change. I realize the president has on bright clothing as well, but it looks nicer on a normal human being.

The label seamstress makes me think of an older woman. I don't like anyone stereotyping me, so suppose I shouldn't do it to others.

"Hello, Penelope." Esther stands. "Thank you for coming so quickly."

"It is my pleasure," Penelope says, smiling.

I notice Samuel takes that as his cue to exit the room. I also notice the two women are on a first name basis, so they must be good friends instead of mere acquaintances.

"Is this her?" Penelope asks, looking me up and down as if I'm a doll, instead of a real person.

"Yes, this is her. Stand up, Emma."

I stand, and Penelope walks toward me as if I'm a mannequin that she can't wait to dress.

"I have to take a few measurements," she says, looking me up and down again.

She carries a black purse. She rustles open the zipper and pulls out a long tape measure the color of the sun. Then, she pulls out a notebook the color of midnight—a color I'm sadly familiar with around here.

"We'll start by measuring your neck and your bust area."

She says we, as if I'm a part of what is going on instead of a hostage, following orders. She wraps the tape measure around my neck, and I feel like a rope is choking me. She moves down to my chest, telling me to hold still. The tape measure feels soft. Now, I know how rich people feel when they're getting fancy dresses made for special parties.

"Now, we'll move on to your waist," she says, as she leans over.

The president eyes everything that is going on with a wicked smile on her face.

The seamstress pulls up my shirt and wraps the tape measure around my waist. My knuckles feel better, but I still feel a twinge in my side while she is measuring me. I'm relieved that the purple bruising along my side has faded. She writes down something in her notebook and continues on.

"Next, I'm going to measure from your neck down to your waist."

She walks to my back, takes the tape measure, and stretches it out near my spine. It tickles, a little, on my neck, like a feather would if someone rubs it against me.

"Almost done," she says.

Her eyes widen as she looks up at me, as if I should be grateful she is a fast and efficient worker.

After she measures what seems like every inch of my body, she looks at me and says, "I need your shoe size."

"Eight," I say quickly.

I'm now tired of the whole charade, and I'm ready to go.

"We're done now."

Penelope stands. She walks over to her bag and places the tape back in. She closes her purse with a swish.

"I should have the garment back to you in a few days."

"Thank you," President Esther says. "Your excellent, expedient work is always appreciated. Let's keep this matter discreet."

"Yes, of course," Penelope says, as if they are making an illegal transaction.

"Emma, you can go now." Esther glares at me. "Samuel is outside the door to take you back to your cell."

"Yes, ma'am."

I turn and walk away. It will be good to get out of here. I felt like I was stuck in a bubble. The bubble has finally popped. Now, I can breathe.

*

"Why would you do this?" Samuel says to me, as soon as the elevator doors whizz closed. "You're almost out of here. None of this makes any sense to me."

He scratches the top of his head and stares at me, like I'm a puzzle and the last piece won't fit.

"You don't understand."

"Then, help me to." His eyes are sad.

I want, so badly, to confide in him; but Eric thinks differently. For the time being, maybe he's right; no one should know about our plan.

"I'm sorry. But I can't." I look away, hoping he doesn't ask again.

Samuel is quiet until we reach my cell. After he closes the screechy bar doors, he looks through them at me. His light brown eyes look darker than before, and he acts as if he has lost his best friend.

"If that's the case, and you're dead set on living here, are there any questions you need answered?" He grips the bars, tightly.

"The president said she is moving two guards out of a room in the west corner of the fourth floor. Where will they live?"

"They'll move in with two other guards, so four will have to bunk together."

"Do you know the names of the ones losing their rooms?"

"It'll be the last two that arrived. Since they don't carry much seniority, it is only fair. One will be your friend, Eric." His knuckles bulge as he clutches the bars tighter.

"And who is the other one?"

"It's a guy name Julian. He arrived over a year ago. But, he was the last one before Eric, good enough to acquire a room in the mansion."

There is loud talking coming from around the corner.

"I should go, now." Samuel glances around. "Take care of yourself."

His eyes are sad again. They seem to look right through me, as if he is searching my soul for answers. He walks away, as if this is the last time he will ever see, or speak to me, again.

Anguish riddles my insides. A pang of guilt echoes within the walls of my chest. I don't know if I'm making a mistake, or not. I do know, there is no way I will read the speech she has written out for me. I have to find a way around it.

CHAPTER EIGHTEEN

"Is THE ROOM TO your liking?" Rich shifts his eyes toward mine. He wears his black suit proudly, along with his six silver buttons.

The room is dark. There are no windows. The air is stale and dry. Out of all the guards here, I don't know why he is the one who has to bring me to my new living quarters. My foot twitches as I look around. It has to be no more than 168 square feet. I know this because it looks about the size of my room at home, a home I may never see again. There are four walls and a bed, to the left of me. Yes, it's a bed, not a cot, like down in my cell. Next to the bed is a small, brown table with a clock on it. It ticks loudly. I'll have to get used to the sound. There is a door, on the right, that looks like it leads to a small closet; but, I'm sure that is where the bathroom is. The space where the second bed must have been is now bare.

"You shouldn't ignore me when I'm talking to you." He walks closer to me. "Do you realize two men had to give up their rooms for the likes of you?"

His hot breath is on my neck. I feel like my feet are stuck in quicksand, and I can't move.

"I realize one of them was your boyfriend," he continues his rant. "But Julian didn't deserve what he got. And, the other two guys don't deserve to have two more beds shoved into their rooms like they are at some kind of boy's camp."

"I'm sorry about what happened to them." I turn to face him. "And, I'm sorry about your loved ones. But what happened to them wasn't my fault."

"What are you babbling about?"

"I know that's why you hate me. Your sibling died, and I didn't."

"I don't want your apologies. There is no way to bring him back now, so your apologies mean nothing to me." I see rage building up in his eyes. There's a crease splattered along his forehead.

"I didn't ask for any of this." My nerves are prickling as if a feather rubs them. "I don't even want to be here."

"And, I don't want you here." His nostrils flare. "So, what are we going to do about this situation?"

I hold my own. My stance matches his. I remain strong, until he shoves me and I fall into the wall with a *thump*. It feels as though I've received a blow to my back with a hammer. Before I have a chance to let the pain sink in, he picks me up by my collar and throws me on the bed. I land with a *thud* and air wafts up in the opposite direction. His eyes expand. He growls, like a grizzly bear, as he comes toward me. He is much bigger than me, and all I can think about are the moves that Eric taught me. I need to stop Rich before he reaches me because once his weight is on me, I'll be pinned down like a rat caught in a trap.

I kick my foot straight out as hard as I can, and I aim for his face. I'm not sure if I got him in his eye or his nose. I do know I hurt him, somewhere. He clutches his face and doubles over in pain. His body crashes down on the hardwood floor. I know this is my chance to get past him before he hurts me, or worse, pulls the gun or the Taser from one of the holsters on his hip. My heart falls into my stomach as I jump to my feet. I run past him as fast as I can. Before I make it to the door, I feel his hand clutch my ankle, as if a rope is tangled around it. I fall, with a clank, to my knees.

"Let go," I say, screaming as if my lungs are on fire.

"You think you're man enough to hurt me, little girl. Well, think again."

He pulls my ankle, and my body slides along the floor to where he is. My fingernails screech along the floorboards like nails along a pavement.

"You think you're special. I'm here to tell you, you're not."

He turns me over to face him. I'm on my back now. He straddles my waist and the pain in my side throbs, but I try to ignore it.

"I'm not special," I say. "I'm just me."

My body shakes. I don't know what's coming next. His weight is unbearable.

"Get off me," I scream.

The door flings open and Samuel stands there with a black plastic garment bag in one hand and another small plastic bag in the other. "What's going on in here?"

Rich quickly moves off me. He stands and wipes the moisture from his brow.

"Are you crazy?" Samuel yells.

He releases the bags. They clank, dropping to the floor. He walks over to Rich and gets in his face.

"If she is going to be a guard here, she has to learn her place," Rich says.

"And, I take it you think you're the one to teach her that place?" Samuel says.

Their eyes are at the same level.

"I don't want any trouble with you." Rich rubs his hands through his hair.

"The next time you make trouble for her, it will be with me, too."

"Fine…fine. Whatever." Rich holds his hands up. He walks around Samuel and glowers at me. The door bangs behind him.

I know my face is flushed. I have sweat coming from every pore of my body. I sit up, a little, but I can't stop trembling, as if I was almost hit by a bus.

"Emma, are you all right?" Samuel kneels beside me. He brushes a strand of hair behind my ear.

"I'm fine." My lip trembles.

"I'm going to report this to the president." He pulls on my arm and helps me to stand.

"No, please don't," I say. I'm wobbly as I try to balance my weight. "I don't want to be seen as a troublemaker. I'm okay." I brush my uniform off. "What's in the bag?" I ask, trying to change the subject.

"I know what you're doing." I see sympathy in his eyes.

"You need to know it's okay to cry. No one's going to fault you, if you do. You don't have to be tough, all the time."

His words are nice, but I know I can't walk around here with red, puffy eyes—no one would take me seriously.

"I'll let it go, for now, but if it happens again—"

"It won't. Even if it does," I say, shrugging. "I can handle myself."

I don't know if I'm saying it to reassure him, or myself, but he looks at me as if he doesn't believe me.

"What's in the bag?" I ask again.

"I went down to your cell to bring you your new uniform, and I was going to show you your new living quarters; but when I got there, they said Rich had already taken you up."

"Was he not supposed to?" I ask. The frown on his face tells me everything I need to know.

"No. The president assigned me to get you settled. But somehow, Rich got to you first."

"I guess he had his own agenda." I blink.

"I suppose he did. I'm sorry he is such a jerk."

His eyes are caring. The room is quiet, for a moment, until he speaks again.

"The smaller bag has the clothes you arrived in inside. I noticed they were balled up in the corner of your cell. I also found this under your cot. We have to clean it for when new inmates arrive."

He unfolds his hand and the silver necklace my mother gave me is inside, along with my ID card.

"Put it over there." I point at the table. "Thank you for bringing it."

In such a short time, I have learned to love that necklace. Now, I don't feel much like seeing it because it symbolizes hope, and I don't have much right now.

"Are you sure you're all right?" He touches my chin.

"Yes, I am." I shiver and turn away. I pick up the long garment bag from the floor. The plastic swooshes in my hands.

"Do you mind if I open this alone?"

"No, I don't mind." He shakes his head. "If that's what you want."

"Yes, that's what I want." I hate it that my voice quivers, but it does. "I think I need some time to myself."

He walks toward me and kisses my forehead. That's something he has never done before, and I don't know what to make of it. My chest stings as he places the necklace and the card on the table and leaves the room.

I've never been kissed before. I know it was only the forehead, but still, it was a kiss. I feel warm. I can't dwell on that now; I have bigger issues to deal with—like what just happened with Rich and the impending announcements.

I splat down on my new bed and the springs creak underneath me. It feels soft like butter, and is nothing like my old cot downstairs. There is a comforter on top and it bunches as I move. I lay the garment bag beside me and take in a breath. My hands go numb as I touch the plastic bag. It is cold and slippery. It feels like there's a weight at the bottom, holding it down.

I stand and the anxiety in my stomach moves into my entire body. I can't exhale. I slink down the plastic and it swishes as it falls. There, before me, is a black uniform. It looks just like the others. The bag is still crumbled on the floor, and I reach inside to retrieve what was weighing it down. There are black boots inside that look as heavy as the ones on all the other guards.

A knock at the door startles me and my shoulders jump. I'm not used to my surroundings yet, and I didn't expect to have any visitors, so soon. The door swings open and, to my surprise, the president is standing there. I didn't think it was customary for her to visit the guards on the fourth floor. I thought they were always summoned to see her. My first thoughts are Samuel must have told her what happened between me and Rich. I wish he hadn't.

"How is everything?" she asks, walking inside. She wears a black pants suit with gold high heels. Her silver hair hangs down to her shoulders.

"Everything's fine," I say, and then swallow hard. "Have I done something wrong?"

"No, why would you think that?"

"I thought when you wanted to see someone, they came to you, instead of the other way around."

"Well, you're an exception to the rule." Her eyes are fixated on mine.

Her words make me shudder. I keep saying I don't want any special treatment, but I feel as though no one is listening to me.

"I want you to take a walk with me. We have some things to discuss before you make your announcement."

"Okay," I say, softly, even though I haven't exactly agreed to read her announcement.

We take the president's elevator and end up on the third floor. Is she taking me to the training room? Maybe she wants to see what I've learned, before she approves of me being a guard.

As we get closer, I hear screaming and hollering from the guards practicing inside. I pray no one sees me. I'll surely be pummeled for walking around with her as if we're friends. But we walk past the training room and continue down the dark hallway.

My fist tightens because we keep walking until we end up in front of the room I never wanted to see again. She wraps her thin fingers around the knob and the door creaks open. The room hasn't changed since the last time I was here. It's still dark and smells musty, like no one ever comes in here. The big screen is still on the wall.

But now, the wooden chair that was in the middle of the room is not the only chair. There is another chair along the wall. The second chair is black and metal. My knees sway and my palms sweat.

"I will sit here," she says, sitting in the black metal chair. "You can take the other chair." She glares down at the wooden chair that reminds me of an electric chamber.

I feel dehydrated as I sit down. I wring my hands. I don't know why we're here. We sit in silence, for a few moments, until the door scrapes open and Rich walks inside. I feel like I'm trapped on an elevator and my throat is closing. I look at him. Our eyes meet, so I quickly turn away. My attention turns to a silver box that has several buttons on it. I didn't notice it before, but now I see him standing next to it.

"Now, we can begin." The president clasps her hands together.

Begin what? I think. *Are they going to kill me and dump my body somewhere in this room?*

I'm thinking crazy thoughts, and I take in a deep breath to calm down.

"The ceremony is almost at hand, and I don't feel you are ready."

I have the speech she demands I read, and I have my new black uniform and boots. What else could she want from me?

"I'm sorry to hear that." I squirm in the hard chair. "What else do I need?"

"I know you don't believe in the speech. I need you to believe." She leans forward. "Do you believe in what you will say?"

I don't understand her line of questioning. She knows I don't believe, so what kind of stunt is she pulling now. I haven't even confirmed to her that I'll read it. I feel like I'm waiting for the firing squad to emerge and start shooting at me.

"No, I don't. But you already know that. You're forcing me into this. Otherwise, my stay in the jail will be extended."

"Yes, that's true." She twists her fingers around as if she is holding onto an imaginary ball. "You could have decided to stay in jail."

"Why would I do that?" I feel fire burning in my ears. I know

I would've been okay staying in the jail. But now, Eric and I have a different plan, and I don't want her catching on to it. "Who in their right mind would want to spend all their time in a dirty jail cell?" I say, forcefully.

I hear Rich clearing his throat in the back of the room, as if he is annoyed with what I'm saying.

"I want you to be passionate during your speech. You shouldn't have to lie. I like to feel passionate about everything I do, and I want the same for you. If you don't believe in what you are saying, the people won't believe you. That is why we're here. Rich…" Her eyes enlarge as she looks toward the back of the room. "It is time."

Time for what? My throat scrunches.

Rich comes over to me.

"Place your hands on the armrests."

"Why?"

"Just do it." He glares.

"Nothing will hurt, dear." Her mouth curls up.

I take my arms from my lap and place them on the armrest like he asks. He clamps the brown leather handcuffs around my wrists. The handcuffs feel tight and heavy, and the leather is thick and hard. The chains that lead from the chair to the handcuffs are long enough to dangle. My entire body shakes, as if I have stepped into an oversized freezer. I feel his scorching breath on my forehead, as he leans in and places round, black headphones over my ears. Then, he gives me a wicked smile that sends a streak of tension up my spine.

"Thank you." President Esther nods at Rich.

He turns and walks to the back of the room. No doubt he'll be controlling the silver box that I noticed earlier.

"Keep your eyes on the screen. Do not move them. Some of the images you see will be disturbing, but do not look away," President Esther says.

"Are you trying to brainwash me?"

"No, Emma. I do not brainwash people. I like people to think for themselves. If a little persuasion is involved for them to get to the correct conclusion, then that is a different story. Rich, you may begin." She nods at him.

My heart pounds through my ears. I wish I was a bird that could slip out of these handcuffs, spread its wings and fly away. My eyes stretch wide as the screen turns on. The room grows darker, as if it wasn't already dark enough.

I hear eerie music start to play over the headphones, like she is trying to set the mood. A black-and-white photo shows on the screen. There is a dark-skin baby with its mouth wide open. I'm not sure if it is a girl or a boy, but it looks to be around twelve months old. The baby is bald and has dark eyes. Its chest is bare and sunken in. The baby wears only a diaper. I can tell the baby is crying because tears stream like a waterspout. It looks as if the baby is lying on a table in a large, bright room. The photo goes away, but as quickly as it disappears, another one appears, as if it is popping through the screen.

The next photo shows the same bright room, but now there is a dark-skin man, standing beside the baby, photographing him-self with the camera. He has on jeans and a white t-shirt. He has something in his other hand that looks square and fluffy. It's a white pillow. Another photo shows the man placing the pillow over the baby's face. The man suffocates the baby, and I feel a pang in my side. The next photo shows the stilled baby on the same table. The baby appears to be dead, and the man smiles at the camera.

"This makes no sense." I rip off the headphones and stand. But the handcuffs yank me back to my original seated position in the chair. My shoulders *thump* as my spine hits the hard back of the chair.

"Who would kill a baby and take pictures of himself while doing it? None of this is real," I manage to say.

"These photos are real." Her eyes glare at me. "But they're from another era—a time before the war. Back then, news was broadcasted daily, and sometimes, hourly. It was back during a time when people photographed everything. This particular man killed his child and photographed it, so his wife would see what he'd done. His wife was divorcing him, and he wanted to get back at her, so he left the photos for her. When she returned home that night, the baby was dead; and the photos were left beside the corpse, so she would see that her estranged husband was the killer."

"No one in their right mind would do that. He was obviously crazy." I frown. "Why would you have photos from another era?"

"I have a lot of things from the eras before ours. The city council building used to be a police station, years ago. I found a lot of old crime photos and newspaper clippings in a locked room. But that is neither here nor there." She shifts in her chair. "Rich, go on with the photos."

I wish she hadn't said that because my stomach is queasy and I don't want to look at anything else. I place the headphones back on my ears.

The next photo shows a small, dark room. There is a light-skin baby, lying on the floor, next to a light-skin man and woman. The baby is probably one or two. The baby is fully dressed, in a green jumper. The man has on a blue suit. The woman has on a pink dress. They have blood on their chests and faces. There is blood all over the floor and the walls.

"This photo was taken from some police files. It was classified as a murder-suicide. The father shot the mother, the baby, and then himself," President Esther says. "Next slide, please." She clasps her hands together, as if she is pleased with what she is doing.

I hear humming and beeping. A new photo appears on the screen. It is a little girl, around five. She has two pigtails, like I had when I was little and my mother braided my hair. She has on a blue dress. Tears stain her cheeks. Her lip is as big and as puffy as a ball; and, it is bruised. Her head has a big gash on it.

"This little girl was beaten by her mother. If you don't believe me, I can show you the police files."

She looks down at a manila folder that's sitting in between her thin body and the arm of the chair.

"It's all in here."

"No, I believe you." I shake my head. "May I go now?" I ask.

I want to stand again and rip off the headphones. I want to run out of the room, but I know the handcuffs will jerk me down like before, so I remain seated.

"No, dear. We've only just begun." She chuckles, as though we're working together and I just agreed to stuff the ballot box during her election. "Keep looking ahead." She points at the screen.

The eerie music plays again. The screen brightens. This time it looks like a video of some sort. The photos are gone. There is a moving picture. A man sits behind a gray desk in a bright, white room. He looks straight at the camera. He reads from a white sheet of paper.

"A young man was robbed and killed while walking home from school today. His killers are still on the run. If you see someone matching the description of…"

The video cuts to the same man, but this time, he is reading a different report.

"A seven-year-old little girl was found dead today in an abandoned building. It appears she was raped, first; and then, her throat was slashed…"

"A thirteen-year-old girl was bullied at school today because of her race. Her bully brought a knife to school and cut her face…"

"A single father was shot to death, and now his young, three-year-old son will be put in foster care…"

My hands sting and my face feels hot, like a match is under my skin.

"A pregnant mother of four was killed in a car accident. Now, her children have no home…"

"A ten-year-old …"

I wish I had braided my hair today because the strands surrounding my neck feel like they are strangling me.

"I don't want to do this anymore," I say. My eyes water, and there is a hollow feeling in my chest. "Can we please stop now?" My voice shakes, like every other part of my body.

"These are videos from another era, when news was always on television. The news is just as horrifying now, but I try to shield my people from most of the violence that goes on here. That is why it is not displayed in this fashion anymore. When I do my Monday night broadcasts, I put in bits and pieces—those who have been murdered and those who have been sent to jail. If I told everything that goes on in this territory, it would be maddening, just like these tapes. Do you understand, now?" She advances toward me.

"I may understand, but that doesn't necessarily mean I agree." I swallow hard. "I realize our world isn't perfect for children, or for adults, but it's still not fair for you to make it so children can't be born. As human beings, it should be our decision, not the government's choice."

"So, you would rather have children suffer?" She narrows her eyes at me, as if she's annoyed that after all of her videos, I still don't agree. "You would rather have an innocent child, who didn't ask to be here, go through hurt and pain?"

"No, that's not what I want at all." I sit up, straighter. "That's why it's up to you, as the president, to make things better for all children, so they won't have to worry about that. It is your job to make the streets safer and to make sure young ones are protected." I feel fire burning in my belly. "Your whole concern is that children shouldn't hurt, and the poor can't take care of them, so that is why they shouldn't be born; but you're doing the same thing as every monster in those photos or videos, you're killing them, as well."

"I try to stop the hurt, before it gets to the stage in the videos." Her chest puffs up, as if she is proud. "That is why I try to get the ingrates of this territory to stop having them; and if they do get pregnant, to get rid of the babies, while they're too young to understand what is going on. You need to understand that, fully, before you make that speech."

"Well, I don't understand. I don't care how many photos you parade in my face, I'm still not going to change my mind." My teeth clamp. "Don't you see, if no more children come after us, then once we die off, there will be no one left? There'll be no one to carry on. Territory L will be gone, forever. Is that what you want?" My eyes adjust to hers. I'm trying to appeal to the human side of her.

"From what I can see, you don't even want to live in Territory L. So, why do you care?"

"Just because I want to move ahead, doesn't mean I want this territory to be non-existent. I want everyone to be treated equally, in all the territories."

"You think that I'm heartless and cruel. Well, let me show you something else. Maybe this last video will convince you." She turns toward the screen.

Rich must have hit the button because, once again, the dark screen lights up and the eerie music plays into my headphones. But this time is different. There are no photos and no video. There is only what looks like a white piece of paper with words on it. Whoever shot this, didn't do a very good job. The camera is not focused well, and I cannot make out what it says. They refocus it, and like a washer cleaning the windows, the words become clearer.

"Dear President Esther,

My name is Tiffany, and you are my hero. I'm twelve years old, and I want to be president so I can be strong like you. But that will never happen because tonight is my last night in Craigluy.

My father hurts me and my mother lets him. I have bruises on my neck, and I hide it with my clothing. I'm scared to tell my teachers because they won't do anything. I tried to cut my wrists, but my mother caught me before I could finish. I took some pills from my mother's dresser and I…"

"Can we stop now, please?" A tear graces my cheek. "I have seen enough." My fist is clenched so tight I can feel my nails digging into my skin.

"This letter was sent to me during my first term in office." She glares at me. "Before the no more children law went into effect."

"Is this why you started the law?"

"It is part of the reason, but I have others." Her eyes are cold and dim.

"What are they?"

"You needn't worry about that. You should only concern yourself with what you want to do."

"You mean there are no more photos, no more videos to scare me into doing what you want?" I wipe my face with the back of my hands.

"No, that's over." She twists her hands again. "Now, I need your answer."

"I can't feel passionate about that speech." My hand trembles, taking off the headphones.

"I'm sorry you feel that way." She tilts her head to the side. "Rich, bring her in."

I grab my forehead with my fingers and squeeze. My head is pounding, as if someone is jabbing me with a hammer. I don't know what is about to happen, but I know it can't be good. I hear the door rustle open, and I hear Rich's footsteps as he exits the room. I glance down at my lap, and then up at the blank screen. I can't stomach looking at the president. The door swishes again, and I hear loud footsteps and whimpering. It sounds like a canine that is being punished for disobeying its owner.

I glance down and see Rich's boots, off to the side of me. In front of me are small white gym shoes, like the kind I wore when I was an inmate. I succumb to the darkness in the room and tears catch in my throat.

"Look up, Emma," President Esther says.

I glance up and see Cassandra standing before me. I haven't seen much of her since she was first brought in. She looks paler and weaker. She looks as thin as a pencil. The biggest thing on her is her stomach, which is extended out toward me.

Her eyes are wide, like saucers, and as red as a tomato. Her hair is disheveled and tears stain her face. Her neck has sunken in so much, I can see the bones piercing through her skin.

"Em-Emma," she says.

Her breaths are rough, and her voice is raspy. Her blue uniform doesn't fit her anymore. Silver handcuffs surround her wrists. Her face shows anguish, and her body shakes. She needs my help.

"Cassandra," I say, and my throat feels raw. "I'm sorry."

"Why are you sorry?" President Esther stands.

I know something bad is coming, and my whole body aches, as if I've just splatted on the ground after being pushed off a ledge.

"You have no reason to be sorry, unless you disobey my orders. I'm sure you know what I mean." She shifts her eyes. "That will be all, Rich. You can hand her back over to Samuel. He will take her back downstairs."

Hearing Samuel's name makes my ears perk up, like an animal hearing a high-pitched noise. He can't do anything about my situation, but knowing he is so close calms me, somewhat. I listen as Rich's footsteps stomp across the floor. The door opens and then slams closed.

"Have you seen enough?" Her eyes are trained on mine. "You should know what comes next."

"Yes," I say quietly. "I'm sure you'll hurt Cassandra, if I don't comply." I wipe my forehead.

She remains silent.

Rich is standing over me. The handcuffs click as he puts the key in the tiny lock and takes them off.

"May I please return to my room now?" My knees ache, as if I've been sitting for several hours, instead of minutes.

"Yes, I'll have Rich take you."

"No." I shake my head and stand. "I would prefer to walk back on my own. I mean, I'm no longer considered a prisoner but a guard." My mouth goes dry as soon as the words are released. "So that means I should be able to walk by myself."

"That's true, dear." She places her hand on my shoulder and squeezes. "Go ahead, take your time walking back, clear your head. You have a lot of decisions ahead of you."

I'm grateful for the alone time. I can't get those disturbing images out of my head. I feel like the metal handcuffs I used to drag around are still holding me down as I travel back to my room in slow motion.

My head spins and my ears won't stop throbbing. My eyes feel as if they're bleeding, but they aren't. The wetness I feel is tears streaming down my face. Esther didn't come out and exactly say it, but I know if I don't comply with her wishes, she'll hurt Cassandra—or worse, maybe kill her. I can't let that happen; I have to do what she asks.

So, I'll stand and read the words she wants me to say. I'll go against everything I believe in to save Cassandra's life. My tears make a haze appear before my eyes, but I can still see the metal necklace my mother gave me, on the table. Samuel placed it there earlier, and now I wish he would have left it under my cot in my jail cell. I want to rip it apart. It doesn't symbolize hope or peace. Instead, it should symbolize death and destruction. That is what I feel right now and, at this moment, I don't know how to feel any other way.

CHAPTER NINETEEN

BEING A GUARD IN training is better than being a prisoner; and, it has its advantages. I don't have to wear handcuffs anymore. I don't have to have a guard follow me around everywhere I go, as if a third leg is attached to my own. And, I can go down to meet Samuel and train in real workout gear.

"You ready?" Samuel says, turning to me.

"As ready as I'll ever be." I shrug.

Its early morning and I haven't quite gotten the sleep out of my eyes. I try to forget the speech ahead of me and take out my aggression in my workout. Everything that has happened has made the small pain, still jabbing at my side, seem minimal.

"I'm still having a hard time seeing you without your blue uniform on." He grins.

"I'm having a hard time myself, but I must admit it feels nice having workout clothes on, instead of that heavy garb. Penelope brought these over from Territory U for me to wear."

"Well, they fit nicely," he says, pulling on the sleeve of my gray sweatshirt. He stares at me for a minute, and then walks away.

I'm not sure if he asked the president if he could be my trainer, or if she assigned him to me. Either way, I'm glad it's him and not one of the others. He's always so levelheaded, and it makes me feel calmer.

"I thought you said you were ready." He smirks.

"I am."

"Then stop daydreaming and follow me."

We walk inside the gun range, and I hear booming sounds like cannons are going off. This is our second day of training. Yesterday, my stomach bounced all around and my shoulders jumped at the sounds. But today, things are different. My stomach doesn't feel nauseous, like I'm seasick on a large boat. And, I no longer want to hurl into the nearest garbage can. The popping sounds have a weird, calming effect over me. I'm not sure if that is a good or bad thing.

The room is a gray-silver color, reminding me of the president's hair. I walk up to one of the bays and take my stance. I put on the bulky, red headphones and the clear, plastic glasses. I pick up the small black gun that is in front of me. My hands itch as I load it. I lift it in front of me and point it at one of the heads of the paper figures. I don't believe in violence, but I have to say, the coldness of the metal feels good against my skin. Although my hands still shake, a little, they embrace it like it has always been there.

"Go ahead." Samuel touches my shoulder. "Remember the muzzle faces down, and no rapid fire. Wait two seconds—" he shouts at me.

"I know, two seconds between each shot," I shout back, finishing his sentence.

I hear the bang of the gun going off, and the force doesn't push my chest back, like yesterday. I feel stronger, and my grip around the weapon feels tighter. I hit the paper target right in the chest, and that's good, since that's what I'm aiming for. The first time I tried this, I aimed for the chest but hit the head, which wasn't so good. Like a teacher would say when you're learning to read and write, I'm progressing nicely.

I feel a tap on my shoulder. I take off the headphones and glasses.

"Are you sure you've never used a gun before?" Samuel asks.

"Yes, I'm sure."

"You're doing pretty well for only your second day of training."

He beams. "One day you'll be able to guard the president, or take outside duties, like the rest of us."

"I'm surprised you're pleased. I thought you didn't want me to do this—become a guard, I mean."

"I didn't." He shrugs. "But you seem determined to do it. The least I can do is be supportive. And it's nice spending this time with you. If you'd gone home that wouldn't have happened. I'd never see you."

His gaze is hard, making my insides spasm and I don't know how to respond. But before I can gather my thoughts, Eric walks in.

"We need to talk," he says, roughly.

His black uniform looks brown and dusty, and his boots are covered in mud.

Samuel steps up to him. "We're still in session."

"Can we take a break? This seems important," I say.

"As you wish." He steps aside, looking annoyed.

"Not here." Eric squeezes his eyes together. "Up in your room, where we can have some privacy."

*

"I didn't mean to take you away from your session," Eric says. "But I didn't know when we would have another chance to speak. They've loaded me up on outside responsibilities, so this may be our only time together."

He brushes off his black pants. Dirt falls on the floor of my room.

"I know you accepted her offer, but I must say, I was surprised to see you training with a gun, so soon. I thought that would come later." He frowns. "You kind of looked like you were enjoying it."

"Don't look at me like that," I say.

"Like what?"

"Like I'm a different person. I haven't changed."

I reach under the collar of my sweatshirt and feel for the

necklace Mother gave me. I decided to put it back on, hoping it would help me remember what I'm doing this for.

"You looked comfortable, holding that weapon in your hands, is all." His eyes squint. "And, I want to make sure you remember our deal—we don't kill, we only maim. If we went around killing people, we would be no better than Esther killing babies."

"I haven't forgotten. I'm only doing it because it's a part of every guard's training. I need to know how to defend myself. If push comes to shove, I would still rather use the Taser. You know that."

"I do know that." He moves toward the opposite side of the room.

I see mud on the floor, where he had previously stepped.

"What's really going on?" I ask, walking closer to him. "You didn't come here to talk about my weapons training."

"No," he says, shaking his head. "I know she's making this into some major event for the Monday night announcements. I wanted to see how you're holding up." He brushes his hand across my cheek.

"Not good." I shake my head. The warmth of his fingers calms me, but only a little.

"She plans for me to read some awful speech. She wants me to say that she's only looking out for us. That she's our friend, and we have to trust her. The real kicker is she wants me to say that during my brief time here, I've gotten to know her, so now I'm retracting everything I said about her the night of my party."

The words coming out of my mouth make my skin crawl, as if bugs are running all over me.

"It'll be okay." He rubs my cheek again.

"No, it won't," I say, removing my face from his fingers.

"If I say those words the territory will hate me. It contradicts everything I said the night of the party. I will appear like some fool-ish teenage girl. No one will ever trust me again. I only wanted to become a guard, not make a stupid speech."

"Then, when you get up there, say your own words." He places his fingers under my chin this time and grips my face. "Tell everyone that she tried to force you to lie, so she would look favorable in their eyes. Once they know what she has done, it will push them over the edge, to your side."

He releases my face, but his gaze remains strong.

"Since I've been working on the outside, I've heard that the people may be trying to stage another protest. Like they did a while back at the medical facility. It's only a rumor, but I believe it's true." There's a glimmer of light in his eyes.

"I thought the people were too old and set in their ways to try that again." I bite down hard on my lip.

"I'm not talking about the older ones. I'm speaking about the young people, the ones around our age or a little older. They agree with you, and they want things to change, so they can have a future. If we can accomplish this, it's only a matter of time before the older ones take a stance as well. They just need someone to lead them."

"I take it the president is not happy about this turn of events."

"No, she's livid. That's why she needs you to speak again, as soon as possible, so you can set the record straight."

"And she thinks by making me speak, the young people will back off."

"Precisely. They trust you, and if you've changed, then they will change."

I believe what he's saying. The girl who whispered thank you to me that day in the hospital caught me off guard.

"I wondered why she was rushing me into doing this. Now, I understand the urgency." I grit my teeth.

"So, you see, this can work for us. If you speak your mind again, the most she will probably do is put you back in jail, for a longer term, which I know you can handle. But at least the territory will be against her."

"I'm glad you have such faith in me. But I haven't had a chance to tell you what happened." The weight bearing down on my chest now feels unmovable. "The president, and Rich, threatened me. They took me to that death chamber room and showed me a bunch of pictures of little kids dying, in hopes that I would read her words during the announcements." I close my eyes and take in a much needed breath. "Then, she said if that didn't convince me, she would hurt Cassandra. I couldn't let that happen, so I had to comply with her wishes."

"Did she say she would kill Cassandra?" He steps closer to me. "Did she say those exact words?"

"No." I shake my head. "But it was implied." My side aches. I don't know what he is getting at.

"You can't assume anything." His eyes harden. "I'm sure she tricked you, and she was never going to hurt Cassandra. She'll take her baby, as she does with everyone's babies; but as far as harming Cassandra, I don't think it'll happen. Cassandra will have the baby, serve her time, and go home like everyone does."

"How can you be so sure?" A lump is in my throat. "What if it doesn't play out that way? I don't know if I can take that chance, she reminds me too much of…"

"Too much of what?"

"Nothing," I say, knowing I cannot tell him about Taylor and baby Abigail.

"I don't know if you should destroy thousands to save one."

"What else would you have me do?" My voice quivers.

"We need to help the territory, by making them see they're stronger than they think. If you get up there and tell everyone what Esther has done, I believe it will bring a backlash on her. That is what we need right now." He leans in and whispers in my ear, "It's your choice, but you need to know, I'm here for you, no matter what you decide."

"I don't understand how all of this became my problem. I'm just one girl." My eyes water.

"No, you're more than that." He raises my chin. "And, I think you know that."

His arms lace around my waist, like rope intertwined together. The light in his eyes is unlike anything I've seen before. It's as if he feels my pain and wants to take it all away. He pulls my chin closer to his and presses his mouth against mine. His hand moves to my cheek, and it feels warm. I tremble.

The butterflies in my stomach flutter faster. This truly is my first kiss. I feel a warmness surge within my body and a pulsating inside my chest. I feel the leanness of his body through his uniform. I don't want our closeness to end. I know as soon as it does, I'll have to face my reality. I want to enjoy this moment for as long as I can, so I hold on to it, until he leans away.

"I'm sorry." My voice shakes. Maybe this isn't the time for it, but he stares at me with caring eyes, and I feel the need to say it.

"What would you have to be sorry for?"

"I know you were kicked out of this room, so I could have it."

"None of this is your fault."

"I'm sure the other guy who lived here doesn't think so."

"Don't worry about Julian. I talked to him, and he's all right with it."

His arms are still wrapped around my waist, and the bond I feel with him is unlike any other I've felt before.

"It's going to all work out," he says. "I know it will."

He speaks to me as if he really believes in what he is saying. I feel the butterflies in my stomach calm down and rest, for a minute.

"Can you sit with me for a moment?" I ask.

"Of course." He takes my hand.

We sit on my bed, and I hear the floor creak. I glance back at him, and there is a spark in his eyes, like the moonlight at night. I want more of this, more quiet time with him. So, I lean in again. His chest is pressed against mine. He feels solid. I kiss his cheek. He kisses my neck. The warmth engulfs me. I've never felt beautiful, but in this moment, he makes me feel like my skin color has no bearing on anything, anymore. With him, I see no color at all. I rest the side of my face against his hard chest, while his strong arms gather around me. Everything is nice and quiet, like the calm before the storm. I could stay locked in this moment forever, but I know we can't.

CHAPTER TWENTY

ERIC'S VOICE IS SOFT in my ear. "I have to tell you something."

I've been lying on his chest for what seems like hours. He smells earthy, like wood.

"What's that?" I ask, peering up at him.

The bed squeaks, as I shift my weight. The earlier light in his eyes has vanished, and I have no idea what he is about to say. I shiver, a little, because of his quiet stare. The covers bunch beneath me and I smooth out the wrinkles with my hands. I'm trying to distract myself. I fear it's something bad.

"I should have told you this earlier." He removes his arms from my waist. He takes my hand in his and stops me from what I'm doing.

"You're scaring me."

"I don't mean to." He sits up straighter. "I wasn't sure if I should mention this or not. But I don't want there to be any secrets between us, so it's best if I say this now."

He clears his throat and glances around the tiny dark room as if he can't bring himself to speak.

"I can handle it." I rub his knuckles. "Whatever it is just tell me," I say, softly.

"I know about your sister and the baby. I know they've been in hiding."

"I don't understand." I shake my head. "How could you know?" I quickly move away from him. "How is this possible? How long have you known?" My chest throbs, like my insides are about to explode.

"A few of the outside projects I was assigned to involved me working with your brother. We had to go around and collect the monthly payments from all the shops."

This reminds me of when Cassandra's grandfather was beaten up because he was behind on his payments. But I still don't know what this has to do with my sister, and I'm finding it hard to swallow.

"During the past few days, President Esther instituted a new rule. It used to be that we only searched abandoned homes that we knew no one owned; or, if someone owned them and they looked torn down, had broken windows or screens, we were to search for anything suspicious."

"That's why we made sure the house Taylor is in was boarded up nicely and that there were no windows broken." My heart is beating loudly in my chest. I feel beads of sweat on my forehead.

"While I was out with your brother, we got word from one of the patrolmen that your mother was seen coming and going from an abandoned home after dark, when no one should be out. Every time they questioned her, she said her husband normally kept up on the repairs of the old place; but he had been working a lot lately, and she had to do it. They found that suspicious, so they handed the case over to us to check out the place."

He stops to take in a breath. I need him to keep going. I feel warm, as if I've eaten a hot pepper and I'm about to pass out.

"I got the call and told your brother about it. He had to tell me about your sister and the baby, so we wouldn't go look over the place. We filed a false report saying that the place was empty, just as your mom said."

"Why was my mother going there after dark?"

"Your brother said your mother went to visit earlier in the day and saw that the baby was sick. By the time she went to the hospital, picked up medicine, and got back to the house, it was after dark."

"Did you tell anyone?"

"You know I wouldn't do that." He squeezes my hand. "I care about you. I would never harm you or your family."

I know that in my heart, but my head gets defensive when it comes to my family.

"This is my fault," I say. A haze appears over my eyes. "It was my job to go and take my sister food and clothes. Once I got myself locked in here there was no one to do it properly. My mother wouldn't have been put in that position if I'd been there."

"None of this is your fault. You can't blame yourself."

"I know you're right, but it's hard not to."

"As far as we know, they filed the report we took and have moved on to other things."

"I pray you're right," I say, even though I have an uneasiness in my stomach, as if I'm about to fall into a black hole.

*

I wake up alone in my room. I must have fallen asleep after Eric left. The stressful events of the last couple of days must have gotten to me. I still have on my workout clothes. Instead of changing, I smooth out the wrinkles with my hands. Now that I'm considered a guard in training, I can walk around wherever I want to. My every movement isn't monitored—at least I hope that is the case.

I have to get my mind off my sister and the baby, so I decide to go for a walk, outside on the grounds. This is only my second time leaving the mansion since I arrived here. I don't see many guards around as I make my way down to the first floor. I use the guard's elevator. Instead of feeling pride, I feel like a rat stuck in a small hole.

I decide not to take the front door route. Two guards always stand there to protect the front entrance. They question those who are coming and going, and since I'm the one most hated around here, I rather not walk past them. I go out one of the side doors that Samuel told me about. The sky is gray, and the air is thick. The grounds, around the back and side, are as beautiful as the grounds in the front. There are multicolored flowers and shrubbery as green as a toad's body. The air smells citrusy as though an orange tree is somewhere close.

I walk about thirty steps from the door and stare at the wall. The wall that surrounds the entire territory also surrounds the back of the mansion, but the right side of the mansion is a different story. I see a stretch of grass that looks to be about a half a mile. This stretch goes from the mansion to a fence. I believe that underneath that half mile stretch of grass the underground prisoners are kept.

From here, I see the fence. It is a black, electric, chain-link fence that has barbed wire at the top. To get over the wire, you would need protective gear or very heavy clothing; but no one would ever make it to that point, since you can't get over the electric fence. I've heard that it's thirty feet tall. I see the right side of the fence attaches to the black gate that leads to the street. The gate can only be opened by the guards, for those allowed to go back and forth between the territories. On the opposite side of the gate is where the 124 foot wall starts up again.

"You know why there's a chain-link fence there, instead of that enormous wall that surrounds the rest of the territory?"

I hear a raspy voice that interrupts my thoughts. A light-skin guard in a black uniform walks up next to me. His smile seems friendly, and his eyes are bluer than the color of the sea. He rubs his hand through his full mane of brown hair and looks at me.

"It's because the president doesn't like staring at a wall when she opens her bedroom window. She likes to be able to see over into Territory M. A wall would obstruct her view."

"It doesn't seem like there's much to look at." I shrug, and engage in conversation, "From here, all I see are trees and wilderness."

"It's more than that once you get a few miles in." He points his finger in the direction of the fence. "You thinking of climbing it?"

"Do I know you from somewhere?" It's a stupid question because I don't recognize him, but he talks to me as if he knows me.

"No, but I know who you are. Everyone does." He winks.

I remain silent and stare back at the fence.

"I guess I should introduce myself. I'm Julian." He extends his hand.

"Julian." I repeat, extending my hand to his. "Are you the guy who had—"

"To exit his room because of you." He finishes my sentence. "Yes that would be me."

"I'm sorry about that."

"No need to apologize. I was a little upset, at first, but now I realize it's all good."

"Thanks for that," I say. The wind splays a strand of hair in my eye, and I push it back behind my ear. "Why did you ask if I planned on hopping the fence?"

"You were staring at it so intently, I wasn't sure."

"I have no plans on going over the fence."

"I knew a guy who tried it. He knew someone on the inside that was willing to turn off the fence, but he never made it over the barbed wire." He scratches the back of his neck. "He's in prison now, and so is the guard who tried to help him."

I'm not sure why he's telling me this; but it's all new information to me, so like a puppy listening for his master to call him for dinner, I listen intently.

"I used to live in Territory M," he says, continuing his rambling.

"I never knew anyone who came from Territory M. I thought once you were there you stayed there for life." I turn to him.

"That's never mentioned in the president's speech. She never tells you if you mess up, you can be kicked out and placed back here."

"Is that what happened to you? Did you mess up?" I don't know if I should believe what he is telling me. "I mean, how did you make it into Territory M in the first place?"

"You have a lot of questions." His eyes shift to mine.

"You're the one who started this conversation."

"That's true. So, I suppose I should answer you. First, my father was a senior accountant for one of the hospitals. When the president divided the territories, we were automatically put into Territory M. Second, if you don't stay on your best behavior, or you slack off and don't work hard, you can be placed back here." He pulls on his collar as if the conversation is making him uneasy. "I wasn't too eager to go to college; but if you're 'privileged' enough to be in Territory M, you should make every effort to go." He uses air quotes. "That's what my parents kept telling me. But I didn't see it that way."

"So what did you do?" The wind howls, making me cough. "I mean, how did you get sent back here?"

"I messed around and got a girl pregnant. My parents wanted us to marry and be this big happy family. They wanted me to be responsible, follow in my father's footsteps, and be an accountant, like him. I wanted to be a patrolman."

"There are patrolmen in Territory M?" I ask.

I never thought about it, until now, but I don't know much about the people in Territory M. I only want to go there so I can attend college. And, that is where you end up if you're privileged enough to continue with your studies.

"Yes, there are patrolmen to watch over the people there. They make more in wages than the ones here."

"I'm sure they do." I roll my eyes.

"Anyway," he continues. "The people in M are not allowed to have children either, since they don't make the required amount of money." He rubs his fingers together as if he is rubbing two sticks. "The difference is if they do become with child, they have the option of working harder. If they get more schooling and try to land a better job in Territory U, they can keep their babies and move there. The people here are not given that option. Their babies are taken away and killed."

"What happens if someone doesn't work harder to get into Territory U?"

"They're given a year to show they're improving. If they don't show signs of bettering themselves, the babies are taken away, like here."

"And killed?" My voice is high-pitched.

"As far as I know, yes." He cocks his head to the side. "Territory U is the only exception because they have the money and resources to take care of their own."

"If you don't mind me asking, what happened to your child?"

"Since I went against my father's wishes and refused to go to college, he turned me in to the patrolmen. He said I did nothing all day but mess around. I had no focus or purpose to my life. But that was a lie. I had hoped to get accepted to the training facility for patrolmen, but my father ripped up my application. I was kicked out of the territory before I could try to reapply."

He puts his hands in his pockets and takes them back out.

"As far as my ex-girlfriend and the baby go, I know my ex…" His voice trails off. "Whitney is her name. She is in school and doing well; so, our baby, Adam, is still with her. I try to visit them whenever I'm over there, if I can." He glances down.

"I don't understand how you're able to visit them, when no one is allowed over there unless they're accepted. You just said you were kicked out."

He looks away from me.

"And how does Esther choose who gets accepted? What do they do to get picked to go?"

I've been wondering that for a while now, but can never get a straight answer from anyone. Since he has been so forthcoming with information up to this point, I thought he would tell me. But maybe he has decided he has already said too much to a stranger, because he remains silent, like his voice box has been ripped from his throat.

"I've been looking all over for you."

I turn away from Julian when I hear Samuel's distraught voice.

"You should get down to the jail cell, something has happened."

He's running toward me. His voice is jagged and he's out of breath.

"To Cassandra?" My first thoughts go to her.

"No," he says, shaking his head. "Word is they just brought your sister in."

My heart drops to my knees. I'm not sure I heard him correctly.

"W-what did y-you say?"

"Your sister is downstairs."

I feel like I'm in a nightmare and my worst fear has come to life. Why is Taylor here? How did they find out about her? And, the question I most feared: where is baby Abigail?

*

I race down to the jail. The jail feels colder and darker than when I occupied a cell. I hear guards whispering and the sounds of crying. I know it is my sister's cries and a shockwave goes up my spine. Samuel is in front of me, but I rush past him.

I see her behind the very cell that I lived in for weeks. Her face is red. Tiny tears grace her cheeks. She looks weak and pale. The tiny tears turn into a flood. Her thin fingers grip the bars. Her voice shakes as she argues with Rich. I know she is the older sister; but in this light, I feel like she is the baby and needs consoling.

"P-please, give me my baby back," Taylor screams. "You can punish me, but please don't punish her."

Her eyes are as red as her face.

I want to run to her and wrap my arms around her, but I know I can't. Rich glares at me as if he is a shark and I'm a fish he wants to devour.

"Do you have to keep her locked up?" I say. I'm trying to remain strong, but my knees buckle underneath me.

"This is what happens when you don't follow rules. You should be in there with her." He cocks his head to the side. "But for some reason, the president wants to see you upstairs."

"Please, let me stay with her. Let me take her place." My eyes swell. "Please…"

"I said you're needed upstairs." He growls, ignoring my cries.

I know by the look on his face he means business, so I shakily mouth 'I love you' to Taylor and leave the room.

*

"You see what happens when you disobey my laws," President Esther says.

Her eyes burn a hole through my chest, and her mouth curls up like a witch's.

I wiped my tears away on the elevator ride up here, since now, I have to appear strong. Esther sits on her sofa, sipping tea that smells of vanilla. She has on an all-white pants suit, as if she is dressed for a wedding, as if nothing catastrophic is going on down in the jail.

"You and your family have had your sister in hiding, all this time." She shifts her weight on her sofa. "This is grounds for all of you to be remanded to jail."

"Why aren't we?" I ask, in a rough tone.

"I need you for other things and, to accomplish them, you can't be locked up."

"And my parents?" My eyebrow rises.

"I need them for other things, as well."

"What things?"

"That is no concern of yours. All you need to know is that your brother, and Eric, will be dealt with accordingly, for placing a false report. We now know that the house was occupied with your sister and her baby."

"Where is the baby?" My jaw tightens. I'm tired of her gibberish. I need some answers. "What have you done with Abigail?"

"There is no need for you to get upset over things you can't control. I need you to get ready for the speech you'll read tomorrow."

I'm still standing because she hasn't invited me to sit. My legs feel weak. My chest throbs.

"Why can't you let my sister go? She has already lost her baby. Please, don't make her endure anything else." I don't like to beg, but I will for Taylor. "We had a deal. If I did what you asked, you wouldn't harm—"

"That deal was for Cassandra, not your sister." Her tone is brash, and her eyes are narrow. "But maybe, if you do a good enough job convincing the territory that your views are the same as mine, I'll have a change of heart. I suppose there wouldn't be any harm in letting your sister go, if you do as I ask." She purses her lips together and blows on her tea. "You should leave now and return to your room. I want you well-rested for tomorrow night's events."

She turns her head away from me, and I know the conversation has ended. No matter how much I plead, she won't listen to anything else I have to say. All my family's efforts at hiding my sister were for nothing.

CHAPTER TWENTY-ONE

I STAND IN FRONT of the bathroom mirror, looking at myself in my new black uniform. I couldn't sleep at all last night. My once hazel eyes are now red. I have opted to wear my hair in one long braid; that way, the strands don't suffocate me as they surround my neck.

I have one silver button plastered on the left side of my chest; but more will come later, depending on how well the president thinks I'm doing. I have an empty gun holster on my right hip; the gun will also come later, after more training, along with a radio. But my left hip is graced with a small holster with a Taser in it. I suppose it is an object they think I'm worthy of carrying.

I walk to my bed and collapse on it. These new pants feel tighter than what I'm used to. Maybe it's not the pants at all, but the situation I find myself in. I'll be lying to thousands about what I feel is right, and the thought disgusts me. My stomach feels raw, as if my insides are bleeding. The chain my mother gave me is around my neck. My earlier thoughts were to discard it. Instead, I wear it, praying it'll give me the strength to believe there is still a tiny bit of hope for us all.

I had made the decision to protest during my speech instead of reading her words, but that has changed now. Eric thought Esther wouldn't harm Cassandra, but now that my sister's involved I can't take that chance. I'll stand like a robot and read her words, for both their sakes. I want to cry, but there is no time for tears. I have to be stronger than that.

My jaw flinches when there is a banging at my door. I'm used to guards walking up to my cell anytime they want, so knocking is a sound I'm not familiar with.

"Yes," I say.

"Emma, it is Penelope. May I come in?"

"Yes," I say, grateful for her politeness.

The door swishes open and she rushes in, as if her feet are on fire. Her blonde hair is up in a bun and her gray eyes protrude out at me. She has on a pants suit, much like the one from the other day. Only this suit is dark like the walls, instead of yellow like the sun. Since this is a Territory L function, maybe she was instructed to wear dark colors, like the rest of us.

"I need you to stand, dear," she says. "The president wants me to make sure you look appropriate for the ceremony."

How much more appropriate could I be, I think, while standing. I have on the thick, hot uniform she wants me to wear, along with the bulky, black boots. The only addition is my necklace, but no one can see that. It's hidden away underneath my uniform.

"This won't do," she says, with a high-pitched squeal, as if I've sat in paint and messed up my uniform.

"What's wrong with it?" I glance down at myself and then back up.

"It's not the uniform. It's your face and hair." Her eyes are wide. "That braid will definitely have to go, and you'll need makeup."

"I'm only giving a speech. Why do I need makeup? I wasn't in makeup the night of my party."

"This is different." Her eyebrow rises, as if I should already know this. "Not only are you the last eighteen-year-old, but now you are the first—and the youngest—female guard. And don't forget, Esther wasn't in charge of you then, but she is now."

My whole body quakes, as if I'm in a downpour of cold, wet rain. She says in charge, as if President Esther now owns me.

She unclicks her briefcase and takes out a brown case that has powder in it. She takes out a small, brown brush, wipes it over the reddish brown powder, and applies it to my face. The powder's mist floats around the air, and it makes me want to sneeze. It smells like cocoa, the kind we have at home when my mom says it's a special occasion. I have never worn makeup before. It makes my skin feel tight, as if someone is stretching it out of place.

"Poke out your lips," she says, while she grips my face in place, like I'm a screw and she is holding a clamp around it. "This shade should go nicely."

She applies some kind of thick, brown liquid on my lips.

I frown. It is sticky to the taste and it smells like medicine. If this is lipstick, I don't care for it.

"Now, I'll have you unbraid your hair, and then we can go. The ceremony starts in thirty minutes, so we need to get moving." She glances down at her watch. "Hurry," she says, as if we're running to catch a bus, and it's about to leave.

The city council building is only a little ways down, so I don't know what the big deal is; but I unbraid my hair as she asks. The thick strands surrounding my fingertips feel like rope twisting around me.

"That's good enough." She brushes my hair back as if I'm a child. "It will have to do," she adds. "I'll leave you be, but a car waits for you downstairs."

"It's just down the street. Why can't I walk?"

"You can do whatever you want, dear. But make sure you're there on time. And, if you do decide to walk, don't get all sweaty on the way there. You want to look presentable over the information box. Thousands of people will be watching."

The door closes with a *bang* behind her.

*

I hear grinding metal as I ride down in the guard's elevator. Maybe it's not the elevator but the screeching of voices in my head. Everything's a blur as I walk toward the front door. The air is dry and odorless. I don't see, or hear, anyone. They must all be down at the city council building already.

I'm not used to my boots yet. They're heavy, like lead weights are holding my feet down. I push the front door, with force, and it swings open. It's cool outside, and the gray sky is cloudy. The air smells damp like rain. I should be used to it by now, since it is the norm around here. A downpour of water is what I need right now to wash the stench of betrayal from my skin.

Penelope must have informed them I wanted to walk. I don't see a black car waiting by the curb. I hear a bird squawking up above; besides that, the area is clear. I'm used to gravel and mud, where I live. The streets here are straight and smooth. The sidewalk has no rough spots or bumps, and I walk without stumbling. My jaw winces, seeing the maple-colored building up ahead. Once I arrive, all eyes will be on me, and it will be my time to shine for the president.

My brain stops scrambling, when I hear the squealing of tires behind me. I turn to see a black car. I wave my hand so they know I don't need a ride. I'm almost there. The closer I get to the building, the more my blood boils. I grit my teeth at the task I must perform. My eyes want to leak, but I blink, refusing to let that happen.

"Whisper, it's me." I hear Eric's voice. "Wait up a minute."

I shake my head, not caring what he has to say. I don't want him talking me out of this, so I keep walking.

"I said hold up." I feel his strong hand grip my arm, and he yanks me around.

"You don't understand," I say, shouting. "You don't know what has happened." I pull my arm away.

"I know about your sister, and I know you're going to give in to her demands." His gaze is strong. "But you can't do that."

"I know what I have to do. You can't stop me." I turn from him and continue my stride. I feel as though fire is burning in my larynx.

"You need to listen to me." His voice is rough.

He grabs me by my waist and turns me toward him.

"You cannot give that speech."

"You should let me go." My eyes slant. "My family's imprisoned, not yours."

I hear another voice, as someone walks up to us.

"Listen to what he has to say."

My eyes widen because it's Theodore.

"Yes, if you won't listen to me, listen to your brother." Eric lets me go.

I stand with my fist clenched, trying to take it all in.

"You can't make that speech."

"But…" I try to speak.

"I know she has Taylor and she took the baby," T says. "But she has a plan."

"She wants the people to listen to me and stop the protests."

"No," he says, shaking his head. "That may have been the plan at first, but things are different now."

"Different?" I say, stepping closer to him. "How?"

"She no longer wants the people to agree with you. She wants them to hate you," T says.

"She wants to destroy your reputation, so they'll never listen to you again," Eric chimes in.

"How can she do that?" My throat has a lump in it.

"If you make that speech saying you now agree with her laws, she'll spin everything to make you look foolish," Eric continues.

"I already know that. I said the very same thing to you the other day, and you told me to protest, instead."

"I know, but things are different now that she has your sister. If you say you have seen the error in your ways, and now see the good in her, she will tell the people you're lying and only saying that to get your sister out of jail—"

"And that's the truth," I say, cutting Eric off.

"Yes, but she will twist things. She will say she tricked you into believing she would release your sister to see whose side you're really on. If you choose to read her words, it will look as if you only care about your family and nothing about theirs."

"It will look as though I'm willing to lie to save my sister, while leading the people to believe they should still follow her laws and not protest for freedom from them. It will make me seem like a hypocrite who would sacrifice them to help my family." It's as if a fog is lifted and I can see. "She also wants me to tell the territory that if they have any family in hiding, make them surrender, which will make me look like I want their families to suffer even more, while mine goes free."

"And since Mother and Father weren't imprisoned at all for help-ing to hide Taylor—"

"It will seem as though our family is being shown special treat-ment for knowing the president," I say. "You're right, the people will never trust me again. They'll probably hate me."

"And if you do the opposite and decide to protest, there is no doubt in my mind, Taylor will be moved to the prison and labeled a lifer. And you'll be put with her. You won't be able to help anyone from in there," T says.

"How do you know all of this?" I ask.

"None of that matters. We can't stay here. We have to go," Eric says. His eyes look dim and his hand is on the gun in his holster. "We need to follow the plan we put together."

"Make it to Territory M." My chest burns like coal on a fire.

"Yes." Eric's gaze is strong. "But we have to go now, while the Territory's eyes are glued to the information box and no one's paying attention to us."

"He's right." Theodore steps closer to me. "You have to go now, before they notice you didn't show up to make your speech. Once they realize you're gone, they'll come for you. She'll have every patrol-men and guard searching for you."

"What about the rest of the family?" My lips quiver. "I can't leave them, or you."

"There is nothing you can do to help them. Taylor will serve her time, and Abigail is gone now."

"Don't say that." My heart drops because he means dead. "Abigail can't be gone for good." I shake my head. "She just can't be." My body shudders.

"You know it's true." His eyes are strong. "You'll do more good by leaving than staying. I'll look after them."

"But she knows you placed that false report. Who knows what she is planning for you?"

"I can't dwell on that now. Besides, someone needs to stall them, so you'll have time to get away. There is a shipment of hospital supplies coming in tonight," T says. "The guard driving the truck is a good guy. He'll help you."

This is the strongest I've ever seen Theodore.

"One of our outside duties was to make sure the shipments came through the gates safely and were delivered to the hospital," Eric says. "We unload the supplies, since the president doesn't trust hospital employees to do it. They might try to smuggle over things that aren't allowed in our Territory."

"Now that she knows we lied on the report, she assigned two other guards to that task," T says. "So, you'll have to fight your way past them. You should take this." He pulls his gun from his holster. "You'll need it."

"If she's after you, then you may need it more." I blink. My eyes sting. I'm trying to stop them from watering.

"I can get another weapon."

My fingers tingle as he gives me the cold piece of metal. My hand trembles, placing it in my holster.

"Take care of yourself." Theodore leans in and gives me a hug.

"You do the same," I say, in a whisper. "I love you."

"We have to go now."

I feel Eric pulling my arm, making me release the hug. I watch T as he mouths the words back. This may be the last time I see my brother, my family. But I know they're right. This is the way it has to be, for now.

"We can't take the car. They have trackers in them. So, we'll have to go by foot," Eric says.

CHAPTER TWENTY-TWO

"It's good that no one's around," Eric says, once we reach the hospital.

There's sweat on his brow and he's a little out of breath. The hospital's about a half mile down; so my breaths are fine, but my heart beats fast like a hummingbird's. The gray skies are gone now, and the darkness is setting in, which helps us hide without anyone seeing us.

"The shipments come in back," he says.

I follow him around the building; but we stay low, so no one will see us. Most guards are summoned to the city council building on Monday nights, except for the two who have to watch over tonight's shipment. Patrolmen aren't as privileged. They still have to be on watch while the announcements are going on. I don't see any patrolmen around, but I still remain low and close to the building.

We get to the back of the building, and I see a white truck in the parking lot. It's being unloaded at a dock that leads into the back of the hospital. I see two guards unloading. It looks like Jason and Rob.

"Stay down until they finish." Eric is crouched down in front of me. "Once they're gone, we can get in the truck and go."

I nod.

"I don't know why we got stuck with unloading, while everyone else is at the weekly announcement," Rob says.

"Why do you care? Who wants to see some stupid female become a guard, anyway?" Jason says. "She doesn't deserve it, like her brother."

"I heard her father tried to make a plea deal with the president. He would be her personal doctor, if she let Emma out early," Rob says.

My stomach has a pang in it. I thought the job offer was her idea.

"What he doesn't know is Emma wasn't getting out early because she wasn't getting out at all," Jason says.

His laugh is high-pitched, like a hyena, and it makes my shoulders cringe. What do they know that I don't?

"You two need to stop gossiping like schoolgirls. Less talk and more work."

It's Rich's voice. My hand twitches.

"There are normally only two guards," Eric mouths to me. "I don't know why Rich is here."

Whatever the reason, it can't be good, at least not for us.

"Rob, you can go to the announcements. I'll stay and finish unloading." His voice is rough.

I place my hand on Eric's shoulder, and his eyes are strong as he turns to me.

"We can handle this," he mouths.

"I know," I whisper back.

I place my hand on the gun in my holster. I feel better knowing it's there.

We remain crouched and watch as they bring in big brown boxes. The two men are quiet, as if they don't like each other. All I hear is the scuffing of their boots on the dusty ground.

"Once this is done, you can go to the meeting. I'll meet you there, later. I have newbie business to take care of," Rich says.

"How much time do you think we have before they are done unloading?" I ask Eric.

"I'm not sure. It's too dark to see how many boxes are left on the truck."

"I'll be right back."

"Are you insane? You can't save your sister. The jail will be guarded." His eyes are wide.

"That's not where I'm going." My throat is dry. I wish it was. "I have to get something. It's important; otherwise, I wouldn't leave."

"Whisper, we only have a small window of time. What if you miss it? What if you don't make it back?" His eyes are soft. "Be careful." He grips my arm.

"I will, I promise," I say, turning on my knees to crawl away.

Once I clear the hospital, I sprint across the street and race to the mansion. There are still no guards around. I enter the front door and get on the elevator to make my way up to the fifth floor.

Once I'm in front of Esther's chambers, I take out my gun. I point it at the knob and pull the trigger. The pops are loud, but that's the only way I can get the door open. The knob falls off, and I walk inside. I know her hallway is guarded, and the few guards left watching the security monitors will be here any minute.

I've noticed Rich saying the word newbie a few times, and just now it clicked that I saw newbie written on the map in Esther's drawer for Territory M. I know it's a long shot, but what if newbie stands for newborns? What if newbie camp is where they take the newborns to kill them? And what if midpoint burial is where they bury them?

I dash over to the table where I saw the maps. The drawer whizzes open, but I don't see that map, or any maps at all. I have to hurry, so I rustle papers around, but there are no maps, only files. I see dozens of green file folders. The first file says adoption papers for baby Miller. I open it and there's adoption papers that say baby Miller goes to the Robinson family in Territory U for $50,000. My heart is thumping. I don't understand, but I scoot that file aside. The next one says adoption papers for baby Smith. Inside it says the Smith baby will go to the Johnson family in Territory U for $70,000.

My lungs feel warm. The next file I see says adoption papers for baby Whisperer. My lungs turn into fire. The file says baby Whisperer goes to...it's blank. There is no name. What does any of this mean? My hands tingle and my eyes blur as I look toward the bottom of the document. It says baby Whisperer's adoption or execution to be determined.

I hear the elevator swirl open, so I shakily put the files back in their original position and slam the drawer closed. Then, I duck behind the sofa. My hand jiggles as I place it on the gun in my holster. I hear footsteps bounding forward.

"I know you're in here," a loud voice says. "Give yourself up."

I stay still, but the footsteps come closer. I reach for my weapon as a guard, with blond hair and gray eyes, peers over the sofa. It's Mike. Before I can pull my weapon, he draws his.

"On your feet," he says.

My leg spasms as I stand.

"Let's go." He holds the gun on me and cocks his head toward the door.

I step into the hallway. I feel the gun jabbing into my uniform. I hear a sizzling noise, and the gun releases from my back. I unsteadily turn around to see Samuel standing there. He used his Taser on the guard. The guard falls to the floor. His muscles contract, and he closes his eyes, like he is dead to the world.

"He'll only be unconscious for a few minutes," Samuel says to me. "You need to go."

"W-what are you doing here?" I ask. My nerves are on edge.

"A couple of guards stayed behind to watch the jail and monitor the security cameras. I volunteered for security. I didn't want to go to the meeting and watch you make the biggest mistake of your life." He looks down then back up. "I saw you come through the front door, and then the cameras spotted you stepping onto the fifth floor. I knew your plans must have changed. Mike saw you first, so he got up here before I could. But I would never let him harm you. I waited out here, so I could knock him out."

"Thanks for that." My eyes find his. "And for everything you've done for me during my time here."

"I take it you're leaving with Eric?"

"Yes, but I don't have time to explain. I need to get back into Esther's quarters. I saw something—"

"There's no time for that. Mike called in a break-in up in Esther's quarters. Others will be coming."

"But you don't u-understand." My lips tremble.

"You need to go." He grabs my arm. "Take the commoner's elevator. They'll be using the guard's."

"But Samuel," I say, trying to get my point across.

We see the up arrow is lit up on the guard's elevator, and I know there is no time. He is right. I have to go.

"I wish I could go with you, but—"

"You can't because your father needs you." I finish his sentence as the commoner's elevator doors swish open, and I step inside. "How will you explain this without getting in trouble?"

"Don't worry about that, just take care of yourself."

"I-I will," I say, as the doors merge.

*

I manage to slip back out the front door while the guards are on their way up on the elevator. Once I reach Eric, I see he is still crouched down in his original position. My stomach is in knots. I try not to dwell on what I just saw, and I am pleased that he hasn't left without me.

"You made it back." He gives a quick smile.

"I told you I would."

"They're still unloading." He looks back toward the truck, then turns to me. "Where'd you go?"

"To Esther's quarters to get a map she had of Territory M." I squat down and watch Rich carry more boxes. "But I couldn't find it."

"Don't worry about it. The driver can instruct us on where we need to go. You look pale. Are you okay?"

"I'm fine," I say, even though I know I'm not; but there's no time to tell him what I discovered, right now.

"That's the last one," Rich says.

I hear grinding metal as the dock leveler goes back up to the building. We watch as Rich and Jason walk away, disappearing into the hospital. The truck engine roars and the truck drives off. We stay down. We're waiting for the truck to turn around and come back for us.

It seems like hours have passed, although I know it has only been a few minutes. All of a sudden, I hear tires squealing as the truck backs up, at lightning speed, in our direction. It stops, a hundred feet away, with a screech, and I see someone jump out of the front. He comes around and lifts the back door, but it is so dark, I can't make out who it is. I know this is as close as he can come without causing suspicion as to why he has returned.

"Get ready," Eric says.

The dark figure searches around and then nods in our direction. "Run," Eric says.

We both take off as if fire is under our feet. I run as fast as I can, and it reminds me of my race to take food to my sister when darkness was setting in. I hear the crinkling of gravel and rocks under my boots, and the sound of my own heart beating in my ears. My breaths are jagged, not because I'm not used to the run, but because of the situation we're in. I'm twenty steps in, passing Eric on my way. I see the back of the truck, but I still have a ways to go to reach it. I stop when I hear the click of a gun cocking. I turn around, and so does Eric.

"I had a feeling you would try something." Rich stands with a gun on us. "But I thought it would be Eric and your brother," he says, tilting his head to the side. "Since they lied on their housing report. I never thought the *chosen one* would be trying to escape. The president is probably boiling over right now since you're not there making your speech."

I stand quietly, and Eric does the same.

"Now that you're caught, no one has anything to say." He stands with the gun still pointed at Eric, so I can't make a move toward him.

His eyes are so dark I see the light of the moon glistening in them.

I wonder where the driver is. The truck is still a few feet away. He should be able to see what's going on.

Rich's attention turns from Eric to me. He has a smarmy smile on his face, as though he has won a prize. He steps in front of me with the gun pointed at my chest. My mouth goes dry.

I hear an array of bullets and my heart beats erratically.

Jason is running at Eric, as if he is a dog pouncing on a cat. His gun is pointed above Eric's head, and he doesn't let up on the trigger until he reaches Eric.

I know Eric can handle himself, so I turn to face my own attacker.

"I knew you didn't deserve to be a guard. And now, like some scared little girl, you're running away." Rich's gape is hard. "I'm going to put this down and then we'll see what you're made of."

He places his gun on the ground. His eyes are dead as he walks up to me. His first instinct is to go for my face, but I move back and his swing misses me. My hand shakily grabs the Taser from my left hip. Rich knocks it from my fingers before I can get a good grip. I reach for the gun on my right hip. He grabs me around my throat. I know my face is red. He is choking the life out of me. My body shivers, as if I'm naked in a cold river. I use my fingers as a weapon, poking him in the eye. He grunts and lets me go. I wobble but hold my stance. I watch him stumble back and grab his face. Before he can gain his composure, I kick him in his groin. He grunts louder this time and stumbles onto the ground.

"Whisper, let's go!"

I hear Eric's voice screaming at me. I see Jason's lifeless body lying on the ground. In the darkness, his face looks purple and badly bruised. Eric has done him in and is on his way to the truck. I want to follow, but I notice Rich has gotten up and is walking toward his gun. My hand shudders, yet I manage to pull my gun from my holster and point it toward his leg. I have to stop him before he reaches his weapon or I know he'll kill me.

Pulling the trigger on a real human feels different than at a poster on the gun range. The force pushing my body back is strong. My heart beats as if a bomb is exploding in my chest. I pull it again, since the first time I missed. This time I know I've hit him in the leg because I see blood spurting from it.

"Whisper…" I hear Eric's voice, drifting off. The truck's motor blares again.

I unsteadily put the gun back in the holster, and then search the grounds for my Taser. I may need it later, and I don't want to leave without it. I almost tumble over it trying to bend down to get it. My whole body quakes as I tremble, gripping it in my hands. I run to the truck.

I only hit Rich's leg, so I'm surprise he isn't shooting at me. The wind blows my hair in my face, but that doesn't stop me from seeing the truck pulling away.

Eric holds out his hand to me and I run with ragged breaths until I reach him. He clutches my arm and pulls me inside. We hit a bump and I land on him. I quickly slide over. He reaches up and pulls the door down with a *bang*. My heart crumbles in my chest, and my throat feels as though it is closing.

We're in the back of a cold, empty truck. The interior walls are dark, and the air is stale and dry. I slide to one side, while Eric slides to the other. The truck bumps up and down for a while as we drive. We're both silent, distraught over what just happened. The next thing I know, I hear the driver talking to the guards at the gate that leads into Territory M.

The guards don't bother to look inside. I guess it is always the same driver, and they trust him. Even so, we stay crouched down and hidden. It's hard to believe we're at the gates. Sometimes after school—before I would get on the bus to go back home—I used to walk to them and stare at the traffic that was allowed in and out. I now hear the gates screech open. The truck's motor revved up as it moves. Eric and I don't look at each other. It remains quiet, until I hear the driver's voice.

"We made it across before Rich had a chance to radio this in. You two okay back there?"

I know that voice. It's Julian, the guard from the yard, and Eric's roommate. He said he goes back and forth to Territory M. Now, I know how he does it.

"We're fine, man," Eric says. "And thanks for fulfilling your end of the deal. I told you we could handle it, and you wouldn't have to get involved."

"I wasn't so sure, at first, but you two work well together."

"I agree," Eric says. "Are you okay?" His voice gets softer.

I can feel his gaze on me.

"I'm fine," I mumble.

"You're not mad at me for not helping you with Rich back there, are you?"

"No, I'm not mad." I turn to face him. "But I did wonder how long you watched me tussle with him."

"For a few minutes, but you weren't struggling. I knew you could handle your own and you did," he says. His hand is warm as he brushes it across my cheek. "I would've helped, if you needed it."

"Is Jason dead?" I ask. "I couldn't tell."

"He was unconscious but still breathing. I stayed true to the pact, and I see you did, too. You could have shot Rich somewhere else, instead of his leg."

"I wanted him gone, but I couldn't justify killing him. But he could have killed me. Only his leg was wounded, so why didn't he? And why hasn't he called this in?"

I feel his fingers move from my cheek to my hand.

"I don't know, but I'm grateful he didn't."

"Me too," I say.

"Now, can you tell me what is so special about that map?"

"It's a map of Territory M. A lot of the structures and landmarks are marked, in terms I didn't understand." I stop and take in a much needed breath. "There were things like mainstream market and midpoint burial and newbie camp. I didn't think anything of it, at first, but I've heard Rich talk about newbies, twice now. So, I thought what if newbie means newborns...?"

"Whisper, you can't—"

"No, let me finish." I shake my head. "Have you ever really thought about where they take the newborns to kill them? Does anybody really know?"

"The level six guards know."

"Level six, like Rich?" I ask, not waiting for a response. "It's strange that our burial grounds here don't have any babies in them. So, where do they put their remains? What if newbie camp is where they take the newborns, to kill them or to do something else? What if this midpoint burial is where they bury them? Abigail hasn't been gone that long. What if we can get to her in time before...?"

"I see where you're going with this. It is a wild theory, but I wouldn't put anything past them." His voice fades in and out when we hit a bump. "I'm sure the camp is kept secret, so Julian probably doesn't know how to get to it."

"That's why I was trying to get the map."

"It's okay." His eyes are reassuring. "If it's out there, we'll find it." He glances away and then back at me. "Whisper, this is a long shot, so I don't want you getting your hopes up."

"I know, but this long shot is all I have."

I turn from him and lay my head back onto the hardness of the truck walls. I close my eyes and feel Eric clutch my hand. Why didn't I tell him everything? Why didn't I tell him about the adoption papers? I can't share it with him, until I let it sink in myself. There were only a few files. What if some babies are adopted, while others are killed? Abigail's file said 'to be determined'. Does that mean she will be sold or killed?

Eric squeezes my hand, harder. I turn to him and smile; but as quickly as the smile arises, it fades. How will my family survive, now that I'm leaving? How will Theodore take care of Taylor when he'll probably be thrown in jail himself? How will things be without my family by my side? I won't receive the answers I'm looking for at this moment, so I try to focus on how warm and reassuring Eric's touch is.

My focus doesn't last. I wish I'd said more to Samuel, but there wasn't time. He's a good guy. I'll miss him. I lay my head back on the wall again, since it throbs as if it's breaking into tiny pieces. Hiding in the back of a truck was not the way I imagined myself getting into Territory M.

I have dreamed of this day, ever since I was a little girl. My goal was to make it to Territory M to go to college, so I could have a future. I never thought I would be going there to start a war—a war to tear down walls that should've never been built in the first place. I pictured myself walking through the gates with my family by my side, and sometimes—selfishly—by myself. But now I sit here, in a beat-up, old truck with Eric by my side. He's sometimes mysterious and carries his own set of demons. I now know, after everything we've been through, that I can trust him. I hope the feeling is mutual.

I have so many emotions washing over me. I'm pleased with myself for being strong enough to fight off Rich. I now realize, I'm tough, resilient, and worthy of love, no matter what color my skin is. But does being strong and independent matter, if I can't save Abigail?

My stomach twinges, wondering what will happen when we get there. Will the people of Territory M welcome us with open arms, or will they hate us for being different? What if the one in charge won't listen to me and all my efforts are in vain? What if we're taken in to custody as soon as we arrive? What if the walls never come down?

I touch the chain around my neck. I'll keep it close to remember the hope I'm looking for. I'll make my family proud. I know I'll see them again. And when I do, the walls will be down. Abigail will be with me. We will start over.

There will be no more extinction of children.

Dear Reader,

Thank you so much for purchasing and reading my novel. I hope you enjoyed reading about Emma as much as I enjoyed writing about her. Her voice was constantly in my head, which made writing about her journey fun for me. In case you're wondering if Emma's quest will continue—the answer is yes—it will continue in the sequel.

I would be grateful if you left an honest review. Let me know if you loved Emma's adventure or hated it. I always love to receive feedback.

If you have any questions for me please contact me through my website *www.ljeppsauthor.com*.

I would love to hear from you.

P.S. Here's a sample of the sequel.

JOURNEY TO TERRITORY M

CHAPTER ONE

I glance out of the rear window and see the gates of Territory L behind me. It's still so close my eyes sting. I can't believe no one is shooting at us. With Julian's help, we just strolled right through the guard's gate; they thought Julian was bringing back an empty truck. He does it all the time when he delivers supplies, so what would make them think today is any different.

It's hard to believe I was cooped up in a jail cell for thirty days because I went against the president's laws. The best thing about my time there was learning how to fight with Eric. I shudder thinking about President Esther and her values. She believes the poor should no longer have children because they can't take care of them. I once thought she killed all of the babies that were born and hidden, but I've since found out that some are illegally adopted.

Territory L is considered lower class, while Territory M is middle class and Territory U is upper class; but the labels are only there because she separated everyone and made up the division of classes. Just because the upper territories make more money than my territory doesn't make it right to send the babies there.

I still can't believe she planned to use me—her first female guard—as her personal mouthpiece, or I could be sent to the prison for lifers. I was able to escape that fate, for now; but what about the others who are still jailed for thirty days or sent to the prison for lifers? Will I be able to get them released or be able to get the walls torn down?

I take in a breath, glossing over everything that has happened. Territory L is my home—the only home I've known—but I need to do this to make things better for my family and all the people who live there. And I need to find my niece, Abigail, who was taken and may be dead or illegally adopted. I know that is my primary goal.

The back of the truck is dark. I am so deep in thought, I didn't notice that Eric moved away from me and is now up near the front, conversing with Julian, who keeps his gaze straight ahead, but nods as he listens to Eric talking behind him. I feel the bumps in the road as my body bounces up and down and I sway from side to side.

"Sorry," he says, turning from Julian to look at me. "I figured you needed some time to yourself. I was right because you didn't even notice me leave your side."

He crawls on his knees, back to where I am.

"You okay?" he asks, as he brushes a strand of hair from my eye.

"I'm fine now that we've made it into Territory M. I never thought that would happen."

"I feel the same and, so far, none of the guards or patrolmen have caught up to us, so we should take that as a good sign." He slides next to me. "Julian and I were listening on our radios and, so far, Rich hasn't reported us gone. I'm surprised but glad he hasn't."

"I'm surprised, too," I say. My chest aches knowing we could get caught and our speedy getaway will be for nothing. For some reason unbeknownst to me, Rich hates me. I think it's because his siblings died when the no children law started and I was the last one to survive. His dislike for me goes well beyond anything I've ever experienced.

I thought he would never stop coming for me but, for some reason, he hasn't called this in. I thought, with him being the president's top guard, he wouldn't have hesitated to make light of what I've done. Was he injured so much when I fought with him he was unable to call it in? My hand trembles thinking about how I shot him back at the gates.

"I didn't know the radios would work over here," I say, trying to get my mind off Rich.

"Julian comes here frequently, and he says my radio has only a small range; but his is set up for longer distances, since he is allowed back and forth through the gates. Once we reach certain areas near the outskirts of the territory, mine won't work anymore but his still will."

"So where are we going now?" I ask, shifting my weight. The truck's floor is hard as a rock and uncomfortable. "Is it somewhere safe?"

"Julian knows a place where we can hide, in case this gets radioed in. No one should find us there—at least not for a while, and at least not until we figure out what our plan is."

He gives a half-smile that comforts me; but only for a moment, because my throat tenses when I hear a loud noise like a cannon going off.

Order your copy today! Click the link below to see a full list of outlets that carry the Extinction series.

www.ljeppsauthor.com

ACKNOWLEDGMENTS

I have to thank my sister and brother-in-law for believing I could write a second novel, and for being excited about it.

Thanks again for the kind words and encouragement from my friend, L.W.

Thank you again to all my hard working beta readers who believed my manuscript was good enough to be published and to Helen, my copy editor, proofreader, and beta reader. Her help always encourages me to do better, and made me believe I could self-publish a second novel.

BOOKS BY L. J. EPPS

<u>Romance</u>

I Wish I Could Remember You

<u>Young Adult</u>

Extinction Series:

Extinction of All Children

Journey to Territory M

Journey to Territory U